Hide and Seek

Titan Protectors, Book 1

Cristin Harber

Mill Creek Press

Prologue

Twelve Years Ago

Two men whom Grace Willoughby had known her entire life watched her and her boyfriend with undisguised scrutiny. Of course they did. Her brother, Hayden, and his best friend, Callum, had never treated her like anything other than a kid. Now that she lived on her own and had returned home with a boyfriend for her family to meet, both were making this family dinner more awkward than it already was.

Her boyfriend, Dominic Marino, sat at the outdoor table on her parents' back deck. Despite the fact that Dominic had insisted on meeting her parents, it was clear he didn't want to be there. If she were honest, their relationship was too new. It'd only been weeks since he'd swept her off her feet. Far too soon for family introductions, but Dominic always got his way.

She tried to ignore the small stirrings of doubt and found herself staring at Callum. She quickly jerked her gaze away.

Callum Hale. Broad shoulders. Powerful long legs. He wasn't family, though he acted like it and probably believed it to be true as he sat next to Hayden and shot the shit with her dad.

She hadn't seen Callum since he and Hayden had graduated from Army Ranger School. His stormy eyes melted her insides, and when he turned his bourbon-brown gaze on her, she wanted to drag him to bed. So she did what she did best: ran her mouth and rolled her eyes and tried her damnedest to treat Callum like Hayden. It might have worked to the outside world but didn't change the stupid-level of arousal that coursed through her veins when he smiled.

Her backup plan was to ignore him. Ignoring him was a talent she'd mastered over the years, because there was only so much world-class sass she could spew before her sarcastic well was depleted. If she wasn't able to shield herself from Callum, her insides turned into a gooey, upside-down tornado. That would have been a terrible problem to have while standing next to her actual boyfriend.

And her actual boyfriend was a verifiable catch.

Handsome: Check.

Wealthy: Double check.

Polite—erm, well, half-check.

He gave excellent interviews, had topped more than his fair share of famous people lists of the likes of Forbes, Inc., and Bloomberg, and once had paparazzi in speedboats follow his yacht while he partied with nepo babies and Los Angeles royalty.

How could she compare Dominic to Callum, who literally never noticed that she had grown up from the kid next door to a woman with a figure that wasn't all that bad? Nice curves and a pretty smile, if she said so herself. But nope. Not even so much as a second glance. That was probably good, because if he had given her a fraction of a thought, he would have noticed that she'd pined after him from the moment she'd noticed boys.

Irony of all ironies, he noticed her now.

Or rather, he was noticing her sitting on a two-person bench with Dominic.

His steely eyes had tracked Dominic since the moment Callum eased into his chair, longneck beer sweating in hand, frowning in a way that said he clearly didn't trust her boyfriend.

That was fine. Callum didn't have to trust Dominic.

Dominic didn't seem to notice Callum. He wasn't fazed by the uncomfortable small talk or broiling summer heat. In expensive khaki pants and a polo shirt, she wondered how he could look so cool and detached. Hayden and Callum wore boardshorts and T-shirts and looked like they might walk to the neighborhood pool after burgers and beers.

She ignored them and focused on her boyfriend. "Do you want something cold to drink?"

Dominic's flashy smile was one more layer of his put-together persona. Dark hair. Dark eyes. Killer smile. "I'm fine, darling."

Darling. Was she a darling? It wasn't the first time she'd asked herself that question. Darling always sounded like he was speaking to someone else. Just as "Mrs. Willoughby" would always be her stepmother, "darling" would be someone else.

Someone more blue-blooded or pretentious.

Someone who wore pearls and sweater sets.

Someone who looked like they should be on Dominic Marino's arm.

The nickname would take getting used to. All new things had a breaking-in period.

Her dad returned to the deck with a tray of burgers for the grill. "These shouldn't take long. Hope everyone is hungry."

She was starving. Between the time zone change and flying into a private airport, she hadn't grabbed a meal all day. The flights were supposed to have been catered, but as best she could tell, that meant champagne, liquor, and charcuterie boards. After more than a few olives and fancy deli slices, she agreed with Dominic that she'd eaten several days' worth of calories. She had still been hungry, but the flight attendant cleared the tray at Dominic's request.

She wanted to disagree, but her boyfriend had a weird way of finagling her agreement. *Manipulating?* No, that didn't sound right, but Grace could never pinpoint how it happened.

"Hayden says you work in finance," Callum said.

"I do." Dominic's lips curved into that effortless smile he used in board meetings and when schmoozing clients. "Crypto. Bitcoin. I specialize in blockchain technology."

"That's, like, pretend money, right?" Distrust tightened in the corners of Callum's eyes. He tilted his head toward her brother. "Everything in Las Vegas is fake."

Hayden's gaze narrowed as well. "Think so."

Dominic didn't spend all his time in Las Vegas. She wished she hadn't told Hayden and Callum that they were flying in from there. It raised too many questions about where Dominic lived. Las Vegas. New York. Miami. Washington, DC.

Dominic chuckled good-naturedly, as if Hayden and Callum weren't acting like over-protective buffoons. "The business opportunities in Las Vegas are as real as the money in my bank account."

Hayden snorted, Callum rolled his eyes, and Grace blushed. Talking about money like that was crass. Then again, it was his money that had been whirling her around the country, gifting her with over-the-top bouquets of flowers, dining her with unbelievable meals. She literally couldn't catch her breath under the weight of his attention. Who was she to judge when Dominic was lavishing her with attention in a way she hadn't known was possible?

Her stepmother shot a warning glance at Hayden and Callum. "That sounds exciting. Don't mind them."

Dominic hooted as though they were all in on a funny conversation. The hint of his thinly veiled condescension echoed with his laughter. If she heard it, Hayden and Callum did as well. Her stepmom, who always saw the best in people, probably didn't.

"No, it's fine," Dominic said. "Digital assets are a complex market. Hard to understand. Takes a lot of understanding. *Not for everyone.*"

Her stomach churned. Dominic's snarky side comments wouldn't help everyone get along. Wasn't that what she had wanted? For everyone to get along? For her family to be swept off their feet by Dominic as she had? Yes? *Yes.* That was why they were here.

She should have known it had been too early for him to meet her parents. Much less Hayden and Callum. She'd never brought a guy home before, and the timing of Hayden and Callum's leave from base was unfortunate.

Wait—what? She never wanted to miss a chance to see her brother and Callum, and nearly exploded from excitement that Callum—*that both of them*—would be home.

Callum is only a family friend, she reminded herself.

She'd let go of her dreams of him years ago, and Dominic had treated her like a precious possession since the moment he'd swooped into her life. She'd never had to fight for Dominic's attention. Never second-guessed what his intentions were. Dominic cared about her, wanted a future with her. Why shouldn't they all meet?

"The thing you have to understand is," Dominic continued, "the bigger the risk, the bigger the reward." He wrapped his arm over her shoulder and secured her close with a possessive hold. "It will definitely provide for a great life."

The churning in her stomach intensified. Her family never shied away from public displays of affection. Dad and Mari snuggled, held hands, and did everything in their power to be near one another when lounging around the house. Theirs was a comfortable love. Terrific role models. Dominic's hold on her now wasn't comfortable. His arm around her shoulder was more a message to her brother and Callum than anything indicative of their relationship.

She wanted to inch away. She needed breathing room. But Dominic didn't do breathing room. He'd barely let her catch her breath since they first met. Las Vegas and New York City. Fancy dinners and shopping. A declaration of love on their third date. Her boyfriend drove fast cars, owned a private plane, and lived life to its fullest. Now she was, too.

Callum's face tightened. The muscles in his jaw twitched. He glared at Dominic's hold. "How long did you say you've been dating?"

"A few weeks," she managed.

"That's pretty fast." He took a pull from his longneck without taking his eyes off of her.

"Why waste time when it's the right woman?" Dominic asked.

She blushed again and couldn't hide her smile. This gorgeous man adored her. He'd offered her the world. Everything had been so right, so absolutely overwhelmingly amazing, that she couldn't see how it could go wrong.

Hayden grunted his skepticism.

"Come on, boys, give the kids a break." Dad flipped burgers on the grill. "We're glad the timing worked so that everyone was here at once."

Kids. Dominic was the same age as Grace. With a three-year age gap from Hayden and Callum, she would always be the youngest in her family. Three years might well have been a decade. Dominic's important job and flashy lifestyle wouldn't change that.

Her stepmom stepped outside with a bowl of potato salad. "Hayden, grab the watermelon from the counter."

Callum took the bowl from her and set it on the table. "What else do you need help with?"

Flames licked from the grill as Dad shoveled the burgers onto buns. "Gracie, hold out the tray."

She pulled away from Dominic and stepped next to her father. Heat radiated from the grill. Still, it was nice not to be pressed against someone in the summer swelter.

Everyone helped set the table except for Dominic. He was a guest, though, and new to their dynamic. Not that they were waiting on him, but more that he didn't know how to lend a hand.

Callum and Hayden sat in their usual seats. Her stepmom topped off drinks and then joined them. Grace returned to her place next to Dominic. Her dad circled the table, dishing out burgers. "Which one do you want, Gracie?"

Mouth watering, she eyed the one with extra cheese melting out the side.

"That little one looks good," Dominic suggested.

"Oh, that little guy is the one we make for Sprout." Dad gestured to the old dog sleeping under the table. "That's not even half—"

"It's fine, Dad. That's good for me. There's more than enough for you to halve a burger for Sprout when we're done."

Dad frowned. His spatula-wielding hand hovered. "Well, uh…" He scooped up the comically small burger with the bun tipped off the side. "Sure. You can always have seconds."

She didn't have to look up to see Callum and Hayden scrutinizing her burger selection. Dinner went downhill from there.

Finally, the night wrapped. When they were alone, she'd explain to Dominic how he made her and her family uncomfortable. She'd point out a few things that would make their next family get-together run more smoothly.

Grace offered awkward goodbyes to her dad and stepmom, ignored Hayden and Callum, and, hand in hand, let Dominic escort her to his BMW. His firm grip was the slightest bit too tight, and he shut her inside the fancy car with a hint of too much force.

All she had to do was ask him to relax. Maybe her unflappable boyfriend had felt ganged up on. Hayden and Callum certainly hadn't made dinner a relaxing time. Then again, Dominic had been combative with subtle condescension and a few straightforward jabs.

Dominic rounded the hood. His brooding dark eyes and set jaw made her nerves bubble. Grace looked toward the childhood home that always made her feel happy and carefree. Until tonight.

Callum watched from the porch. His thick arms were crossed, and his scrutinizing glare followed Dominic. Then his gaze dropped to hers. Her stomach plummeted. Every concern that she tried to ignore was lit up on his face like a billboard in Las Vegas. His angry frown pulled down so far that she worried he would come down to the BMW.

But he didn't.

Besides, she didn't need him to. She was more than capable of having a private conversation with her boyfriend. Dominic needed to ease up. She had a voice, and she'd never been scared to use it before.

Dominic closed the door and turned on the engine. Warm air blasted over her, and the music kicked on. His irritation flooded the car. He slapped at the controls, as if changing the settings would immediately blast cool air on a ninety-degree day.

Grace squirmed in her seat as the air conditioning barely cooled the car. Sweat prickled on the back of her neck. Callum still watched from the porch. "I just thought today would be…"

"Would be what?" Dominic snapped.

She inched away and leaned against the door. "Different." Her tongue pressed to the roof of her mouth as she combed through the most important issues to bring up. "I can pick my cheeseburger out."

"You didn't go back for seconds, so it must have been the right burger to fill you up."

She hadn't because Dominic, Callum, Hayden, and her dad—probably her stepmom too—were watching what Grace ate. She'd wanted another burger but had loaded up on sides instead. "That doesn't matter. Don't pick out my food for me."

He let out a long breath and pinched the bridge of his nose, and after another long breath, he turned and took her hand. This time, his handhold was gentler than any time he'd touched her all day. "I'm sorry, darling. I was overheated. I just want you to be happy and healthy and to take care of yourself."

She was happy and healthy and tried to understand what he meant. So...he was looking after her? Sort of. But choosing her burger wasn't her only issue with the day, and she didn't understand how this perfect gentleman, this well-spoken business executive, had been so rude and arrogant.

"Grace, I'm sorry." He released the tender hold on her hand and reached into the center console. "I got you a little something. I planned to give it to you later tonight, but I can't stand to see you upset."

She eyed the small blue box that she now recognized as being from his favorite jewelry store in New York City and wanted to say she wouldn't need a present now if he'd been kinder to everyone. Actually, she didn't need presents. At all. Period.

Warmth radiated from his eyes and into his smile. This was the Dominic she knew and loved. Still, she hesitated.

"Open it, Grace."

She lifted the top. A keychain wasn't what she expected. Not that she *expected* anything. "What is this?"

"What does it look like?"

Grace lifted it from the box. The metal keychain was heavier than any she'd had before, and if she had to guess, it was real silver or white gold. Her eyebrows lifted. "I know it's a keychain, but—"

Dominic held out a key. "For you."

An empty feeling pitted at the bottom of her stomach. She swallowed hard and looked from the key to him. His smile was almost nervous, almost shy, but it was the excitement in his eyes that won her over. Dominic, her macho boyfriend who commanded boardrooms and made million-dollar deals, was insecure and hopeful. Okay, that was sweet. "You're giving me a key to your condo?"

"I'd like to call it *our* condo."

She had hardly set foot in her apartment since the day they'd met. Everything was happening so fast. She blinked, trying to get a handle on the way he'd acted earlier. They'd been dating for weeks. That was all. Not to mention, she liked her own place. It was nowhere near as nice as his polished properties, but it was her own space. Grace gnawed on her bottom lip. Was he asking her to move in with him? Or was it just a key? It had to be just a key.

Still, she hesitated. "I don't know."

"Grace, I'm sorry tonight didn't go the way you imagined." He brushed his knuckles over her cheek. "But I wanted to meet your parents before I gave you this."

She met his dark eyes. They twinkled as if this was something he needed. Almost like a challenge—no, that didn't make sense. Almost like he was scared she'd say no. The corners of his lips lifted. Dominic clasped his key in her palm and closed her fingers around it, then brought her hand to his mouth, pressing it with the softest kiss. "I love you, Grace."

Her apprehension melted away. How could she doubt a man who saw their future together? He was stable, secure, and he would treat her like she was precious. "I love you too."

"My lawyers will handle your lease. We'll have movers bring over whatever you want to keep. Simple."

Wait. He *was* asking her to move in with him. Alarm bells sounded.

"You're the love of my life." He glanced over her shoulder. Callum was probably still standing there, watching. "Tell me you know that."

"I know that."

"That you'll never break my heart."

"Of course I won't." They were moving in together. A luxury condo. Maid service. Rooftop pool and gym. Concierge and doorman. It was safer than her apartment. It was the next step.

Grace forced herself to ignore Callum Hale as Dominic drove them toward her unexpected future.

Chapter One

Present Day

Almost everyone Grace had ever met thought she was dead. She lived in hiding, yet somehow her ex-husband had found her. Years of lying with the sole goal of keeping Dominic away had been a big, fat failure. The peace that she'd precariously clung to evaporated.

Grace blocked the exit of the grocery store, frozen under the blowing air that cascaded from above the door. Could he see her? She crouched behind her cart. A sleek black Mercedes stood out in the quiet rural parking lot of the Shop 'n' Save like a dark god lording over its thralls. No, Dominic hadn't even seen her yet. That she was sure of. If he had, she wouldn't still be standing.

Her ex was supposed to be in prison.

Well, just like she was supposed to be dead.

But Dominic really *was* supposed to be behind bars. There had been a courtroom showdown and more than one guilty verdict handed down by a hangman judge who was worth his weight in gold. Or rather, cryptocurrency, as Dominic would have preferred.

Dominic's lawyers had been trying for years to throw out his conviction. They'd tampered with evidence, terrified witnesses, and worked every angle the justice system offered. She'd known their playbook. That had been the primary reason she'd "died." Guess his attorneys had finally been successful, because she had no doubt he was outside the grocery store.

But she'd set up warning systems. His release from prison should have triggered a heads-up. No one had called her. No one had warned her. The safety measures that had been put in place to give her time to ensure her safety had failed—unless she was wrong, and that wasn't Dominic.

"Hey, lady, get a move on," a man called from behind her.

Grace looked over her shoulder and wanted to apologize but couldn't get a word out. It was as if Dominic had wrapped his hand around her throat yet again, but this time without even being in front of her.

Maybe he wasn't really here.

No. She wasn't wrong. The black Mercedes sitting like a vengeful menace among the pickup trucks was all the proof she needed.

He was waiting for her. Screwing with her. Hoping she'd run across the parking lot and dive into the nondescript car registered to a shell company LLC so he could chase her. He needed their cat-and-mouse games where she ran for her life and he took her down. It was foreplay. At least to him.

That sadistic game that he relished was the reason he hadn't waltzed into the store and dragged her out of the frozen food aisle. No, Dominic parked in the handicapped spot, wanting to be seen. Everything was a mind game.

"Excuse me?" A woman inched her cart closer. "Can you move?"

Grace furtively glanced over her shoulder. Behind the woman with a baby in the cart, a man in Carhartt overalls, waiting impatiently for her to move, held his deli hot bar lunch sack. She couldn't meet their eyes. "I'm sorry."

They probably didn't hear her. The staccato rhythm of her heartbeat drowned the words from her own ears.

"Lady, get outta the way," the Carhartt man demanded.

"I..." Grace couldn't catch her breath. It was as if her chest was devoid of oxygen while simultaneously squeezed to capacity. Her lungs would burst like a balloon if she said another word to them.

She abandoned the cart and sidestepped past the woman with her baby. Grace pressed her crossbody purse to her stomach and put her hand behind her to smoosh her backpack closer. The baby reached for Grace as she skirted between them and the promotional tower of colas. Her backpack threatened to push a twelve-pack to the ground.

The Carhartt man grumbled. His judgment burned into her ducked shoulders. Blistering shame curled down her back. Grace fumbled with her purse for her burner phone. Her thumb slid over its raised buttons as she tried to decide who to call.

She could call her parents and ask them to check on Dominic's prison status. The Bureau of Prisons' website listed where inmates were located, but hell, what good would that do? It would only confirm what Grace had seen with her own two eyes. Dominic was out of federal custody.

Hayden would know what to do—except her older brother was deployed somewhere overseas and likely incommunicado. On the off chance that he was in the US, Grace was certain Hayden wasn't anywhere near the little rural Maryland town she'd hidden in. Her parents and brother never knew where she was. That was part of the magic of keeping her family safe from her ex's reach.

The only option was to escape from the grocery store and melt into one of the hiding places she'd used over the years. Grace had a safe contact—a protective friend she'd made—who lived relatively nearby and had always helped without asking too many questions. She hurried to the customer-service desk.

The manager held court there, ready to sell nicotine and lottery tickets or take complaints and requests. He pushed his long hair back and shifted behind the battered and bruised counter littered with legal notices and age requirements. "What can I do for you today?"

She focused on his name badge. *Johnny.* Johnny seemed like a reasonable guy who wouldn't ask too many questions. "Can I use your back door?"

His hair fell loose again, and she imagined he played death metal on the weekends. "Sorry?"

Grace twisted the black tourmaline beads on her bracelet and tried to catch her breath. No one would understand her if she mumbled and rushed. Minor mistakes like that would slow her down, and Dominic would pounce. She glanced toward the front exit. No sign of him. Not that she expected him to walk in and find her. Where was the fun in that? Better for her to walk out and straight into his open arms.

She noted that the traffic jam she'd created was gone. Her abandoned cart had been moved out of the way. Did Dominic see it? She licked her lips and forced herself to speak slowly. "I have to—" Breathless, she had to pull it together.

Johnny pushed his hair back again, dark eyes studying her as though she might cause a problem in his store.

"If I use your back door, will an alarm ring?" She couldn't meet his eyes, but his silence bore into her. "Please."

His wariness softened. "Ma'am, are you okay?"

Ha. Not in a million years. She had no immediate plan other than to run. No access to most of her belongings. No place to go without a friend's help. Even her car had to be abandoned. She'd figure out what to do about that and the little place she'd rented under a false name later.

"Ma'am?" Johnny leaned against the marred counter. His hands planted over the taped notices and the stack of Shop 'n' Save coupons.

She couldn't meet his eyes and dropped hers to study the worn grooves where years of use had faded the faux wood. Years of therapy had come down to this moment that she knew would inevitably arrive. She had two choices: get her anxiety under control or have a panic attack at the customer service desk.

Grace inhaled through her nose and held it. An eternity crawled by before she released the breath. "I can't go out the front door. There's someone out there—I just can't."

"I can call the police for you."

"No. Don't. Please. That will make it worse." She stared at his name tag again. A valued employee for more than five years. So much could change in five years. Five years ago, her parents and brother had buried her in a family-only closed-casket ceremony. "Johnny. Please. I need to go out the back. Will an alarm ring if I do?"

His fingers tapped on the worn groove of the counter. He had short fingernails with dark nail polish mostly scratched off and wore several rings. A portion of a tattoo peeked out from his shirt sleeve. If only she could meet his gaze, if she could see what he was thinking, and he could see her desperation, then maybe he would answer her.

"Nah," he finally said. "Come with me. No alarms."

Relief flooded as if a cold rag had been wrapped around her neck on a sweltering day. "Thank you." But he couldn't have heard her whisper that had caught in her throat. She followed him and tried again. "Thank you."

His keys clinked as he guided her down the canned vegetable aisle and past the deli, where the lunch crowd waited for mac and cheese, potato wedges, and fried chicken. They entered a dim hallway and passed the restrooms until Johnny pushed through the old swinging double doors.

Boxes and pallets lined the walkway. They stopped beside two large, closed truck bays next to a beaten-up door with a handmade poster that read, *Don't forget to clock out.*

Johnny swung the door open as though he wanted to catch someone lurking by the dumpster. The bright noon light momentarily blinded her. Grace's eyes watered. She faltered in her escape, but Johnny lifted his hand to block Grace until he'd inspected the space. She appreciated everything the guy was doing for her.

"There's no one out here."

"Thanks." Slowly her eyes adjusted to the sunshine. Grace inched out and surveyed the delivery area as Johnny had. She clung to the door as if it tethered her to safety. No sign of Dominic.

"You sure you don't need me to call the cops? Family? Friends? Anyone?"

"No. Please don't. I won't be a problem—"

"Lady, I'm not worried about you being a problem."

Summer heat baked the back lot. She hesitantly let go of the back door and carefully stepped onto the oil-stained asphalt. The delivery area backed up to the employees' entrances for the grain and feed store, the post office, and a rarely staffed real estate office. Its lone Realtor was a part-time long-haul driver. Grace had used that to her advantage when she'd found her little rental house online and finagled the keys without ever having to meet anyone in person.

"Hey, lady. You need anything? Food? Formula? Something?"

His humanity squeezed her heart. She shielded her eyes as tears pricked, but she didn't have time to tell him how much that might mean to a woman in trouble. Grace just smiled. "Thank you for even asking."

She hurried toward the feed store's delivery bay and climbed the stairs to the employee entrance. With a little prayer for luck, she tried their back door and let out a deep sigh of relief as it creaked open with an overused, under-maintained groan.

The sweet smell of grain and corn hung in the air. Machinery beeped, and voices floated nearby. Her eyes adjusted from the summer sun. Overhead fluorescent lights illuminated the space stacked with boxes and pallets. She'd never been inside the feed store before, but its customer parking lot was always busier than the Shop 'n' Save. Their inventory towered around her. She hurried down the makeshift aisle, searching for a way into the store.

"Hey," a forklift operator yelled as Grace crossed an open space. "You can't be back here."

Grace ducked her head and rushed by.

"Yo, you're going the wrong way."

Shit. She paused and turned toward him.

He wasn't a tenth as helpful as Johnny, but he did lift his hand and point a different way.

"Thanks." She rushed that way and, a moment later, saw the entrance into the store. Grace burst through without any of the hesitation she'd had stepping out of the grocery store's back door. Dominic wouldn't be in the feed store. He was probably sitting in the air conditioning, making crypto deals on his phone, counting the minutes until Grace would stumble out of the grocery store like a bumbling idiot, straight into his clutches. He always thought she was stupid. At least that worked in her favor this time.

The feed store's bright lights beckoned her into its aisles. The merchandise caught her off guard. There was far more than livestock food. She rushed through the section devoted to shoes and boots and farther into the store. A cordoned-off area with large metal troughs held center court. Grace slowed and, curious, glanced down. Little chickens waddled under heat lamps.

She moved next to a toddler standing on tiptoes while her mother focused on the fussy baby in her arms.

"Dwucks." The toddler reached toward the chickens with an outstretched finger. "Dwucks!"

"Chickens," the mother corrected.

A tiny pain panged in Grace's heart. The frazzled woman didn't notice Grace but had something Grace desperately wanted. A simple life. Kids. She realized everyone had their problems. The fussy baby and the exhausted mother were clearly having a moment. But that was a moment that Grace would never have. *Because of Dominic.* She had to focus.

Escape was paramount. Grace glanced around. She'd had no idea what was actually in a feed store. Maybe if she hadn't been scared to leave her rental for anything more than food, she would have known.

Grace ducked behind a display of pest control options. Across from the safety of the baby chickens, she called her brother Hayden.

No answer.

She could leave a message, but what would she say? She'd seen an expensive car parked at the grocery store and had known with every ounce of her being that her ex-husband had tracked her down? Grace would have to admit that she hadn't told him the complete truth about how she'd been living. Staying off the grid had been important. But she'd done something wrong for Dominic to realize that she was alive, much less track her down.

Grace redialed her brother. The voicemail picked up again. She cleared her throat and, after the beep, left a message. "Hey, it's me. I don't know how, but Dominic's out early. And he's here. At the grocery store. *He knows about me.*"

She swallowed the rising wave of panic and inhaled, then let it out slowly. The adorable little cabin that she'd secretly called home for the last few months and her car would have to wait until she returned. *If* she returned. She had to put distance between herself and Dominic. Calling Hayden had been a bad idea. Now he would freak out and have questions she wouldn't want to answer.

The most important question was already reverberating through her thoughts: How did Dominic know? "Actually, Hayden. Sorry. Ignore me. Everything will be fine. If it's him," she said, knowing damn well it was Dominic, "I'll figure out a plan and let you, Dad, and Mari know. Bye."

Hayden wouldn't ignore her.

Damn it. Why hadn't she thought her next move through before calling him? Oh, yeah. Because her brain short-circuited when Dominic was involved. She had places to go; friends who had helped her in the past and would again. All she had to do was get there without being seen.

Chapter Two

Callum stepped into Vivian Maddox's office in the Victorian mansion of polished wood panels and stained glass that Titan Protectors, the new personal security division of Titan Group, had converted into their headquarters. He didn't know why he'd been called into a meeting when no one else, except for their lead tech analyst, was on site.

A few months new to this team, he hadn't been there before when it was so quiet. With its soaring ceilings and oversized solid wood doors, the place felt more like a gothic horror movie set than anywhere he'd worked while in the Army. Those days were gone. He'd been burned and didn't want to look back.

A slight perfume hung in the cold office air. The woman behind the fancy desk, with long red nails and bright lipstick, watched him with a stillness that set his instincts on edge.

"Hey, Boss."

Her eyes narrowed. "Hale."

He'd returned from an assignment late the night before and hadn't had a good night's sleep in his crappy apartment. Exhaustion gnawed despite the coffee he'd slugged back after he read the message to report in immediately.

Vivian tapped her fingers three times. Something else was amiss.

Callum sat across from her, not liking the scrutiny. "What's going on, Viv?"

"How's the transition back to civilian life?"

Meaning, had he gotten over the backstabbing shitstorm that had fucked his world? No. But in an effort to act casual, he crossed his arms, leaned back, and raised his shoulders. "Yeah. Sure."

She snorted. "I bet."

Viv double-clicked her computer awake. After a few keystrokes, the flat-screen wall display lit up with their assignment portal. "I have a job for you."

What kind of assignment came when most of his colleagues were out of the office? A foreboding hummed in the air.

She continued to click through their database until her cursor blinked over the assignment file. Then she waited, finger hovering over her mouse, and eyed him one more time. "I have a special request for you, and I need to make sure you're okay with it before you take the job."

His eyebrows arched. "Me? Yeah. Fine. I'll let you know if I can't pull off a gig."

Though he couldn't think of a single assignment that might come across her desk that he couldn't handle, unless it was something technical like comms interception or interpretation. She wouldn't give him that, though, and no one would ask for him by name. Callum understood his role. He was strategic muscle and tactical ops. Not intel analysis.

The screen lit up with the photograph of a woman he hadn't seen in years, and his heart stopped. "Grace Willoughby."

"Grace Willoughby," Vivian confirmed. "What do you know about her?"

Everything. Callum had spent the better part of his life pretending he hadn't fallen for his best friend's younger sister. Grace was as off-limits as a woman could get for two reasons.

The first was simple and deemed her completely and entirely untouchable: bro code. That unspoken rule that had sealed his mouth shut and glued his hands by his sides had seemed like the most important rule of his twenties.

The second reason was the one that had shown him how stupid his first rule had been. Grace was dead. Losing her shattered him and fundamentally remade him into a different person.

"She died about five years ago during her ex-husband's trial." His throat dried. Anything else he might say simply vanished.

Unless he stepped into the Willoughbys' house, Callum never saw any pictures of her. The photograph on the screen wasn't the way he remembered her. That Grace with vacant eyes and photo-shoot-ready makeup was the woman who had married a very wealthy, criminal-as-fuck piece of shit. His Grace was bold with a smile that could power a nuclear generator.

Once, he thought he hated Grace. She had married Dominic Marino and had transformed into something unfamiliar, with fake long lashes and rouged cheeks that served as a billboard for the man she'd married. Then Callum realized he hated himself for not taking a chance.

Once Hayden told him she'd filed for divorce, a spring of possibilities surfaced in his mind—only for her to die in a fire. They rarely spoke of her again, and Hayden and their parents acted as if mentioning Grace would unearth a pain that their family couldn't process.

The world sucked.

It took more and more and more, and whenever Callum thought it had taken all that it could, it took again. He cleared his throat and could not fathom why Grace's photo was on Vivian's screen. "What's going on?"

"To be totally honest, a lot."

"If there was a problem with her family, her brother would have reached out to me." He jerked back. "Something happened to Hayden?"

"He's fine, and he did."

"What? No." But Callum hadn't had his personal phone on him while on assignment and had dropped into bed the moment he returned home. The ringer was likely off, and he didn't bother to check his personal phone that morning. "Viv, what the hell is going on?"

"Hayden contacted Titan Group—Jared Westin—" she gave him a sharp look, "when he couldn't get you."

Jared Westin owned Titan Group and was the tip-top tier of the Titan hierarchy. Dread settled on his shoulders. "Why?"

She tapped her red nails against the polished wood three times, as if carefully constructing what she might say next. "Hayden connected with Jared, Jared with me. I have already spoken with Dean, and now you and I are talking."

His heartbeat thumped in his ears.

"This has been like a complicated game of telephone, and what I'm about to tell you will hurt."

"*Vivian.* What?"

"Grace Willoughby was supposed to be in witness protection. She was asked to testify against Marino."

The news hit him like a lead pipe. Grace had filed for divorce after Marino had been arrested. Marino's trial had been in the news and prosecutors never seemed to lack witnesses, even as some backed out for fear of retribution. Dominic Marino was nothing if not a wealthy narcissist who never thought he would be prosecuted. The so-called Crypto King didn't bother to hide his tracks.

"She's in witness protection?" Callum asked, unsteady as possibilities he couldn't fathom raced in his head.

"No." Vivian clasped her hands and rested them on her desk. The uncertain cloud still hung over her expression but was tinged with concern. "She was supposed to testify. Another witness died—they were murdered, if we're being blunt—and she called it off. She was scared. Scared of testifying. Scared of living as Marino's ex-wife. *Scared.* Grace slipped from contact with the federal marshals and vanished. Then there was the fire."

None of this made sense. He blinked, as though he might be able to refocus the conversation. "What are you telling me? Is she alive?"

"Hale—*Callum*, look, she's not dead. And she's in trouble. She needs help."

His thoughts turned to putty. Pain squeezed the back of his throat, and he could hear his heartbeat thundering behind his sternum. "I don't understand."

Vivian pressed her lips together and waited until he steadied his breathing. She met his gaze. "Her dad, stepmom, and Hayden have always known she's alive."

His confusion about Grace faltered as the situation reorganized in his head. Hayden called. Hayden knew. Callum couldn't form words, and Vivian grimaced as though understanding the profound betrayal.

"I understand you are close to the family."

His pulse picked up. His body tensed. He would take a swing at Hayden if the man walked into the room. Callum pushed out of his chair and paced the space in front of Vivian's desk. He replayed every conversation. Every emotion. Every lie Hayden had told him. Callum wanted to beat his fist against his chest to lessen the pain filling his lungs.

Instead, he ran a hand over his face. "Yeah. Thought I was."

Vivian waited until he stopped pacing. He stopped behind a chair and gripped its back until he might rip through the fabric. She waited until he remembered to breathe and let go of the chair. "You want some water?"

Callum shook his head and collapsed into the chair again. "I'm good."

"Hayden wanted to talk to you himself, but you know how it goes. He's off the grid and has a time-sensitive problem that couldn't wait for him to talk to you about it."

"What is the damn problem?"

"Hayden received a voicemail from Grace."

"She's alive and leaving voicemails. Got it."

"Rein it in, Hale. Now."

His molars ground. "I'm calm."

"Yeah, clearly." She let out a breath, shoulders dropping. "It's fucked. I agree. But that's the situation, and you've got to pull it together."

Callum ran a hand over the back of his neck. His heartbeat still raced. "All right. *Grace* left a voicemail. What'd it say?"

"She saw her ex-husband."

"He's out of prison?" Callum calculated how long it had been. "That's not right."

"Seems as though a few federal witnesses recanted their testimony, and poof!" Vivian lifted her fist and splayed her fingers. "An appeals court had no choice but to release him."

"Then they should find new witnesses."

"Double jeopardy? I don't know. Maybe they are. But I'm not an attorney, and that's not the point."

The point, the point... "A dead woman sees her recently released ex-husband who she's been hiding from."

"Yeah."

Grace was alive, and her nightmare of an ex-husband was also aware. "Even if Marino is out of prison and knows Grace is alive, that doesn't constitute a call to Titan Group." He lifted his shoulders. "What else?"

"No one can find her."

"She lives in hiding. Of course no one can find her." He lifted his eyebrows. "She went into hiding to keep from Marino once before. She probably did it again."

He still couldn't wrap his head around the situation. In what world did Grace pretend to die instead of facing the problem head-on? And, hell, in what world did Hayden agree to go along with the story? He pinched the bridge of his nose.

"What else do you know about her ex-husband? First impressions. Last impressions. What are your thoughts?"

He forced in a long breath and held it for a five-count. "At first glance, I thought he was a dick. But we didn't realize how bad it was until after the FBI raided Marino's houses and offices and led him away in handcuffs." He dropped his head back and stared at the ceiling. What to say when he couldn't substantiate anything beyond gossip and conjecture? "He probably abused her."

"From the redacted divorce documents..." Vivian nodded.

"Hayden and I knew some details from their stepmom, but not enough. How long has he been out of prison?"

"A few months."

His eyebrows hit his hairline. "That's all it took to find Grace."

"The last known sighting of her was in Maryland more than a week ago at a small-town grocery store, where she asked the store manager to let her out the delivery entrance."

"Hayden knew that?"

"No, her voicemail was only about her ex-husband. Her family has not been able to reach her since."

"How do the grocery store and the voicemail connect?"

Vivian waffled her hand. "That's what Dean is working on. A day after the grocery store incident, the manager reported the abandoned car and interaction with the woman to local police. The car was registered to an untraceable shell company. That might or might not be Grace, but the car was also tied to a nearby cabin where a woman paid upfront in cash for a few months. The name on the contract doesn't match Grace Willoughby, but the description from the grocery store manager vaguely does."

"What about CCTV footage?"

She shook her head. "No security cameras. This was a small place in a tiny town."

"But the manager's description matched?"

"To that?" She gestured to the picture on the screen. "No. About the right height. Hair in a ponytail. But no makeup. Quiet voice. Nervous eyes."

"Quiet with nervous eyes doesn't sound like Grace."

"A lot can happen to steal someone's sparkle."

He swallowed hard. His disbelief was gone, and he wasn't ready to deal with the implications of his closest friend lying, but he couldn't stomach a nervous, quiet Grace. "What else?"

"I had hoped to have something for you pretty quickly from Dean, but Grace knows how to cover her tracks. Hayden provided her aliases, phone number, and emails. Despite all the money she apparently still has access to, she works as a freelance calligrapher and illustrator."

Dean, their resident former NSA-analyst, could find anyone's electronic trail no matter how well they had tried to hide their digital breadcrumbs. That he'd come up with nothing was strange.

"I reached out to Marino's lawyers this morning. They swear up and down that he hasn't left New York."

"What's the assignment? She might be hiding from her ex, but she's not going to resurface in her old life just because he found her. She could get in trouble for faking her death." He worked over the angles. "Skipping out on the marshals, not testifying if she'd been compelled to by subpoena. There are possible tax issues…"

"Hayden wants you to set eyes on her. He wants to know what the hell is going on, and why the family can't reach her, and he wants you to do it while keeping a low profile."

"I bet."

"Says he would do it himself if he could…"

"But he can't." Callum knew the life Hayden lived. It had been his life only a few months ago.

"This will probably be simple. She probably checked into a hotel and is watching trashy movies and bingeing on room service. That's what I'd do if a nightmare ex showed up to scare me."

"No, it's not. You'd kick his ass."

Vivian smiled and shrugged. "I might do both."

"Okay, this is a stupid question, but since we have her contact information, what if I call her until she answers? Hell, I could leave a voicemail. 'Hey, I know you're alive. You're scaring your family. Let's meet up.' No matter what she's gone through, I don't think she wants to scare them."

"Be my guest." Vivian frowned. She clicked her mouse, and the screen turned dark. "Something's going on. If it looks like shit, and it smells like shit, it's going to be a big pile of shit."

"Yeah."

"Give Dean another day to hunt down leads and send you the file. Then, after you find Grace and figure out the situation with the ex-husband, we can decide our next move."

Callum pushed out of his chair. "I'd be good with stringing Dominic Marino up by his balls. Then again, that's always been my attitude toward him."

Vivian snickered but held up her hand. "One more thing. If the ex is a current threat, this might turn into a protection detail until he's handled. You good with that?" She narrowed her eyes. "Anything I need to know about your past with Grace?"

There had been a time her smile would bring him to his knees. She would laugh, and he'd want to get closer. Good thing Callum had a hell of a poker face. He lifted his hands with a shrug. "I literally thought she was dead."

"That doesn't matter if there was a past between you two."

Memories flashed through his mind. The time he and Hayden ignored her when the three of them played tag in the dark. A few years later, when she was a freshman in high school, they'd watched out for her as high-and-mighty seniors. Callum recalled the way she watched him with those beautiful brown eyes at his and Hayden's Army Ranger graduation. And the time Callum watched her drive away in Marino's fancy-ass car, knowing he should have said or done something the first time he met the prick. "There's not."

"You sure, Hale?"

"Absolutely nothing. She's always just been the girl next door. Come on, Viv, don't look at me like that. I just thought she was dead. Cut me a little slack."

Chapter Three

Callum closed his apartment door with a dull thud. His bootsteps echoed, reminding him of how alone he was in Granite Creek. The floor creaked under his feet, making the space feel that much emptier.

Grace was alive.

Grace was in trouble.

The truth looped through his head. He and Hayden needed to speak. Callum had tried, but every call went straight to voicemail. Likely out of pocket with his former teammates. He could call their parents, but what would he say? Nothing that would help the situation.

He crossed the apartment in a few strides. The empty space was all the reminder he needed that he was Titan's new guy without roots. The air conditioning kicked on to fight the August heat and break the overwhelming silence in his apartment.

He didn't like the quiet. It reminded him of everything that was missing. No chatter from the guys he'd risked his life with for years, no clatter of weapons being broken down and cleaned, no smell of chow that was half-plastic and half-edible. Just the faint hum of cool air blowing, the small fridge purring, and the occasional groan of old floorboards beneath his boots.

He dropped onto the couch that had come with the apartment. The furnishings were cheap and foam and inconsequential. The generic brown couch and chair matched the uninspiring four blank walls, which at one point had been a neutral beige. After years of wear and tear, the walls were more like a collage of scuffs and fingerprints.

His basic one-bedroom came with a monthly lease. No commitment to go with his lack of personal details. No pictures, no mementos. Just furniture he hadn't cared enough to replace when the landlord offered the basics.

He didn't have to live in this shoebox of an apartment. When he first arrived, Vivian had promised him housing to complement the hefty paycheck until he found a place that he wanted to call home. He ignored the offer, not knowing why, and chose this place instead. It wasn't a shithole, but it wasn't far off.

Callum's head ached. He should throw a party. Grace was alive. But he hadn't arrived at the point of celebrating yet.

Why in the hell hadn't Hayden looped him in? The anger and betrayal flared again. He wanted to get in Hayden's face and, if he saw Grace—*when he saw Grace*, he would… Would do what? Fuck, he didn't know. Demand answers. Shake her until she apologized. He'd said goodbye. She was just gone.

Except she wasn't.

Callum pinched his eyes closed. Not that long ago, he'd messed up enough for the Army to unceremoniously boot his ass to the curb. Vivian offered him a job when plenty of others wouldn't touch him. Even if he didn't think he had done anything wrong, Titan was Callum's second chance.

Maybe he deserved it. Maybe he didn't. That largely depended on who was asked.

Did Grace deserve a second chance?

Of course.

At least, probably.

He couldn't compare their second chances, though. His was simple: an order ignored. He'd do it again—no hesitation—even if the memory still haunted him. Wrong on paper. Right in every way that mattered. The kind of thing that branded him a liability.

Callum leaned back and stared at the ceiling. White paint of varying shades was patched over stains and scuffs. No matter where he went, he always looked at the damn ceiling like it could tell him a secret.

What did this place say? Nothing he wanted to admit.

He exhaled hard. The sound bounced back off the bare walls.

Tomorrow, he would find Grace. Save Grace. Be whatever Grace needed. That, at least, he understood. Protecting others was in his bones. The rest—figuring out if he belonged anywhere outside a battlefield—he'd learn on the fly.

The next morning Callum woke with a better attitude and a refreshed sense of the world. The drab apartment and his new job didn't bother him as much. Sleep was a miracle drug. He needed to remember that anytime sleep deprivation came calling.

He planned to check in with headquarters first thing for an update, but Dean beat him to it with a plan of action and a location pinpointed in Maryland.

According to Dean's research, the library was an hour's drive from the grocery store where she'd last been seen. Seemed promising. He scrolled through the report. Devices that Dean believed were associated with Grace had logged hours using the library's Wi-Fi. She had used the library's internet to communicate and submit work on a freelancer website.

He checked the drive time. The location in Maryland wasn't close. He'd get there in a few hours.

Callum packed his go bag with fresh clothes and work essentials and searched his sparsely filled kitchen. Pretzels and beef jerky would have to do for breakfast on the road.

The bright summer sun reflected off the interstate. Traffic was surprisingly light, and he made good time. Callum spotted the public library on a semi-busy main drag lined with mature trees and pulled into the large parking lot.

Grace might be in there.

He thought about the photo he'd found the night before after spending far too much time scrolling through his personal phone's album. The picture was from the summer he and Hayden had graduated from West Point. She had just finished her first year of college, and the way she looked at him had Callum crawling out of his skin. There was not a single quiet or nervous bone in her body, and she'd given Callum and Hayden hell for simply existing.

They were too loud. Too cocky. Too muscle-headed. Too much of everything.

Her mouth had been running a mile a minute, but he had heard little of what she'd said because he'd been staring like a moron. Grace had told him to take a picture if he was going to stare. Hayden had snorted, missing Callum's reaction to her, and Callum had said, "Fuck it," and taken the picture.

He'd probably looked at that picture a thousand times later that night. But he had been by himself. To the world, he hadn't betrayed a single thought about Grace. It had taken all his self-control, but that's what West Point had trained him to do. Control everything.

Maybe that was why he had no more pictures of only Grace since that day.

Control everything, and everything would be controlled.

Except this was as far out of control as he could imagine. He needed to find that focus again. He had a job to do: locate Grace.

The early afternoon sun beat down. Heat radiated in wavy lines at the far corner of the parking lot as he rolled over a speed bump. Why did Grace spend so much time at this library? Given how she could hide her tracks, she was more than capable of setting up a VPN and using the internet from anywhere.

Callum mentally ran through Dean's report again. Her online footprint was negligible for a woman whose livelihood depended on the internet. She had evaded them all.

He eased off the gas and waved across a woman dragging a red wagon in one hand and a wriggling kid in the other, then parked in a shaded spot where he could see everything: the entry to the lot and the library and every minivan fighting for the spot nearest the entrance. The whole scene served as another reminder that this wasn't his usual assignment.

Then again, he hadn't worked here long enough to have a usual assignment.

He called the control room at headquarters.

Dean picked up on the first ring. "You there already?"

"Yeah. Learn anything else that might help?"

"Grace was surprisingly good at staying out of sight. I've been sifting through her previous clients and found a nearby residential address where she sometimes transmitted work from. The homeowner works at the library."

"That sounds like more than a coincidence." Callum rubbed his chin. "So we're moving in the right direction."

"Affirmative, though we can't find a connection between her and the owner, a woman named Alicia Jackson. But here's the kicker: other than time at the library and at this woman's house, we don't have a single connection between Grace and this area. No lease. No bills. Not even a gas station fill-up." Dean grumbled. "I called the library to confirm Alicia's employment, but whoever answered the phone was unsure."

"This place doesn't look that big. You'd know your coworkers."

"That's what I thought, too. Let me know if you get anything."

"Roger that." Callum ended the call and headed inside.

The double doors whooshed open and wrapped him inside with a cold burst of air. Bright signs directed him to the children's section, periodicals, and the circulation desk in front of the adult section. There was more noise than he had expected, though he hadn't been in a library for longer than he wanted to admit.

His casual clothes hid his purpose, but he couldn't help but feel out of place. Callum bypassed a teenager with a volunteer badge at the returns desk and headed toward the computer stations, which occupied two large tables. He swept the terminals for Grace.

Most stations were in use. Lady Luck would have been on his side if Grace had been sitting at one of the computers. But no, that would have been far too easy. He eyed the study desks that lined the walls. Again, no Grace, and wandering through the small space, he stopped at the circulation desk.

The librarian, a tall woman with umber skin and loose coiled hair, offered a welcoming smile as she nudged her glasses up her nose. "Can I help you?"

"I'm looking for a friend." Callum pulled up Grace's picture on his phone. "Have you seen her in the last few days?"

Her smile faltered. "No, I'm sorry."

"Are you sure? It's important."

Her lips pursed as she pointedly looked *him*—not the picture—over. "I haven't seen her. Anything else I can help you with?"

His gaze narrowed on her. Callum tried to get a read. Protective? Cautious? No, something more. Perhaps worried. This was a woman who was protecting another woman, or maybe even a friend watching out for a friend. "You sure?"

She squared her shoulders. "*Positive.*"

"Her name is Grace Willoughby. Maybe you've heard of her?"

"Never."

"She sometimes uses other names." He lifted Grace's picture again, only to be ignored. Callum double-checked the woman for a name tag and found none. "Do you know someone who works here named Alicia Jackson?"

Her eyebrows arched. "She works here?"

This wasn't working. Callum ran his hand through his hair. Schmoozing people wasn't his forte. He should have partnered with someone else on his team for this. Viv could've sent Wes Wilder, the charmer, or even Eli Landry, who was laid back unless someone looked too closely. Callum's patience didn't lend itself to the softness that was required to pull information out of people. "Like I said, it's important."

"Are you the police?"

"No. I swear." He smiled, but that did nothing except add a hint of mistrust in her eyes.

"Either way." She shrugged. "I haven't seen her."

"She might be in trouble."

"You don't say?" Saccharine disregard dripped off her words. "That's a pity. Still haven't seen her, but I'd be willing to take down your name and number if she comes in. I'll pass it along. What's your name?"

He pushed a hand into his hair and tried a different angle. "Let me ask you another question."

"I guess that means no to *your name*? But by all means, what else can I help you with?"

"How many people have come in here looking for her?"

"Just you."

"Would you tell me the truth?"

"Don't see why not."

No, Callum definitely wasn't the best person to send to the library, and forget Wes or Eli. Vivian should have sent their social media maven. Scarlett Wu had a magical effect on people, whether in person or online. This librarian would love Scar. Everybody did.

Callum rocked back on his heels and thought about why Grace would come here again. She could have used the internet anywhere. But she'd come back to this library. Maybe the community was safe and anonymous. Maybe she'd made a personal connection. "Fair enough. If you haven't seen her, you haven't seen her."

"Like I said—"

"But if you have seen her, and you're keeping your mouth shut because you think she's in danger..." He tilted his head. "Good on you."

The librarian kept her expression blank, a stone-cold alibi. He liked that for Grace, even if it made his job that much harder.

"Grace called her brother for help. Said she was in trouble." He studied the woman's face for anything. Still, nothing. "Her brother's deployed. We served together, and he asked me to find her." The blank stare didn't change. "All I want to do is check on her. Just let her brother know all is well." Callum rolled his lips together and tried one last time. "Are you sure you haven't seen her?"

"If I had, and I'm not saying I have—" Her gaze skittered behind him. "I, uh—would—uh, could I see that picture again?" She concentrated on him as if every ounce of her being wanted to look over his shoulder.

Callum turned. His breath caught. Her back was turned to him, but he had no doubt that was the woman he'd known most of his life. With wavy honey-brown hair tied into a messy bun and a cute ass clad in yoga pants, Grace was rushing from him toward the front doors of the library as though someone had entered her into the speedwalking Olympics. "Grace!"

Chapter Four

Someone hissed at Callum to lower his voice.

"Sir," the librarian called. "Wait!"

He ignored her and followed Grace, hot on her tail. Something hit the back of his shoulder. A pen hit the floor. Then a pencil. "What the—" He looked over his shoulder and sidestepped a flying magazine. "Jesus Christ, lady. I'm the good guy."

She launched a paperback at him. "Leave her alone."

"I'm here to help." Callum pivoted, but Grace was gone.

"Wait!"

He ignored the librarian's call to stop and hustled into the parking lot. No Grace. He called her name. She was so damn close but slipping farther away. His heart hammered. He couldn't screw this up for Hayden. Not to mention, she was clearly on the run. More was wrong than they knew. Callum could fix whatever she was hiding from. She just had to give him a chance.

Think. She ditched her car a week ago. Nobody stood at the bus stop. Maybe she had another car. Hell, maybe she had Alicia Jackson's car. Clearly, she had roots here that hadn't turned up on Dean's cyber analysis.

Callum scanned the parking lot and came up empty. All right. She wasn't *that* fast. Especially not on this sweltering day. There weren't any vehicles speeding from the parking lot. She was still there. Somewhere.

"Your brother sent me," he called to the empty sidewalk. "Grace?"

She didn't magically appear.

A man with an armful of books walked out of the library and gave Callum a wide berth.

Callum itemized his surroundings: a bus stop, a pollinator garden, a shaded cluster of benches, and a path that disappeared around the side of the building. He rushed in that direction.

Hayden wouldn't like how he was handling this, but hell, Callum didn't either. He rounded the corner of the building. The summer heat baked him as if Satan had left the oven door open.

Liquid sprayed over his face.

Fuck.

Pain brought him to his knees. The sharp, spicy chemical seared his eyes and nose. The white-hot agony was nearly paralyzing. "Son of a—" Hands on his face, Callum folded over.

"Leave me alone!" she cried.

"Grace." Damn it. He couldn't see. He choked on tears and snot and fuckin' pepper spray. "Hayden—" Adrenaline coursed through his body. Every nerve in his head screamed for action. Run. Water. Anything to stop the searing burn. "—sent me."

Callum couldn't see if she'd sprinted away or watched him keel over. Fire licked his burning lungs. His throat screamed. The overpowering urge to rub his face and eyes was too much. He'd been trained for this. The intense pain would stop, but maybe not before he could see again. He tore off his shirt and pressed it to his face, praying for a reprieve. Hell, the shirt probably had pepper spray on it, too.

He forced himself up and backed until he hit the building. He peeled the shirt from his eyes and tried to get his bearings. Then he saw Grace through his blurry, crying eyes as she backed away. The sunshine intensified the burn and his tears. Callum re-covered his face.

"*Hayden* sent you?"

Mopping his eyes, he battled the burn and labored through each fiery breath. He nodded and should have identified himself but couldn't. Hell, he needed to string words together to say something, anything, but the effects of this fucking spray had him brain-dead. Not to mention, that was Grace. *Alive.* It blew his mind to see her, even as it aggravated him to no end that she'd maced him.

"Why did he send you?"

"Why the fuck do you think?" He wiped his nose and rapidly blinked as he lifted his gaze. She hadn't run. That was about the first good news he'd had since Viv sent him chasing shadows. "I need to..." Fuck. His face hurt. "You gonna run if I go wash my face?"

"I...uh, I don't know. Maybe."

Callum snorted and immediately regretted breathing through his nostrils. Did he have to talk to her? The assignment had been to set eyes on her. He'd set eyes on her. Sorta. And could report that Grace Willoughby and her can of pepper spray were doing just fine.

He peered back in the direction he'd come from. If he walked into the library, the pen-throwing librarian would call the cops. That wasn't what either he or Grace needed.

Grace inched closer. "How do you know Hayden?"

"Fuckin' hell, Grace." He pulled the shirt away from his face. "Look at me."

"I *am* looking, asshole—Oh God. Callum?"

He grunted. The years sharing a backyard fence should have left her with a few memories of him, even if he was currently red-faced, choking on snot, and blind. He covered his face with the shirt again but found no relief.

She rushed to his side. "I didn't know it was you. I'm so sorry. God." Her hand rested on his shoulder. "What are you doing here?"

He pulled the shirt away again and narrowed his irritated eyes. "What the hell do you think I'm doing? Trying to help."

She touched his elbow but backed up as if he were a powder keg that the peppery spray had just primed. "Cal, come with me. I can help. I'm so sorry. I didn't know it was you. Just come with me."

"Where?"

"To the bathroom."

Callum snorted again. Again, that was another massive mistake. His nasal passage throbbed as if he'd been snorting lines of dried habaneros. At least the pain was dulling, or he was growing immune to it. The cyclical nightmare of breathing and blinking wasn't as bad as it had been. That didn't change how badly he needed to wash his face. "The librarian threw office supplies at me. I'm not welcome."

"It'll be fine." She walked backward, as if she didn't trust *him* not to run away. Grace gestured with large movements. "This way."

"I can see." *More or less.* The pain had somewhat dulled from white-hot agony to a general, all-consuming fire, enough that he could semi-function.

They returned to the library's main entrance. He couldn't stop the tears or blinking, and with his chin tucked to his bare chest, he followed her inside.

The cold blast of air conditioning rolled over his sweating shoulders, reigniting the burn on his face. His muscles twitched and shivered.

"This way." They turned into the hallway off the main entrance. "The bathrooms are over here." Grace lifted her hand to the door in front of the men's restroom like a very quiet tour guide who hadn't just brought him to a standstill with a bottle of pepper spray. "Here you go."

He itched to rush inside and let cool water rush over his face, but wanted to keep an eye—more or less—on her until they were able to talk. She was in a predicament that he could quickly fix. If only she would give him a chance. "You gonna run off again?"

"No," she admitted in a rough whisper.

He didn't trust her quiet lilt. She was a runner and far better at hiding than expected. "You're going to stay put. Right here? Right outside this door?"

"Yes."

Still, she didn't meet his eyes. He scrutinized her as best he could. The longer he studied her, the more she avoided eye contact. That could mean deception. Then again, his red, swollen eyes and irritated face probably weren't offering much comfort.

Callum backed against the door to the men's room without entering. "I'll be back in three minutes or less."

She studied the posters on the wall above the water fountain. "I'll be here."

He didn't trust her but needed to wash his face. After one last look, he stepped inside.

The bathroom sinks had spigots with barely enough room to stick his face under the stream. He managed and let the cool water run over his skin until his eyes didn't weep continuously.

His shirt had seen better days. It was gross enough to scare Grace away if he tugged it back on. Good thing for the change of clothes in the truck.

"Better?" she asked when he emerged.

Callum nodded. "Much."

The librarian stood a few feet behind her like a bodyguard. He held up his hands in a show of good faith. Clearly, she knew Grace well enough to mama bear her, though Callum suspected she would throw office supplies at any man asking for a woman that set off her internal worry meter.

"Much?" The librarian stepped closer to Grace. "Then you must have been pretty bad to start with."

"She got me good."

The woman continued to assess him. "Must have, because you look a hundred times worse than when you strutted up to my desk."

"I don't think I strutted, but..."

Grace quietly snorted.

"I want to grab a change of clothes. Then can we talk?"

The librarian crossed her arms and lifted her chin, not hiding her glare. "Are you sure this is your old neighbor?"

"It's him." Grace twisted her fingers together. "Callum is my older brother's best friend."

"I knew Grace for as far back as I can remember," he added, wanting to lessen the librarian's dislike for him. He wasn't a people pleaser, but this lady was the ticket to Grace's trust.

"Grace says you serve in the military with her brother?" the woman asked.

"We did." Callum pressed his molars together. The how and why they didn't anymore wasn't up for discussion. "I work for a private company now. I'm based out of Virginia."

"I did my undergraduate at the University of Virginia." She extended her hand and shook like she meant to impart her willingness to go to the mat for Grace. "Alicia Jackson."

Alicia Jackson. He gritted his teeth but managed, "Nice to meet you."

She offered a slight shrug, brushing off their initial meeting when she laid no claim to her name.

"Good school," he offered like a peace branch.

"Great school," she corrected, stubbing out his goodwill as if she'd tossed a cigarette to the ground and smashed it under her shoe. "We'll stay here. You get your clothes, and then we can sit down in a study room. Are you okay with that, Grace?"

Grace nodded.

The women entered the library. Callum made a quick run to his truck and changed clothes. A minute later, he spotted Grace in a small study room. Its glass wall had the privacy shades drawn back, offering a direct line to the circulation desk. Alicia saw him and moved in like a heat-seeking missile until she blocked the door.

"You going to let me in?" he asked.

Almost as tall as him but slight and slender, she placed her hands on her hips like a force to be reckoned with. "Are you going to do something to hurt or scare her?"

Again, he tried to appreciate Alicia's protective role and didn't want to spook either woman. "Hadn't planned on it."

"If you do, it will be something a lot heavier and sharper than a pen or magazine that hits the back of your head."

He held up his hand like a scout. "Honest, Alicia. I'm here to help."

She pushed back her glasses and scrutinized him in a way that would make most people wilt. Finally, Alicia inched aside. "Then good. She could use more help than she'll ever ask for."

That struck a nerve. She had money for security and a family she could trust. What didn't he know? "I'll do my best."

Chapter Five

Callum walked into the tiny room and took in the pale woman he believed to have died in a fire. Part of him hurt, but most of him wanted to pull her into his arms and rejoice. But they were far from there. She reminded him of a scared, caged animal all too familiar with the ways she could be abused. "I'm not going to hurt you."

"I know that." She rolled her eyes but didn't look at him.

Now that the painful effect of the pepper spray had mostly diminished, and with his eyesight back to normal, he could get a look at the woman he hadn't seen in years. She didn't resemble the picture Vivian had shown him. Without makeup, she wore a thin-strapped tank top and yoga pants. Braided and beaded bracelets were stacked on her wrists. Her honey-brown highlights looked more sun-kissed than salon-placed. She was prettier than he recalled, even if there was a hesitant cloud of worry hanging over her.

"Can I sit down?"

"Of course." Grace cracked the top open on a bottle of water and sipped. "You don't have to treat me like a lost child."

"I'm not. I—uh, Grace, I thought you were dead. I don't know how I'm treating you. Carefully, I guess."

"You don't have to."

"Honey, you faked your death. So..." Maybe he was treating her like a lost child because she looked like a scared, lost puppy. He hated that his mind went back to the hurt animal analogy, but her evasive eye contact and hard voice were too much like a fearful dog that growled when offered help. "I'm trying here."

She rolled the water bottle between her hands and wouldn't make eye contact. "I should explain, but I need time to think about how to say it." Her gaze skittered to his face and shot away again. "It's complicated. You said you're not in the Army anymore?"

"I'm not." Callum pulled out the chair across the table from her and eased in. He leaned back and tried to give her space, tried to give her as many reasons to trust him as possible. They'd known each other for a long time, but that didn't mean shit when he only had the barest details on what had happened to her in the years since she "died" and Marino had been imprisoned.

"Are you mad at me?" she asked quietly.

Furious. "I'm figuring it out."

"That's fair." The water bottle crinkled as she toyed with it. "Don't be mad at Hayden. He had little choice."

"Everyone has a choice."

Her half-laugh rang sad and lonely. He thought she was about to defend her brother, but the silence ticked by.

"I'm sorry I didn't recognize you." She pushed the water bottle away but immediately toyed with the beads of her bracelet, as if she had to fidget.

"It was probably hard with my face full of pepper spray."

She cringed. "I'm sorry. I thought you were...I wasn't trying to hide from you."

"From me. But you are hiding."

"I'm supposed to be dead."

"That's not the reason you're hiding."

Her fingers picked up the pace as she worried over the bracelets. "You look different. Bigger than the last time I saw you."

Years of working special forces assignments would do that.

She opened the bottle of water and took a slow sip, as if she were using the drink to collect her thoughts. Grace was wary of him. Of that much, he was sure. Her eyes darted around the room, on him and off him again, and she rolled the bottle between her hands again. Nervous tics and fidgeting. He couldn't recall her ever doing that.

"Can I ask you a question?" she said.

"Sure. Shoot."

"I get that Hayden sent you, but how did you find me?"

Callum pushed the chair onto its back legs and threaded his hand through his hair. An NSA-like dragnet wasn't likely to comfort her. Saying too little would add to her distrust.

The plastic bottle crinkled in her hands. "It shouldn't take you so long to answer."

"It's not that," he said. "Just trying to figure out how to explain it."

"The problem is, if you can find me, my ex-husband can find me again as well."

"Not likely." She didn't have to live this way. Divorcing Dominic Marino would have set her up financially. She could easily have put security measures in place. If she didn't want to testify, she could have employed lawyers who would have been able to help. There were so many options.

"Appease me, Cal."

A memory skipped over him. No one called him Cal except for Grace. He wasn't sure how he'd never noticed that before now.

Callum rolled his shoulders and focused on her question. "I was unavailable when Hayden tried to get ahold of me. He talked to my boss and basically said you needed help. That you disappeared from the grocery store—"

"I didn't disappear."

"I don't know what you want to call it." He tilted his head, sizing up her reaction. "Did you know the grocery store manager called the cops?"

She bit her lip. "I should have done things differently there." Grace fidgeted with her bracelets. "But I left a voicemail for Hayden saying that I was fine. I told him to ignore me. Now I'm telling you, I'm fine."

Worry shadowed her eyes. Tension tightened the corners of her pinched lips. She was in a defensive position, and he didn't even understand the threats. "I've gotta tell you, sweetheart. This doesn't look like the life of a woman who is fine."

Tears brimmed in her eyes until she rapidly blinked them back. "It was easier before Dominic got out of prison. Now? It doesn't matter." She shook her head. "Back to how you found me. Hayden called you, then what?"

Then the NSA-like dragnet. "You submitted a project to a client earlier this week. A business card design for a private chef, right?"

Her mouth parted in genuine surprise before the uncertainty in her eyes intensified. "How on earth would you know that?"

"That's what my company does. We specialize in personal protection and have the technology that allows us to keep our clients safe."

"I'm not your client." She didn't hold back but wouldn't quite meet his gaze.

"Hayden is."

"Hayden is being ridiculous."

"Look, Grace, why are you fighting me on this? Just tell me what the hell is going on. We'll get everything squared away. If you want to stay dead, then who am I to stop you? I don't know the situation, but there has to be a better way. You're causing the people you love stress, and the last thing Hayden needs is to be distracted over there. All right? Give me enough to fix this."

Her frown deepened. "I don't even know what fixing this would look like."

Faking one's death was a hard problem to overcome. It wasn't insurmountable, though.

The more pressing issue was Dominic. They needed to confirm that he had been at the grocery store, and only then would Callum know the full extent of the problems they had to handle. "I want to help you, but I need to know what that means. What the threats are. Where the problems are hiding. Whatever you're not telling me."

She rubbed her temples. "I don't know."

"Yeah, you do." His frustration was piling up. All Grace had to do was spit out the problems so he could fix them. None of this hiding or stressing about an ex-husband.

Callum rocked on the back legs of his chair. She probably needed him to be calm and patient, and those weren't his best qualities.

When she gave him nothing, he set all four chair legs on the ground and tried a more direct approach. "Why don't we start at the grocery store? You saw your ex-husband and then what?"

She turned the water bottle over and over in her hands before shaking her head. "I saw his car. Sleek black Mercedes sedan that looked like a million bucks sitting in the Shop 'n' Save parking lot. That car probably cost more than their inventory of fresh produce."

"You saw his license plate, or...?"

"I don't know his plate. Why would I know his plates?" Irritation edged into her voice. "I just know it was him. No, no, do not look at me like I'm an idiot."

He lifted his hands like a white flag, not wanting to lose the small amount of trust that he'd garnered. "It was him. Marino was in a black Mercedes sedan. Got it. It was him, and," his eyebrows arched, "you ran?"

Bottom lip between her teeth, she nodded. "Out the back door."

"Just like the police report said." She'd ditched her car in a quiet small town in Maryland and ended up in this library. He wanted to know how she got here. Alicia could have picked her up. She could have access to another surreptitiously registered car. Hell, Grace could have taken an Uber. "How'd you get here?"

"Alicia."

"Why'd you come here?"

"It's a safe place. Alicia has helped me on and off for years."

He could have been the one to help her. Why didn't Grace reach out to him? "Why does your ex want to see you?"

"You wouldn't understand."

"I can't if you don't talk to me. Maybe he wanted to set eyes on you, confirm that you were alive?" That would be top of his list if he had a hint that Grace had faked her death. "Maybe—"

"He didn't want to see me. He wants to take me."

That had his attention. "*Take you*?"

"Probably to New York City or Las Vegas."

"Has he been in contact with you?" Marino's lawyer had emphatically said no, but Callum trusted them as much as he trusted Marino.

Dean's report included a summary of their divorce proceedings. At the very least, Dominic had psychologically abused her. The details weren't explicit, but reading between the lines wasn't hard. There hadn't been a restraining order issued while Marino had been in prison. No need until now—though how could a legally dead person file a restraining order? They couldn't. "Has he threatened you?"

"No." She pressed her water bottle between her hands and focused on its cap. "You don't get it."

"I might if you give me a chance."

"You won't. *You can't*."

"Grace, try me."

"I already am. And you don't get it. I can see your face. You're not thinking about Dominic. You're trying to figure out why I did what I did, and how you could have fixed things and made everything better."

He snorted. "Sorta have me pegged there."

"Hayden was the same way." Her gaze flashed to his for a heartbeat. "Don't be mad at him for doing what I asked."

Callum wouldn't agree to that. "Then explain it to me like I'm a five-year-old."

Grace uncapped her water and stared at it for a long moment before taking a quick sip in that same way to buy time. Carefully, she recapped the bottle and studied the way the water swished against the sides as she turned it. She liked to hide her face behind it.

"This is going to take forever if you say nothing."

"Dominic wasn't a sicko who liked to hurt me. He doesn't *want* me the way a husband wants his wife. He's not in love. Not pining for me." She hazarded a quick glance up. "That's what you need to get. I am a *possession* he lost. And he wants me back. He doesn't care that I faked my death. If anything, I made this more fun."

Grace Willoughby was objectively a catch. Dominic Marino was objectively an asshole. He was also a charming, wealthy prick who could easily convince another beautiful woman into his bed, but the way Grace said "possession" made a chill go down Callum's spine.

She tipped her chin back and stared at the ceiling. A hopeless expression fell over her. She pinched her lips and refocused on the water bottle once more. "I've always known this would happen. I just thought I'd have a warning before he was released."

"What would happen?" Callum scrubbed a hand over his face when she didn't answer. His nerves were as raw and frayed as his skin still felt from the pepper spray. "Why do you use burner phones and a network of forwarded numbers?"

"How do you know about that?"

"Like I said, we've done a little bit of looking around. The phone number that your family calls has been forwarded to dozens of numbers over the years. Same with the numbers you give to clients."

She gnawed on her lip. "I didn't realize that was something you could tell."

"That's not an answer."

"I don't trust anyone but myself."

"And Alicia," he suggested, nodding to the window with a direct line to the librarian's desk.

"Well, yeah. I have a few close friends who have helped me keep a low profile over the years."

Jesus shit, why wasn't he on that list? "But not Hayden. You gave him the same information as your parents."

"I trust him, but there's only so much I can share with my overprotective brother, who's never around anyway. Besides, as you said, if I gave him more, he'd be distracted. Distracted puts him in danger."

She could have told him. It's all he could think about. But even if she had, Callum would have told Hayden, thus confirming Grace's worry about creating a distraction for her brother.

He studied her, nervous and avoidant, and wanted to press his luck by asking more technical questions, but it was enough that she was still sitting in this room, sharing her secrets. "You're doing all this to avoid Dominic? Is that the gist?"

She nodded. "Dominic's a gamesman. He needs the thrill of the chase—and *I* am the quarry."

"A possession." He repeated her stomach-turning word.

"Yeah. Part of his collection. It's all a game, and no matter what I did, who I hired, or where I lived, everyone and everything can be bought, turned, changed, or destroyed. His people reported to him while he was in prison. He still ran his company from behind bars. I couldn't just divorce him."

"Yes, you could."

She shook her head. "That's what you don't understand. I would never be free of him. I thought I had more time to figure out what to do when he was released, but now that he's out early…" Her words hung in the room like a blanket smothering out the oxygen. "If I stay still," she said quietly, "he can get to me. It's that simple. Do you know why he's out?"

"It has to do with the witness who recanted their testimony."

"Yes. Literally, a guy who testified and was hidden in witness protection changed his story. That proves my point. Dominic can get to anyone. He had to think I was as gone as gone could be."

A knot formed. Callum tried to swallow. "Well…" He cleared his throat. "Your family can't be bought. I can't be either."

"That just puts you in danger while everyone else is up for grabs. I did what I did for a reason."

A knock sounded on the door. Callum straightened. Alicia walked in, automatically glaring as if she wanted to throw him out with the trash. "My shift is up, and I'm taking Grace home."

Grace pushed her chair away from the table.

"Hold on. Hang on. Give me a—"

Alicia tossed her coiled hair over her shoulder and crossed her arms in the same manner as earlier. "Who knows you're here?"

"Her brother."

"Who else?" Alicia pressed.

He liked that Alicia went to bat for Grace and wouldn't relinquish the role of Grace's protector without a fight. Alicia was a headache, but a good problem to have. He'd figure out how to work with her later. For now, he had to keep their lines of communication flowing. "Why?"

"I would offer to let you come back with us," Alicia studied Grace, "if that's okay with you? We're still trusting him?"

"That's fine. We still trust him."

"Fine. You're still in the tightly held circle of trust." Alicia was laser-focused on Callum. "But I'm not letting you within a hundred miles of my place if Dominic's goon squad could follow or find you."

Callum pulled out his phone and rattled off the nearby address where Dean had tagged. "That you?"

"Well, fuck me," Alicia muttered. "I have pets that will eat you alive if you pull anything."

He almost smiled. Even if she didn't like him, Alicia had won him over.

Chapter Six

Grace could feel every beat of her heart the entire time Alicia drove toward home. Her friend peppered her with questions she didn't want to think about.

"Every time you shrug instead of answer," Alicia pulled onto her quiet street, "I'm inventing answers. It would be easier if you just spoke up."

"I don't have any answers."

"That would be a lot easier to believe if that man wasn't a sexy six-foot-something built like a mountain."

Her heartbeat thumped, thumped, thumped its agreement.

Alicia did a doubletake and cackled. "Some answers you don't have to say out loud, and that face, Grace, was an answer as loud and clear as you've ever given."

"Not true."

She laughed again and pulled into her driveway. Her beautiful home had been a refuge over the years. Now Grace ran to it for different reasons the second Alicia came to a stop.

"Running inside won't make him less—"

Grace shut the door before she heard the rest of what Alicia said, but her mind filled in the blank with "good-looking." Actually, now she was lying to herself. Calling him good-looking was like calling a hot fudge sundae with all the toppings a little treat. He'd always been the hero she'd imagined, and there he was. Good-looking to another level, even after she'd maced him.

And, God, she felt like a horrible person for noticing him like that when he had just learned she lied and was alive.

Grace didn't know what to do inside Alicia's house. She wanted to hide until she had total control over her reaction to him. A totally justifiable reaction. He'd ripped his shirt off after she'd maced him, and holy mother of muscles, Callum Hale was ripped.

Not in a 'roided up, scary way, but in that way a man could send shivers straight to a woman's nether regions simply by walking into a room. She hated how he had always done that to her. She hated even more that he'd never noticed that she thought he walked on water.

The biggest problem with Callum and his good looks and protective bossiness was that she had temporarily forgotten about Dominic. Her ex was always at the back of her mind, but she'd been living like this for years.

She hadn't seen Callum for just as long. The man could still block everything else from her mind.

Alicia followed Grace inside, laughing as though she could read her mind. "You can't run from a man like that."

"Just giving myself space." She kicked off her shoes and tucked herself into an accent chair, wishing to God she could shut herself in a freezer. "And obviously, I'm not running. I said he could come here."

Alicia hummed and pushed her glasses up her nose. "Uh-huh. Sure."

"Don't look at me like that." Grace wrapped her arms around her shins, glad to be in Alicia's charming house that was as sweet and comforting as a homemade pie. She hugged herself tighter and waited for the invisible security blanket that was this living room to cloak her from the world.

Alicia dismissed that with a "we'll see" look. "I'll make tea."

Late afternoon light flooded through the gauzy, draped windows. The living room's cottagecore décor soothed Grace's soul with its wallpaper that could have been in a dollhouse. Houseplants sat in every nook and cranny where books didn't take up residence.

There were so many books, and they always shifted and changed, as Alicia picked up and read whatever was within arm's reach. From the moment Alicia had opened her home, it was one of the safest places Grace recalled being in.

And now Callum was knocking on the door. The dogs barked, and he let himself in before Alicia reached the door.

"Take a nap," Alicia said to Argos, the German shepherd, and Toto, the Corgi.

Both dogs obediently stood down and wandered away.

Grace could hardly believe he was in her sanctuary. His gaze darted around the space as if he couldn't figure out where to rest his eyes. "Nice place."

"Have a seat," Alicia called as she walked back to the kitchen. "Make yourself comfortable."

He eyed the furniture. To be fair, it wasn't just the wallpaper that looked like it should be in a dollhouse. The furniture was delicate and highly customized. The cushions were silk-covered, embroidered, or wrapped in handwoven tapestries. The furniture, carved with custom inlays and intricate designs, brought whimsical touches into the cheerful room. Callum eyed each piece as if deciding where he'd do the least damage.

He actually loomed over the living room. His jawline could cut glass, and sinewy muscle stretched tight over his forearms. This Callum Hale wasn't the one she'd last seen at her parents' house. "Just sit down. You're not going to break anything."

His eyebrow crooked as if he didn't believe her, but carefully lowered himself onto the couch.

Sherlock, Alicia's inquisitive cat who never approved of guests, hopped onto the coffee table and locked his green eyes on Callum like he was a danger that needed to be dragged out.

He lifted his hand to stroke its orange-and-white fur.

"I wouldn't do that—"

Sherlock had no problem speaking up for himself.

Callum snatched his hand from the hissing cat. "Regal little fucker, isn't she?"

"He," Grace corrected. "His name is Sherlock. Well, originally Purrlock Holmes, but he's too dignified for a punny name. Of all the alarm and early warning systems I've come across over the years, Sherlock has been the most cuddly and reliable."

His eyebrow crept up as he looked dubiously at the cat. "There are far better security options out there. I could recommend—"

Alicia tsked as she walked in with a tray of iced tea and her dogs by her side. "It's not your life, and you're not the one who had to live in hiding. You don't get to Monday-morning quarterback her choices."

The muscle in his jaw ticked as he eyed the dogs. "There are personal protection options more dependable than a friend's pets."

"You work in the personal protection business," Alicia pointed out. "That's what you're paid to say."

The personal protection business. That wasn't a far stretch from the Army, but still another world entirely where he and Hayden lived and breathed with insurgents and roadside bombs. Grace wanted to ask him about it. Later, maybe, when she could pivot his attention from her problems.

He continued studying Argos and Toto, frowning at Grace's security decisions. There were things she could have done differently, but the legal system that was supposed to have upheld the law always fell prey to Dominic's moves. His release was just another piece of proof that her ex-husband would always have the upper hand.

He blew out his breath. "I'm only suggesting a better option than dogs."

"You don't know my babies," Alicia said. Argos and Toto flanked her as she set the tray on the coffee table and shooed Sherlock away. "And before you walk in here, making assumptions and judging what you don't know, why don't you keep your mouth shut, Mr. Big Muscles, and listen to what Grace has to say?"

Inwardly she collapsed. Exhaustion rolled through her body. Memories ached, and trauma ricocheted. She'd already said more than she wanted to, but explaining the decisions she had made and the ordeal that Dominic had dished out over their years of marriage wasn't Alicia's responsibility. "I've already shared most of everything with him."

"Yeah, I don't know about that," he disagreed.

Whatever she said to him would make its way back to her brother, and Hayden would have covered her in bubble wrap and never let her live her life. She'd determined long ago that a life-in-hiding was better than a life in a fishbowl where Dominic could find her. There had always been a balancing act between being scared, staying tucked off the grid, and letting her big brother bury her under an avalanche of protection.

Callum cleared his throat.

Alicia shoved a glass of iced tea into his hand. "It's sweet. But if you need more," she gestured to the tray with simple syrup and sliced lemons, "doctor it up."

"Thanks."

Alicia stared at him until he took a drink. That was probably her way of giving Grace more time to organize her thoughts.

Finally, under Alicia's unflinching study, he got the message and sipped. "It's great. Thanks."

"Coaster." Alicia tilted her head toward the hand-tatted doily coasters next to the tray, then signaled for her dogs to sit next to Grace.

Argos and Toto took their places on either side of her chair and folded themselves to face Callum and Alicia. They pinned their sharp gazes on Callum as if he were the boogeyman come to harm their home.

"Stay," Alicia commanded.

They didn't move a muscle. The dogs had hearts of gold and more smarts than she'd ever come across. Grace scratched behind Toto's ear.

Callum assessed their hyperfocus and slowly set his glass on the coaster. "They look like a friendly bunch."

Alicia added a slice of lemon to her tea. "They are to my friends."

"Maybe we'll be buddies by the end of the night."

"Maybe," Alicia said doubtfully. "Grace?"

"What more am I supposed to say?" The shock of seeing him—of macing him—had faded, and she was even readjusting to the way he made her insides spin. Good thing she had a handle on that. He'd barely acted as if he'd known she was alive for most of her life. All the while, she'd been *very* aware of him. If this had been any other situation, she might have dreamed that he could be her white knight. But nothing and no one could outrun Dominic Marino. "I'm safe here, Callum. What do you need to know so that you don't start a five-alarm panic with my brother?"

He snorted. "Think you did that all by yourself."

Argos rumbled with a quiet growl.

"Easy." Grace petted his head.

Callum eyed the two dogs and then Sherlock. "For discussion's sake, let's agree that you're safe here for the time being. The bigger problem is that you're hiding and that, in theory, Dominic knows your location."

"I'm always going to hide from Dominic. That's par for the course. I've accepted it. Now that he's out of prison, I have to stay clear of him even more."

"That doesn't work for me, Grace. It wouldn't work for your family if they truly knew what was going on."

"What do you mean? They've known. I explained the risks of staying alive on my own and existing in witness protection where he could find me."

He held out a hand as though she had presented his case for him. "Do you even hear yourself?"

"I've got it handled."

"Bullshit. Hell, half the time you can't even look me in the eye."

"Maybe you should leave, Cal. There's not much for you to do here."

"I can't leave you like this. I won't."

"Sure, you can."

"Then I won't for Hayden, who hired me to assess, locate, and if needed, protect you. The first two objectives are met. Done. Finished. But we're not anywhere near the third. There is so much mess to clean up—"

"I didn't make a mess that needs cleaning up. This is my life!"

"You need help."

"Alicia helps. I have friends like Alicia. Places I can go. I've built a system to protect myself."

"He found you at the grocery store. He'll find you again. I found you, and if you seriously think Dominic wants to *collect* you as if you're some ornamental belonging of his, then this is a problem that needs a long-term solution."

She twisted the black tourmaline stones on her bracelet.

"He's not wrong," Alicia said quietly.

Grace turned to her friend, surprised by the sharp feeling of disloyalty. Alicia would never mean to hurt her, and she would never betray Grace's confidence, but the idea of her siding with Callum hurt.

Alicia shrugged. "Well, he's not."

Callum was nothing like Dominic and would never harm her, but as big and tough as he was, he didn't look like a safe harbor. He looked like the red flags that she had missed when she first fell for Dominic.

Safe harbor didn't exist. It was mythical.

Which was why she was always on the run.

He shifted uncomfortably on the couch. "Let me help you figure everything out. You don't have to hide."

Grace picked up her iced tea. The ice cubes clinked against the glass. There was no reason to be mistrustful of Callum, and she'd spent so many years wanting so much from him. His time. His attention. Him to see her as anything other than Hayden's little sister. Now he was offering her his complete attention, and she was terrified.

Both dogs tilted their heads. A delivery truck rumbled to a stop in front of Alicia's house. Alicia moved to the window. Callum joined her. They peered through the gauzy white linen curtains.

Grace's stomach turned.

"It's the FedEx lady," Alicia said. "It's fine."

Argos and Toto sat on their haunches. Their heads turned toward the front door, and they barked after the doorbell rang.

"Expecting a delivery?" Callum asked.

"No." Alicia pursed her lips, as though questioning the trust she'd put into Grace's hiding skills. "But I smash a preorder link on paperbacks like some people drink wine.

Then there are review copies, book merch. I enter a lot of giveaways. It's a constant stream, and unless it's for work, I don't track book release dates. They arrive when they arrive and make my day."

Alicia was talking too much. Grace could hear her nerves. The dread curling in Grace's stomach multiplied even as the delivery truck revved to life again and pulled away. There had to be a hundred reasons—a hundred books—why a delivery had arrived, but the timing didn't help her feel safe.

Callum removed a gun from the small of his back, where it had been secretly tucked.

Alicia put her hands on her hips. "Oh, no, sir. We don't do that in my house. No guns. No way."

"Callum. Wait." Anxiety spiked in Grace's veins. "It's nothing. Put that away."

He stalked through the living room. "Stay put."

"Telling me to stay put in my house." Indignant, Alicia recoiled but didn't move.

Neither did Grace. Adrenaline coated the back of her tongue. She needed to apologize to Alicia for bringing problems into her precious home.

Callum glanced over his shoulder to make sure they hadn't moved.

The deep seriousness in his eyes drained Grace's last remaining nerves. She and Alicia stepped closer together as he checked the door. Their elbows touched. Alicia grabbed Grace's hand. "Everything is fine. He's doing what he knows how to do."

Callum disappeared toward the front of the house. Shouldn't he call out something? *The coast is clear? False alarm?* Her heart hammered.

"Come on." Alicia tugged them back to the couch. "It's nothing."

Argos and Toto repositioned to bookend them.

"I'm sorry I brought this into your home."

"Don't be ridiculous." Alicia squeezed Grace's hand. "There is nothing to be sorry about. Let the big guy with the gun check things out, and all will be fine. It's probably not even a fun delivery of books. More like a tax return or something."

"You're such a shitty liar."

Sherlock sailed onto the couch and exercised his paws on a throw pillow that once upon a time had an embroidered profile of Sherlock Holmes.

Callum returned with a standard delivery box in hand. Thank God the gun was nowhere to be seen. She couldn't believe he had a weapon hidden on him. He'd been expecting that level of danger—or maybe he had a gun on him all the time. Was that comforting or terrifying? The Army had trained him to fire everything from handguns to tanks, but seeing it was something else.

"Who's it from?" Alicia asked.

"A P.O. Box." He snapped a photo of the address and tracking information, flipped the box around, inspected every side, then typed a message on his phone. The *whoosh* of a sent text message sounded before he looked up.

"That's awfully bold of you to text someone a photo of my delivery," Alicia said, but her voice wavered.

His lips pressed into a flat line. He assessed them like a general might inspect his troops, and judging by his deepening frown, he wasn't incredibly pleased. "It wasn't addressed to you. Maybe you should let me do my job."

An uncontrolled wave of nausea rolled from Grace's stomach into her throat. "Me?"

Callum didn't answer.

That was all the confirmation she needed. "Oh, God."

Part of her hadn't believed Dominic could ever find her here. Callum had found her, though. If Callum could, Dominic could. He had more resources and money than she could imagine. Even after their divorce, she was certain that he'd ratholed gobs and gobs of crypto and money in offshore accounts.

Callum gave the box a little shake. Grace perched on the edge of the couch and listened for the contents. Nothing.

His phone dinged, and after reading the text, he stared at the box as though he were finally appreciating that Dominic Marino had unexpected resources. "The tracking information was legit, and the return address is the post office next to the Shop 'n' Save that you ran out on."

She wanted to vomit. "Everything's a game with him."

Alicia laid a hand on Grace's back, rubbed it like a mother soothing a sick child, and asked Callum, "Well, are you going to open it?"

His index finger tapped on the box. Callum laid it on a chicly distressed accent table next to the tray of iced tea and removed a knife from his pocket. "Guess so."

"Wait." Alicia's hand froze. "What if it explodes?"

"Too lightweight. The box sounds empty."

"That doesn't sound like a professional opinion." Alicia scootched back. "What if it's anthrax?"

Callum raised an eyebrow. His gaze narrowed on Alicia and bounced between the women. "If you two are legitimately worried about bombs and anthrax, it's time to cut the charade and have more than a cat-and-dog menagerie to protect you."

Grace's lungs didn't take in enough air. A lightheaded dizziness made the room tilt, and she couldn't tear her eyes from that stupid box. "He doesn't want to kill me. He wants to own me."

"Well, fuck that." Callum sliced the blade through the cardboard and tapped out the contents onto the coffee table. A folded piece of paper fluttered out. It didn't take him long to read. He looked over.

Her gaze locked on the paper. "What does it say?"

"Until death do us part."

Chapter Seven

Callum snapped a photo of the note and texted the eerie message to Viv and Dean. Nothing about the previous forty-eight hours made sense, and, rubbing the back of his neck, he wasn't sure that would change. "It's confirmation that Dominic knows you're still alive and where you are."

The color had drained out of Grace's face. She dropped onto the couch. "This is bad, isn't it?"

New intel should have made him more confident, but one glance at the dawning realization of fear on Grace's face, and he knew he could have handled the FedEx another way. Hell, he could have bitten his tongue and communicated only with Viv and Dean. Whatever Grace thought she had under control was obviously not.

"Worse than I expected," he admitted.

Alicia glared and patted the back of Grace's head. "Think you could have sugarcoated that a bit?"

"That's not really what I do." Lying wasn't what Grace deserved. The woman he'd grown up with wasn't a shrinking violet and wouldn't want him to lie to appease her nerves. Grace had faked her own death. She could handle a stupid fuckin' note from her ex-husband.

"I can't believe this is happening." Grace crossed her arms over her stomach. Her shoulders hunched.

At least, she used to be able to handle it. Anger flared in his chest. So many things should have been different, but he could fix this for her. All he had to do was get his hands on Dominic.

"In your professional opinion," Alicia muttered. "What are you thinking?"

Callum cleared his throat. "That Grace is correct. Marino has more resources than I gave him credit for."

"Well, fuck." Alicia harrumphed and joined Grace on the couch.

His phone vibrated with a text message.

Vivian: Well, fuck.

He concurred with Alicia and Vivian. Their sentiment summed things up, didn't it? He tapped his molars. He hated being surprised.

"Do we need to dust for prints? Call the cops?" Alicia asked. "Get a restraining order?"

"It's not against the law to send someone a letter," he pointed out.

"It's obviously a threat. Only a moron would miss that."

"Let's not forget." Grace's unsteady voice barely registered above a whisper. "It *is* against the law to fake your own death."

True enough. "Let's set the faked death issue aside and deal with it later."

For that, he didn't have answers. She hadn't done it fraudulently, and the feds had been involved in her initial plans to disappear. So long as they weren't still upset about her leaving them high and dry without testifying—something that would have been infinitely easier for them to swallow before Marino had been released early from prison—all would be okay. Either way, not a problem for today.

He stared at the ceiling as if hidden answers could be found there. After a few seconds and no answers, Callum rubbed a hand over his face and admitted, "I have no idea about the intricacies of restraining orders when the..." *victim* wasn't the right word for this conversation, "...when someone is supposed to be six feet under."

"That complicates matters," Alicia agreed.

"But Titan has lawyers. We have people who know people. Important, well-connected people."

Grace frowned. "That sounds too much like Dominic's network. Well-connected like the Mafia."

He turned to her. "Obviously, Grace, we're not the Mafia. We can look into it quietly. Before the grocery store, had you ever thought that he or his people had found you?"

She shook her head. "When he was first arrested, I was certain he was tracking me. His goons knew where I was and what I was doing, and his lawyers would pass cryptic messages to mine. On the surface, they were fine, but I always understood the deeper meaning."

"Which was?"

Her shoulders scrunched. "Stay home. Be quiet. Do what I was told. Which was to do nothing." Her breath shook. "I'm positive he knew when I met with the federal marshals."

"How?"

"I don't remember exactly. Relayed messages with hidden meanings. I tried to explain it to my attorneys, to the feds, but I couldn't prove it."

"They thought you were being paranoid."

She nodded. "Even if I were, who was I kidding? I knew Dominic's reach. If he wasn't already keeping tabs on me and my family, he would have started before I testified."

The more Grace talked, the more Callum could see the multiplying effect Dominic had on her. Callum saw why Hayden had agreed to Grace's fake death.

He paced the living room. He didn't know everything yet. "I know there was some..." Guilt thickened the blood in his veins. "... strife in your marriage. Your divorce proceedings didn't go into detail, but—"

"You read it?" Grace flushed. The embarrassed pink colored her cheeks. She shuffled her feet and dug her toe onto the pink area rug that lay over the dark wood floors. "I thought that was sealed."

"I read a summary."

"Yeah, there was some strife."

"Can you give me any more than that?"

"Why?" Alicia snapped.

"I've obviously missed a whole lot of what's happened." A truth that would probably always haunt him. "I've been caught off guard, and if you give me some background, maybe I'll have better footing."

Alicia didn't look convinced. "It was a shitty fuckin' marriage. That's the background you need to know."

"I get that. I do. I swear. I'm just looking for—"

"The divorce attorneys negotiated an agreement that was intentionally vague. I never had a restraining order. I never went to the hospital. I didn't document anything he did to me." She pinched a bead between her fingers, then twisted the bracelet again. "Given his vast control over *everything* in my life, there was nothing I could do until they arrested him. When they led Dominic away in handcuffs, a world of possibilities opened up."

Did to her... His molars clenched. Grace wouldn't look at him.

Alicia squeezed Grace's hand and glared at him in a way that said he needed to shut up and move on.

"Take a drink." She handed Grace her glass of iced tea and then took a long drink from her own glass. "Maybe we need a little bourbon to top these off."

Grace rolled her eyes. "You don't drink."

Alicia snorted. "Well, today seems like a good day for a bad habit." She poured the simple syrup into her iced tea and used the spoon to smash the lemon and mix the sugar, visibly more angry than with the intent of stirring. "That will have to do for now."

He focused on Grace. She hadn't looked at him since he'd read the note aloud. Even as she leaned into Alicia for support, her eyes fixed on the pink rug like it offered her a way out of this mess.

"I don't need to know any more," he said.

Her iced tea trembled in her hand. Grace wrapped both palms around the sweating glass and rested it on her knee. "How long has he known where I am?"

The Grace that Callum used to know would not want kid gloves. This Grace? No idea how the truth would hit. This was a balancing act he wasn't sure how to pull off. "Longer than I did."

She didn't react. Silence lingered in the living room.

Alicia broke the quiet, cursed under her breath, and stroked one of her dogs. "I don't get it."

Callum dropped into a chair that didn't look sturdy enough to hold him. "What's not to get?"

"If he wants Grace to go with him, why didn't he just knock on the door and take her?"

"You know the answer to that." Grace rolled her eyes. "What fun would that be?"

Callum tried to see all the moves in Dominic's 3D chess game. "Alicia makes a good point."

If Grace were property to be repossessed, the game wasn't needed. If the game was needed, Grace wasn't the collector's item she feared. That made the situation worse.

"Of course I make a good point." Alicia watched the ice cubes in her iced tea swirl as she twirled her spoon. "All right, Mister Man. What do we do?"

"If he doesn't know about me," Callum said, "we need to keep it that way."

"First you wanted a security system and answered the door with a gun, now you want to hang low? Does that make sense to you, Grace?"

Grace shook her head. "Nothing makes sense."

Bigger concerns spiraled into his mind. If Dominic had known where Grace was staying, then he could have gone much farther than simply letting her know. He could be watching. Listening. Playing his games. "I need to make some phone calls."

"How long until Dominic figures out that you're with us?"

He might already know. Callum shrugged. "Like I said, I want to make some calls."

"If you explained who you're calling, what you're discussing, that would probably make us feel better," Alicia suggested in a way that brooked little discussion.

"It's late now, but I'd like to get a team up here to sweep your place. See if there's anything listening or watching."

Alicia scowled and glanced pointedly at her dogs and cat. "You're out of your damn mind. None of my boys would let someone walk in here and hide—"

"None of your boys would be able to tell you if someone tranqued them for an hour and did their business."

Grace pressed her hands to her temples and dropped her elbows to her knees. "Oh, God. Alicia. I'm so sorry."

Alicia scooped the cat into her lap. "You have nothing to be sorry for, Grace. You are always welcome here. Psychopath ex-husband or not."

They were strong words of support, but Callum could see Alicia's wariness cracking her bravado.

Grace pulled her knees to her chest and wrapped her arms around her legs. The color still hadn't returned to her cheeks. "I thought I'd been so careful."

"Don't worry about it. We're all safe. No one's hurt my babies. No one's hurt you or me. We're fine."

"We can't stop Dominic. You know that."

Her flat tone worried him. "I don't know that," he said. "And I don't agree."

"He has more resources than you can imagine." Grace unburied her face from her knees. "He's never outgunned. Never outplayed."

"The man went to prison, Grace. He's not infallible."

"Look at the situation now." She stood up. "I should leave. Just go somewhere else and make it clear that I've left."

"Like hell." Alicia pushed her back down.

Better her than him. He wanted to do the same thing. "I'm looking at the situation with both eyes open. It would have been a hell of a lot easier if I had known what was going on from the beginning—"

"Callum," Alicia warned with a careful shake of her head.

"We will get you to a safehouse." He tilted his head to the dogs and met Alicia's eye. "We can all go."

Alicia crossed her arms. "Look, this might be new to you, but she's hidden from Dominic for years. If there aren't listening devices, we should stay put until you have a plan. We're comfortable here. You and your big gun are here. My dogs and cat are here. We stay here unless he's been in my house. If that's the case, fuck it, I don't know. Burn the place down. Stash us someplace secret."

One dog nuzzled Grace until she petted him.

Callum understood the dog's instincts. Touching her would soothe a part of him he had ignored for years.

Alicia arched her eyebrows. "*Well?*"

He wanted to drag both women—and maybe the pets—to a location where he had control. Where only he and his teammates could pinpoint. Grace concentrated on the dog at her side as if she were waiting for two bickering parents to work it out or walk away.

He drew a deep breath and didn't plan to go in circles with Alicia all night long.

"Okay, decision time." Alicia petted the dog with Grace. "Neither of us will let you run off on your own."

"Her leaving alone wasn't even a consideration. Just so we're all on the same page."

"If there's no listening devices," Alicia continued, "what do you want to do?"

"Stay here."

Alicia lifted her eyebrows defiantly. "Fine. We're staying here."

"All right." He'd make that work. It would give them more time to orchestrate a plan with the least amount of upheaval. "Do you want to call your parents?"

"No. Absolutely not. I don't want them involved in anything related to Dominic. They'll be needlessly worried."

"That's not how they're going to see it." He glanced between the two women, not wanting to admit that Hayden would eventually be given an update. It wouldn't be tonight, but soon. Hayden would do whatever he wanted with that information. Callum nodded. "You're calling the shots tonight." Those were the last words he should be saying. "No parents."

"And Hayden?"

"I couldn't give Hayden an update right now even if I wanted to. This goes no farther than my team for the time being."

She almost met his eyes. "And whoever's listening."

Chapter Eight

Hours had crept by, and giving up on her work, Grace set her computer and stylus to the side. She'd stared at the screen, and nothing interesting had come to mind. There was so much work to be done on the book cover that she absolutely adored, but she couldn't even work on the shading.

This had to be like writer's block. A total distraction had sucked the creative energy out of her like a workflow vampire. She didn't know whether Dominic or Callum was to blame.

Probably Callum.

Definitely Callum.

Callum, who still saw her as a pain in the ass, not to mention the eternal title of Hayden's little sister who always needed help. More than that, now, he likely saw her as a liar who had put her family through unneeded pain.

And... She sighed. He probably hated her. She couldn't blame him if he did. Her lies were impossible to come back from, and he was one of those born-to-protect types who always did the right thing.

God, she had always wanted so much from him and now couldn't even have his respect.

Alicia's familiar footsteps climbed the stairs and snapped Grace from her pity party. She picked up her computer to at least pretend that she had been working, but set it down again before another lie fell from her lips. She hadn't lied to Alicia and wouldn't start tonight.

Alicia knocked.

"It's not locked."

She opened the bedroom door and held an oversized lemon-yellow tray with two cornfield blue plates stacked with food. "You have to be hungry. Chicken thighs and rice."

The bright colors were one of Grace's many favorite things about Alicia's house. Books. Plants. Bright colors. Cute furniture. Delicious food. Oh, and an unbelievable rock of a friend. "Were you seriously cooking down there while," she circled her hand overhead, "people are searching your house?"

The sweep team had been efficient if not invasive. They'd torn Grace's room apart twice before they'd left her to work in peace.

"How hard's rice?" Alicia shrugged.

"Compared to how I make rice? Much harder." Grace washed the rice, boiled the water, and presto. Normal, everyday rice. Alicia did that too, but tinkered and worked her magic, and when she said presto, the rice was enough to make angels sing.

"The chicken was in the deep freeze. Quick and easy in the cast iron." She set the tray at the foot of the bed. "Don't tell me you didn't smell dinner cooking."

Apparently not. She'd been struggling with her book cover, daydreaming about Callum, and lost to the world until Alicia walked in. "I've been distracted."

"I bet." Alicia scooted the chair from the desk and set two spots on the bed with linen napkins and silverware before positioning the tray between them. "It's like a picnic without the mosquitoes."

Grace laughed.

"Now, there's a sound I haven't heard all day."

She smiled. "It's been a strange day."

Alicia lifted her fork. "I made a plate for Callum, and he looked at me like he hadn't seen a homemade meal in his life."

"That's not true. His mom is a great cook."

She pointed the fork at Grace with a little bounce. "That's quite the personal detail to know about someone."

The things she knew about Callum would be embarrassing to list. She'd once known the sound of his footsteps in her home and the way his car revved before he drove away. In hindsight, teenage crushes could be incredibly cringy. Still, college and after weren't any less humiliating. She had memorized the curve of his ass, the cut of his jawline, and the width of his chest. Grace struggled to keep from blushing. "Like I said. Known him my whole life."

"You ever sleep with him?"

Her jaw fell slack. A red-hot flush rocketed up her neck and into her cheeks. "Oh, my God. No. He's Hayden's best friend."

Alicia snorted. "That's a horrible reason not to sleep with someone."

I would never almost fell from her lips, but she'd sworn not to lie to Alicia. "There are a lot of valid reasons I never slept with him, starting with the fact that he has never seen me as a woman."

"Huh." Alicia cut her chicken with the side of her fork and mixed it with rice. "He doesn't like it when I follow around his coworkers and make suggestions."

Grace snickered. "I bet not."

They both heard heavy footsteps ascend the stairs before a knock sounded against the partially ajar door. He stepped in.

"Speak of the devil." Alicia grinned, then gestured toward the floor. "Any updates from the nosy Nellies paging through my romance novels for secret cameras?"

"Actually, I have good news."

Hope swelled in her chest. "They didn't find anything?"

"Not a damn thing. At least on the inside. Outside will take a while longer."

Relief flooded Alicia's face. "Good. I didn't want to burn my house down and salt a circle around it. How was dinner?"

"Unbelievable. Thank you." He stepped into the room and eyed the bright walls and frilly curtains. Sherlock followed him and jumped onto the bed beside Grace. "He's been keeping an eye on me the whole time."

"As he should," Alicia said. "But if he didn't trust you, or he sensed I didn't, he wouldn't just follow you. He'd be making your life miserable."

His eyebrows arched, as if he couldn't fathom how that would work. He said to the cat, "Guess I'm glad we're good, little guy." He wandered over to the floating bookshelf. "That's a wild range of books."

Romance novels. Hardboiled mysteries. Children's classics. New age nonfiction. None matched in genre, size, or color, yet somehow looked as if Alicia had handpicked each book for its aesthetic quality. He pulled *The Wind in the Willows* off the shelf and ran his thumb over the worn pages. "Ever read it?"

"Of course," Alicia said.

Sheepishly, Grace laughed. "Not me."

Alicia studied the book for an extra second, took another bite of her chicken, then scooped Sherlock into her arms. With her free hand, she stacked her silverware and grabbed her plate. "I'm going to let you two talk."

He returned the book. "I didn't mean to interrupt. You don't have to—"

"I have a couple of things I need to do after your people touched every single thing I own." Alicia shut the door behind her.

The bedroom suddenly felt too small for her and Callum. Somehow, sitting on a perfectly made bed covered with her computer and dinner felt too intimate. Grace focused her attention on the chicken and rice and toyed with her fork.

"Can I sit?" He gestured to the chair Alicia had abandoned by the bed.

"Sure."

He inched it back and sat at ease with everything around him, the counterpoint to the anxious, exposed energy that vibrated inside her. His knees pressed against the covers. She noticed the powerful muscles in his thighs and the way his shirt clung to his stomach. Callum stretched, tipped the chair onto its back legs as he inhaled so deeply she saw his chest expand. "It's been a long day."

Tongue-tied, she blinked at a loss for words. His tight muscles didn't match his casual demeanor. She could think of nothing except how she would fit so perfectly in his arms. Grace pulled in a shaky breath and dropped her gaze back to her dinner. "Not even a full day since I maced you."

Callum laughed and rubbed his face as though the mere mention of their run-in brought tears to his eyes. "Hayden will get a kick out of that." He brought the chair back to four legs and leaned forward, an earnest expression on his face. "Look, Grace, I need you to trust me."

"I do."

"The way you say that..." He shook his head. "It's almost like you're saying that because it's what you're supposed to say."

"Well, I am, aren't I?"

"I want you to trust me like you trust Alicia. Trust me like, hell, I don't fuckin' know. Like the person who will get you out of this mess."

Whether she wanted to admit it to herself, she trusted him entirely. But she still didn't think he understood the complexity of the problems she'd created. "You shouldn't say you're going to do that until you actually know what it entails."

"I don't need to know all the details to know what I'm going to do. I'll fix it. I promise."

"Cal, I'm not some pain-in-the-ass kid who got herself in trouble at school. You can't simply fix—"

"The hell I can't, and trust me, I don't picture you as a pain-in-the-ass kid. I haven't in a long time."

Her stomach lurched. She lifted her gaze to his, and it lurched again. The intensity of his stormy bourbon gaze shivered down her back. "I wish you wouldn't look at me like that."

His expression only intensified. "Like what?"

"Like I'm a headache."

The corners of his eyes tightened, but he shook his head. "I moved my truck down the block. As long as the sweep team finds nothing, my involvement likely remains unknown."

"That's good."

He pulled out his phone. "Headquarters sent over a few more questions and a couple of items to clarify. Are you okay with another round of questions?"

She shrugged. If she had questions to focus on, maybe her brain wouldn't remind her how he had just made her stomach flip twice. "Sure. Shoot."

"Our data analysis guy can find intel anywhere it hides. He's mapping your business and personal connections. That includes people you relied on. It would make his job easier if you could provide a list of names."

"I can do that."

"You said that you had a few close friends like Alicia. Is that right?"

She nodded and gave him names and contact information.

"He'll want to know anyone you've dated, slept with." The slightest hint of a blush colored his cheeks. "Hookups. Friends with benefits. One-night stands. That type of thing. If you don't know names, then a location, date, and time."

"*Why?*"

Callum grimaced as though the idea of her dating someone actually pained him. "I guess he looks at that person more thoroughly. I don't honestly know. Loose lips sink ships and pillow talk and—"

"Oh my God, Cal. Stop talking. There's no one like that."

He swallowed hard. "Not just now. The entire time you've been gone."

Now it was her turn to blush. "Got it. No one. Can we move on?"

His eyebrows arched. "None?" He scrubbed a hand over his face. "None. All right." His forehead furrowed as he swiped open his phone and thumbed the screen to the list he'd been reading. "All right," he repeated. "Where was I?" Callum set his phone down. "Grace..." Concern darkened his expression. "You've been incredibly alone."

"Well, yeah. Sorry, I thought I had made that clear."

"An unhealthy amount of alone."

"No one asked for your commentary."

He took a deep breath and blew it out. "All I meant was—"

"You don't have to explain what you mean. What other questions do you have for me and my nonexistent sex life?"

"Grace—"

"I'm serious. Spit them out. Let's get this over and done with."

With one last pitying glance, he swiped his phone open and returned to his list.

The questions weren't as intrusive. Most of them, she didn't have answers to. She wasn't sure Callum believed her, but that wasn't her problem. Callum would feed her answers to Dean, and Dean could confirm what she said.

"That's it." He returned the chair to the desk and gestured to the tray with her half-eaten dinner. "Are you done?"

She nodded.

"I'll take it downstairs."

"Thanks."

"For what it's worth, if I could have seen into the future, I would have done something to change your trajectory. You wouldn't have landed here if I could have helped it."

"Hayden had made a joke the night before I married Dominic that he was going to pull the fire alarm right before the I do's." She half-laughed. "Not that a hiccup like that would have kept Dominic from getting what he wanted."

"Well, I didn't even go to your wedding. I don't know what that says about me."

How horrible had she been to wish the man she'd always dreamed of would attend her wedding to another man? Everyone she'd ever known had been there. Everyone Dominic had met, done business with, or had hoped to had been there. The night had been a spectacle. She never should have walked down the aisle, but at that point had been too scared to unwind herself from the mess.

"Why weren't you there?"

Callum rested his hand on the doorknob for a long moment before he turned around.

"You could see the future dumpster fire that was my life." She let out a heavy breath and shook her head. "You don't have to say it."

He just watched her. She kept waiting for him to agree, for him to pity her all over again.

"I didn't want to watch one of the kindest, most beautiful women I've ever known walk toward a man who didn't appreciate a thing about her."

"I didn't want to watch one of the kindest, most beautiful women I've ever known walk toward a man who didn't appreciate a thing about her."

Chapter Nine

Callum had said too much.

Hours had passed since the sweep team had made quick work of Alicia's house, inspecting around Callum, the two women, and three wary animals. Hours had passed since he'd walked out of Grace's bedroom after an honest moment. He had said nothing that wasn't true. But he had said nothing that would build her trust in him.

Nope. He'd left them both with the same question: Why had he said that?

At least the rest of the one-on-one time before his moment of oversharing had gone well. Definitely awkward, but fruitful. She'd produced every name and location that Dean needed.

Other than that, Grace had not had much to say, and he couldn't get a read on her. She ran hot and cold, defiant and quiet. The conversations swung back and forth, and he was questioning whether it was in Grace's best interest for Vivian to replace him.

Then again, there was no way in hell that anyone on his team would be the one to protect her. That reaction alone was enough of a problem that he needed to recuse himself from this assignment, but he couldn't. She pulled him in like a moth to a flame.

The grandfather clock struck ten in the living room as Alicia and Grace cheered, sliding the final piece of a jigsaw puzzle into place.

"Finished?" he asked.

Stretching her back, Alicia preened. "That has to be a world record."

Grace immediately dismantled the puzzle. Nothing stayed put in her life for long.

He wanted her to linger. He wanted to catch up, but that would only be more of the questions he'd run her through earlier. Those had been clinical, procedural, and he wanted more depth. What she thought and why. Not as it related to keeping a low profile, but how or why she made decisions. Except that everything she did appeared to be only about hiding.

She worked.

She hid.

She moved.

She worked.

She hid.

What a crappy life.

Grace returned the puzzle box to a shelf and tidied the kitchen while Alicia let the dogs out for the last time before bed. Then they picked up their books and retreated toward the stairs, offering goodnights as they climbed.

Callum saluted them as they passed and settled onto the couch. They'd offered to bunk together and give him Grace's guest room, but the living room was better suited for keeping an eye out, and more importantly, he needed all the space he could get between him and Grace. Sleeping in her bed? The chance of sleep would be next to zilch, even if she weren't in it.

And the idea of what might happen if she were in bed with him? Jesus fuck, he didn't need to think about that.

Callum squeezed his eyes shut. That did nothing to erase Grace from his wandering thoughts. Her lips had always commanded his attention. Not to mention the way she smiled with that silly, sassy mouth of hers.

The day washed over him like an ice-cold wave. Anything with her mouth was borderline inappropriate, considering the nervous way she moved through life.

The stairwell hall light switched off. Muffled bits of conversation floated through the air vents. Grace paced in her bedroom as the grandfather clock ticked. Finally, upstairs grew silent. He was alone in a dollhouse, on a couch with too many pillows, and hadn't been more uncomfortable in his life.

Sleeping would present challenges. He eyed the pillow and blanket stacked at the end of the couch and would probably use them to make a bed on the pink carpet.

Callum didn't move. His discomfort didn't change because, hell, it wasn't the sleeping arrangements that were the source of his problem.

Forty-eight hours ago, he hadn't known Grace was alive.

Twenty-four hours ago, he hadn't set eyes on her.

Now he had, and of all the women in the world, this was the one who made him wish things were different. Different ages growing up. Different circumstances with her ex. Different decisions on his part.

Maybe Grace wouldn't have had Dominic as an ex if he'd asked her out first. Him and Grace. Hayden would have flipped his fuckin' mind. At least back then. Would dating have been such a betrayal of their friendship, knowing what he had kept from Callum?

His phone chirped. He welcomed the distraction. The display showed an incoming call from the office. He answered.

"Ready for some good news?" Dean said with far more pep than the last time they'd spoken.

Relief settled in his chest. Callum moved to the large windows draped in a gauzy white linen and pulled back the poor excuse for privacy. "Absolutely."

"I have the final report from the sweep team."

Callum frowned. They hadn't turned up anything inside Alicia's. He'd assumed the same would be found outside.

"The external sweep showed the same thing as the one inside the house. Absolutely nothing. No cameras. No listening devices. Nothing transmitting outside the home."

The anxious band around his chest loosened. "Good. Great." But Callum worked the information over in his head and still wondered why Dominic had shown his hand. It had to be more than creating fear and warning Grace away from the feds. "What else?"

"Now for the bad news."

His head dropped back. The modicum of relief vanished. "How bad?"

"On the surface, it seems like small potatoes, but..." Dean let out a deep sigh. "Considering Marino's resources, I'd say we're dealing with a problem."

"Let's hear it."

"After Vivian asked me to find Grace, I tracked her down with the help of a client she'd submitted work to. Backtracked the IP address to the library, and you walked into a big shiny pile of luck."

"If mace in the face is lucky."

"Best we can tell, Marino didn't have the same luck or access. How did he find her? Maybe he accessed her online accounts and tracked her location from there. But Grace uses a VPN, changes passwords almost daily, and has two-factor authorization or authenticator apps set up for everything. He could have installed malware once upon a time, and it's embedded in an online account. He could—"

"Dean, man, don't walk me through the possibilities. Just tell me how he did it."

"That's the bad news. I don't have a clue. She doesn't have a single dedicated device. She uses burner phones. No online presence except for her freelance work posted on aggregator sites—which were uploaded via freelancers she hired through a VPN." He laughed. "Grace Willoughby had her location and online safety locked down like a pro. I wouldn't have mapped her as quickly as I did if she hadn't given us intel."

"I thought she was just an artist."

Dean laughed again in that way Callum could tell he was shaking his head. "She's mastered the art of hiding online."

Interesting. He never would have pegged her for that. Perhaps he didn't know her as well as he'd thought. Three years of an age gap made a difference growing up. She arrived at middle school when he walked into high school. He and Hayden were seniors when she was a freshman. Then they'd grown up, and she'd had all of his attention. Callum had taken pains to ignore her.

The call ended. Callum lay on the couch and listened to the grandfather clock softly ticking. He didn't bother to make his bed yet. The night was still young, and his thoughts were all over the place. He tucked the pillow behind his head and tried to envision Dominic's next move.

Hesitant footsteps padded down the stairs. His skin prickled with a hyperawareness of Grace.

She padded into the living room. "Are you sleeping?"

He eased up as she rounded the far side of the couch. "Hey. No, I just got off a phone call and was thinking the conversation over."

Her hair was loose over her shoulders, framing her heart-shaped face. In her flannel pajamas and a robe, without her fidget bracelets or protective friend by her side, she looked like the woman he'd known before her ex-husband entered the picture. "Can I sit with you?"

"Sure." Callum waited until she'd pulled Sherlock into her lap. "Can't sleep?"

The cat nuzzled against her fluffy robe and purred. Her fingertips smoothed down Sherlock's neck. "I didn't try. I have too much on my mind. I was going to read something, but then I couldn't focus."

"Glad you came down here."

Her eyebrows scrunched as if she weren't sure she should have joined him.

"I'm sorry I had to ask you those questions."

In the dim light of the living room, finally, she lifted her eyes and locked on his. Hours of fighting for them, and now that he had them, he didn't know what to do. Words caught in his throat. A lecture, a security plan, anything about her safety should have been easy to discuss, but he didn't want that, and she didn't need it.

The silent house hummed around them. His pulse sped up, and swallowing, he liked the little beat of excitement that came from sitting next to her. This wasn't the right time to notice her the way he was, but the right time had never come along. Every time it had, he had shoved it away, and look where that got them.

The corners of her lips upturned, almost as if she had an inkling of his thoughts. Grace tipped her chin down. "Are you tired? Do you want to be left alone?"

He would say anything to keep her on the couch with him. "My sleep schedule has been wrecked. On a job. Off. Travel, one night's sleep, and here I am." He was talking too much. "I don't need that many hours a night. But when I'm ready, I'll sleep like the dead."

Sherlock jumped down. Grace curled her legs under her and leaned against the couch, making herself cozy. She threaded her fingers through her hair, twisted it into a bun, then let it go. Long strands fell loose and framed her face. He wanted to touch her hair. His fingers itched to thread through its silkiness. She remained just out of reach, but it wouldn't be hard to dip his mouth under the spot hidden by her hair and nuzzle until she arched her neck.

A tightness that he'd tried time and time again to forget squeezed his chest. What might life be like if he had simply settled down and had a person to come home to? What if Grace had been that person?

"Do you remember when you met Dominic?" she asked.

The fog clouding his reasoning immediately lifted at the mention of her ex. He managed, "Mm-hm," and dragged in a sobering breath.

"You and Hayden were on leave and visiting home that weekend," she said. "Dad grilled burgers. The sun was baking us alive."

"Yeah, I remember."

She closed her eyes and lay her head against the back of the couch. "You and Hayden knew it wouldn't work out, didn't you? You knew on that very first day."

He rolled his bottom lip into his mouth. He and Hayden had thought the situation with Dominic would run its course within a matter of weeks. If not sooner. Not for a minute had either of them believed she'd marry the guy.

Dominic Marino had been as far from the right man for Grace as Callum could have fathomed. He had struggled with keeping his mouth shut more on that day than he had with Grace in his entire life.

"You can say if you knew, Cal. You saw the red flags, didn't you?"

Red flags weren't the only thing he saw that day. Callum simply saw red. "I mean..." He gestured broadly, not sure how much help hindsight would be. "He told you which cheeseburger to eat."

Her forehead furrowed. "You remember that? Major red flag. I was so, so stupid." Sherlock returned to her lap with a sailing jump and nuzzled against her robe. Grace fluttered her fingers down his arched back. "Do you know what love bombing is?"

"You don't have to explain yourself."

"Every single thing he did was a surprise. Not just a surprise. Like, a *surprise*." She used her hands to mimic explosions. "The extravagance of it all. City hopping. Dining out. Jewelry. Fancy private jets. And it wasn't even the money or the flaunting of everything that had my attention. God, that makes me sound so superficial, but the relationship was just a nonstop onslaught of attention. I was drowning in dopamine. I couldn't breathe. I couldn't think. I couldn't do anything except hang on."

Callum didn't know what to say.

She absentmindedly petted Sherlock and let her eyes roam the living room as if hoping to find comfort or safety. He could offer that. He needed her eyes to lock onto him again. But she refocused on the cat, unable to find whatever she was looking for.

"I don't know why I'm telling you all this." The cat kneaded its paws on her leg.

"Because you trust me."

She tugged her bottom lip into her mouth. "Do you think I'm an idiot?"

"No way."

Her eyebrow arched, and she shot him a pointed look.

"Stubborn, maybe, but not an idiot."

The corners of her mouth lifted, and Grace laughed quietly. "Maybe so."

"The more I learn about how you were protecting yourself—even if I think you should have done it differently—the more I realize how much thought you've put into your situation."

Silence hung between them. He liked her laugh and couldn't remember what it sounded like growing up. He supposed he sounded different as well. But that wasn't where his head should be. Callum licked his lips and refocused on the conversation. "Why won't you update your parents about Dominic?"

Her gaze fell. "That he found me? For the same reason I didn't tell them what was happening while I was married and before Dominic was arrested."

He let the silence hang. She would give him more. He just had to keep his mouth shut. Callum bit the inside of his cheek and knew whatever she was about to say would hurt.

"I'm embarrassed," she finally admitted. "I'm ashamed." Her eyelashes fluttered. "It was such a cliché, and I should have been smarter than I was. And now," her voice cracked, "after everything I've put them through since I left, just to have it all fail? That's too much."

Her shame sliced through him. He ached to comfort her, but a darker part of him ached to destroy the source of her pain.

"Don't look at me like that. I can't stand the pity."

"It's not pity," he promised, though he didn't know what it was.

She reached for her wrist, but the bracelets were gone. "When you were younger, did you ever imagine what your life would look like? Where you would live? Or did you always know it was the Army?"

"I'm not in the Army anymore."

"That wasn't what I asked."

"Good. Because that's complicated." He grinned to play down the topic. He wouldn't explain to her what had happened. Not tonight. Maybe never. It would change the way she looked at him. He shifted the conversation to her again. "I didn't imagine much. But I bet you did. What was it?"

She shook her head with a sheepish grin. "That I'd have a cute house. Flowers in the front. A little vegetable garden in the back. Someplace safe. Like where we grew up. A friendly neighborhood. Not too big. Not too small. With lots of happiness and laughter."

"You can still have that."

She scoffed and rolled her eyes. "I thought you said I wasn't an idiot. Because we both know that's not in the cards for me anymore."

"When all of this is through—"

"Which will never happen."

"Grace—"

"*Callum.* You don't orchestrate your own funeral to—"

"We can fix it." *I can fix it.*

"Even if you could, Dominic is too possessive. He never quits, and now that he knows... It's game on."

"When all of this is through, I promise, you will have your cute house with all the flowers and laughter you want."

She met his gaze and held it. Just like when she first joined him on the couch, his stomach tightened. She searched his eyes. He didn't know what for but would gladly give it to her if he could figure it out.

"You shouldn't promise things like that, Cal."

"Too damn bad."

Her fingers knitted together as she shook her head. "You're wrong."

"You'll have a home surrounded by your friends and family and whoever else you want. Kids? Husband?" *A husband?* "Two dogs and a cat? The whole shebang. Whatever you want. When we're done with this, I promise you can have that."

She stared as if he were speaking another language, as if he were offering hope. The longer she stared, the more determined he was to make it happen for her. Grace Willoughby had her whole life in front of her. Screw the ex-husband. Callum would take care of Dominic and hand over her life back. "I promise, Grace."

The tick-tock of the grandfather clock suddenly seemed too loud.

Her chin dropped. "I'm so tired."

Did she mean tonight? Or tired of her life?

She gave Sherlock one last pet, tugged her robe tight over the flannel pajamas, and offered a quick goodnight as she fled upstairs.

Grace was a runner. A hider. She probably couldn't imagine how things would get better. Fixing her life wasn't Callum's job, but damned if the urge to smooth the edges didn't make itself known every time he took a breath.

Chapter Ten

The sunrise alarm clock eased Grace from a restless night. She blinked, confused that she'd actually fallen asleep, and every part of her wished she'd turned off her alarm last night when she'd known sleep would be so elusive. How was she expected to dream when Callum made promises like that when she'd been awake?

The heavenly scent of coffee pulled her eyelids open, beckoning her from bed like the coffeemaker was the Pied Piper. How was the coffee already brewed?

She tumbled out of bed and snagged the scrunchie from the nightstand, finger-combing her hair into a bun, then hazarded a glance in the mirror. Not bad. Not great. She shouldn't care. Callum was here to help. Not to drool over. She could deal with him. She'd done it for most of her life. But first, coffee.

She slid into her robe and shuffled downstairs. His pillow and blanket were folded at the end of the couch, sitting as if he'd never used them. His coffee mug waited on a hand-tatted coaster. Proof that she hadn't imagined the day before.

She wandered into the kitchen. Callum was nowhere to be found, but he'd left her an almost full pot of coffee. "Callum?"

Not even Sherlock slinked about.

Grace doctored her mug with a hefty pour of milk and a spoonful of sugar, stirring and scanning out the kitchen window. He wasn't in the backyard either.

The front door opened. Grace sucked down a fortifying gulp before she entered the living room again as he walked in, shoving his truck keys into his pocket. "You're up early. Sorry. Did I wake you?"

"No. I'm usually an early bird, though it was hard to wake up this morning. I couldn't sleep." She eyed the couch. It couldn't have been comfortable, but he didn't look sleep-deprived. "What were you doing?"

"I loaded my bag into my truck."

Her stomach dropped. Her coffee accidentally sloshed over the lip of the mug. "You're leaving?"

Grace wiped her hand against her hip and tried to wrangle her emotions. It'd been less than twenty-four hours since he'd tumbled back into her life. Her defenses had been high for almost every question and conversation—*almost*, because they had not been during their chat about promises and the future. At the possibility of his leaving, her panic surged. He had made promises. He said he could solve the Dominic problem. She didn't realize she'd believed him.

And...she would miss him. That didn't make sense. They'd barely spent time together. She barely knew him. Except this was Callum. Part of her life until she left. A dull ache of sadness surprised her, but who was she to talk? He'd grieved her death. At least, she supposed he had.

"No," he said. "I'm not leaving."

"But..." Her heartbeat thudded. He'd packed. He'd loaded his truck.

The corners of his eyes tightened, as if trying to read what she hadn't said. "I didn't want to junk up the living room." He lifted a hand toward the living room. "Everything is so...pretty."

She breathed easier.

He inched closer. "Everything okay?"

"Yes. Yeah. Of course. But, um, I don't think Alicia would mind if you left your belongings stored." She held the mug with both hands. The heat burned her palms. It was the kind of pain she understood and could control.

All she had to do was set the mug down and the pain would go away. She didn't. The burning heat made sense. She knew her limit, and she wasn't there yet. The heat was easier to handle than the possibility that Callum could take off.

Carefully, she blew into the coffee and hid behind the mug. If she gave the mug her complete attention, he wouldn't be able to get a read on the bonkers thoughts ping-ponging through her sleep-deprived brain. Then again, Callum had never been able to read her thoughts when it came to him.

"What are we going to do today?" She sipped her coffee and studied the light brown liquid in her mug.

"What do you usually do?"

Work was always a safe subject, as long as her version of writer's block didn't come back. She eased the mug away from her face. "My days are pretty boring. I usually sketch ideas in the morning. It's quiet. I like the morning light." She perched on the edge of the couch next to his pillow and blanket. "I've been working on a book cover commissioned by a children's author—"

Callum reached for her coffee mug and set it on the coffee table.

"Hey—It's rude to steal someone's caffeine."

"Don't hide behind a mug, and maybe I won't."

She made a face but kept quiet. He wasn't wrong.

"Seems to me," he said, "you've been the queen of avoiding reality."

"That's a *sweeping* mischaracterization—" Grace held up her hand when his lips parted. "Nope. Do *not* make me defend myself before I've had more than a few sips of caffeine."

His slow smile grew, and his bourbon eyes danced. "There's the Grace I've always known."

"I don't know what you're talking about." Except she did. Once upon a time, bantering with him had been as natural as breathing.

"Think you do." He winked and reached for his coffee. "Glad to see the girl I used to know again."

"I'm still me. Just reserved with you."

"Why? I'm not the bad guy."

"No. Actually, I guess I am." Grace slid onto the couch and snagged the pillow on top of the blanket. She wrapped her arms around it. If she couldn't have the mug as a shield, the pillow would more than do. "At least between the two of us."

Her chin dipped—and she caught the faint masculine hint of him.

Callum set down his coffee and sat next to her. "Hey—hey. Come on." He put his arm around her shoulder and gave her a squeeze. "Everything will be okay."

Her stomach tightened with instant recognition. His scent was startlingly familiar and intoxicating and inherently Callum Hale. It wasn't cologne or shampoo or even generic man. It was just him.

"You're not the bad guy, Grace. You're the..." He pinched his eyes shut, as though he should have caught himself.

"I'm the what?"

He pulled his arm back, shrugging like he didn't want to say it. "Victim."

God, she hated that word. Victim was too generic, a catchall for all the wrongs, no matter how big or small. Someone could be a victim of credit card fraud, or they could be a victim of a brutal attack. "I don't feel that way." She could tell it made little sense to him. "What you're forgetting is that I've had years to process what happened to me, despite how I've chosen to live, and you're living it like it's fresh."

"Okay," he said quietly. "You're not a victim."

"Not anymore."

He nodded. They sat in silence, though it seemed like he had more to say. Still, Callum didn't push it.

"I'm still the same person you've always known," she said. "It's just been hard to share everything with you. I'm angry at Dominic and frustrated with how Hayden brought you in without telling me."

His face skewed, but he stopped himself from asking whatever was on the tip of his tongue.

"But I really am glad to see you." She pinched her lips together. "I'm sorry I didn't tell you everything before."

"You don't need to apologize. I heard everything you said yesterday, and...I was coming at you from an angry place. I should have said I'm glad you're here. I missed you, hon."

The air in her lungs shimmered. He had no clue how much she'd missed him.

He squeezed her shoulder. "Are you okay?"

Nope. Not even close.

Sherlock trotted into the living room with a meow. Thank God. A distraction. He hopped onto the coffee table, and Grace reached for him. He ducked out of reach and offered a disdainful feline glance over his shoulder before gracefully perching behind Callum.

He laughed.

"Traitor," she told the cat.

"Come on, kitty. Be nice to Grace."

Sherlock jumped between them. Callum held out his hand and let Sherlock cautiously inspect him. After a momentary standoff, Sherlock stretched closer to him.

"He might like me more than he likes you." His large hand slid over Sherlock's back.

"That's impossible. I feed him the best treats."

Sherlock purred, turning his head to nuzzle Callum's hand.

"Oh, come on."

Callum rotated his wrist and let Sherlock rub his face against his palm. "You were scared I was leaving?"

One hundred percent. "I was curious."

"Your face said a lot more."

"Since when can you read my face?" But just in case, she needed to avoid meeting his gaze. "I'm concerned about bringing trouble to Alicia."

"But not yourself?"

"I've always known what I signed up for. Alicia would do anything for a friend, and I don't want to take advantage."

"I get that. We're going to fix it. I promised, remember?"

She would never forget the promise of a house with a garden. In a neighborhood of friendly faces, where she might have a family one day. Last night, his promise was unfathomable. Today, the idea was the tiniest bit more plausible when he spoke to her with that low rumbling voice.

"Simple, huh?" She sipped her coffee and hid behind the mug again.

"It's what I do."

Her eyes met his. A swarm of butterflies circled and danced in her stomach. "I believe you."

Sherlock tentatively pressed a paw onto Callum's powerful thigh. He tested and placed his other paw, kneading as Callum continued to pet his back.

"Where do your folks think you've lived all this time?"

"I kept a low profile and didn't stay anywhere long."

"That's not an answer. Where do they think you were?"

"Don't ask, don't tell?" She ignored the way his expression hardened and wished she had bottled up the way he'd just made her feel moments before. "They think my home base is a place I purchased through a shell company. It's one of the places I mentioned to your colleague. Dad and Mari never asked questions because I asked them not to. Knowing too much would be close to fraud." Or *was* fraud, if she was honest with herself.

"All right," he muttered under his breath.

"What? I answered your laundry list of questions yesterday."

His phone chirped from his back pocket. Callum checked the time. The lines above his brow deepened. "I have to take this."

He stepped outside to take the call. She hadn't seen him do that with a phone call before. Grace glanced at the grandfather clock.

Who called someone that early? Not work. Her curiosity piqued, then plummeted. For all the discussions they'd had about being alive and about her ex-husband, she hadn't asked about him. Who was he now?

Callum could be married. Would Hayden have told her that? She didn't ask about anyone. That had initially been about self-preservation but then became a habit built out of guilt. Getting updates on others when they didn't know about her felt wrong. Callum hadn't volunteered news of his life when he questioned her, and she hadn't asked. He might have a family. Maybe kids. Either way, he definitely had an entire life that she selfishly hadn't thought about.

She pinched her eyes shut. How egotistical.

Surprise! She was alive.

Surprise! Her ex-husband had found her.

Not once had she asked about him.

Had he been wearing a wedding band? Surely she would have noticed. But the lack of a wedding band didn't preclude a girlfriend at home or even children. Callum as a father? She hadn't pictured it before. He would be a great dad. Stern but understanding. Responsible and fun.

It gave her the warm-and-fuzzies, which quickly fizzled into regret. His life had moved forward. He probably shared it with an amazing woman. Grace's life had stayed the same since she had dropped off the radar.

In all the years since she'd been hiding from Dominic, she'd never been jealous. There had been lonely times, times when she was curious what another life might look like, times when she desperately craved being held in the middle of the night. But she'd never been jealous of what might have been.

Not until now.

He opened the living room door—*and was pissed.* Arms crossed, face scowling, he strode to her as if she'd been hiding Dominic in the kitchen. "What else have you left out?"

"What?" Grace blinked back regretful tears she hadn't realized were pooling in her eyes.

"Forget our list of questions and tell me the important parts you've left out."

"*What?*"

"No. We're not going to pretend here. If I'm laying everything out, you need to also."

"What, exactly, are *you* laying out?"

His glare tightened. Glowering over her, he leaned in and lowered his voice. "You know what I mean. I'm here until this shit is fixed. You keep lying—"

"I'm not."

"You've lied about a whole hell of a lot. So pardon me if we have a trust issue. That's the starting point you gave me."

Grace squared off with him. He tipped his face down. She tipped hers up. Her breath raced, and confusion rang in her ears. "What the hell are you talking about?"

"This is serious."

"Really? You think?" she shouted. "Because, no kidding, Callum. If I hadn't already known that after living my damn life like this every day, I think I would have figured it out sometime after macing you and before the FedEx delivery."

He jerked away. Shoving his hands in his pockets, he paced as waves of anger rolled off him like the aftershocks of an earthquake.

Yelling at each other would not fix this. She swallowed over the ache in her throat and hoarsely asked, "What's going on?"

He halted and turned to face her. With a disappointed shake of his head, he said, "We know about your attorneys. We have the records of the incoming calls."

Her blood ran cold. "What?"

"This will not work if you keep lying."

"Maybe you should listen to me. Because I'm not."

"*Maybe* you're trying to protect them. Maybe you signed a legal agreement. Maybe you have something else going on, or fuck it, Grace, maybe you're just scared. The thing is, I trump everyone. I'm at the top of the pile of people involved in this. Do you get that? Because everyone else you've stitched into your disappearing act? They're beneath me. Under me. I call rank in this crazy-ass world you created."

"You sound like an ass."

"I am an ass right now. Get that through your beautiful brain. Look, I don't care who helped you pull off this gigantic, fraudulent charade. I'm over it with Hayden. I don't care about your attorneys. But starting right now, you have to be upfront with me."

"I don't have attorneys."

"Your phone records say otherwise." Gone was the emotion from his voice. Callum was disconcertingly cold, and the shift terrified her.

She couldn't continue their standoff and reached for her coffee. Her hand trembled. She wrapped her other hand around it to steady the mug. "What part of 'no attorneys' do you not understand?"

He ran his tongue along the inside of his cheek. His jaw sawed, and both irritation *and* frustration burned hot in his angry eyes. "We know that Dominic's not the only one looking for you, babe."

She faltered mid-sip of coffee. "What are you talking about?"

"The attorneys who represented you in Dominic's felony trial—"

Her attorneys didn't know she was alive. They couldn't be looking for her. "No."

"*And* your divorce attorney," he said, lifting two fingers, then added a third, "and some attorneys at the Department of Justice."

"No." Her stomach bottomed out. The coffee mug shook harder than she could hide. She set it down. "They aren't. They don't know I'm alive."

"Your phone records disagree and have almost since the day Marino was released."

That was back in April, and now it was August. "No."

"What's the point of lying? Because you don't want to go into witness protection? Do you know how much of my time you have wasted?"

Her stomach turned, as if her coffee had spoiled in her gut. "That's. Not. Possible. Why would I lie?"

He rubbed the back of his neck and paced again. "I don't know."

Grace grabbed his biceps. "If I have to trust you, you have to trust me."

He looked down. Tension flexed in his jaw, and his pinched lips rolled together.

"Callum." She squeezed her fingers into his arms. "Listen to me. Trust me."

His breath came quicker. "I had no reason not to. Then you left."

"I'm so sorry," she whispered. Tears blurred her vision. "So sorry."

He deflated, wrapped an arm around her like he was angry, until he folded her to his chest. She sobbed. Years of emotions and bad decisions and fear bubbled up.

"I shouldn't have come at you like that." He wrapped his other arm around her. "Take a breath."

But that wasn't why she was crying. She'd hurt him. Hurt everyone. And he was pulling away when they'd just reconnected. "I really am so sorry."

He soothed a hand over her back. "It's okay. C'mere." Guiding them to the couch, Callum pulled her next to him and held her close, still soothing, still rubbing, until she caught her breath and wiped her eyes.

"I shouldn't have yelled at you," he whispered. "I've got a short fuse when it comes to betrayal—not by you," he caught himself. "I've got other shit on my mind." He kept her close, resting his chin on top of her head. "It's okay. Catch your breath."

Again, she wiped her eyes with the back of her hand. They were due for a blowup, she guessed. They'd had them over the years, but it had never ended with her crying.

Grace wasn't sure how long they stayed like that. He let her stay in his arms until she was ready.

"I'm not in touch with my old attorneys. I promise."

He nodded. "I believe you."

"Do you swear?"

He nodded again. "I trust you."

Something was happening with her phone that she didn't understand. This was the same dread that had churned in her gut the day the FBI had raided Marino's penthouse in Las Vegas. "I didn't talk to them, but even if I did, why would they want to get a hold of me?"

He casually rubbed her back. "I don't know. My office is talking to them."

His phone signaled an incoming call. This time she wasn't worried about whether he was married with kids.

"Give me a minute." He swiped the screen on his phone and pressed it to his ear, staying on the couch beside her with an arm still draped around her shoulder. "Hey, yeah. She's not in contact with them."

He pulled the phone away. "Just to confirm, no calls, voicemails, emails? Nothing?"

"Nothing," she confirmed.

"Nothing." He pulled his arm from around her and cradled his forehead for a moment before dragging his hand through his hair. "I'm sure." He glanced her way, then pushed off the couch to stare out the window, lowering his voice. "Doesn't look like it, unless she's one hell of an actress."

They didn't believe her.

But Callum did.

That should have made her feel the slightest bit better. She wasn't sure if it did. Grace was too busy trying not to freak out more than she already was.

"That was my thought, too. When you know more, let me know. But that's the understanding we'll operate under." He ended the call and didn't move from the window, keeping his back to her.

"What's the understanding?" she managed.

He joined her on the couch again and tossed the phone onto the coffee table. His shoulders bunched and relaxed, and he bent over, elbows on his knees, head in his hand as he thought. "Give me a second to think." Finally, he lifted his head. "Did you ever get my voicemails?"

"*No.*"

He nodded, as if he could see the missing pieces. Callum picked up his phone. "Give me the best number to reach you at."

She did. He dialed. "Where's your phone?"

"The kitchen." It was a bare-bones burner, not exactly something she'd keep by her nightstand to scroll social media.

"Is your ringer on?"

"Yeah."

His phone rang through. Her phone wasn't registering a call.

A generic prerecorded voicemail message answered on Callum's phone. A beep signaled that he should record his message. "Hey, Grace. Checking in. If you get this, call me."

Callum ended his call and strode to the kitchen to grab her phone. After a quick glance, he handed it to her.

"No missed calls. No messages," she said.

He rubbed his jaw.

"What's going on?"

"Your ex is a dozen steps ahead of us." He let out an exhausted sigh. "Dean will have to confirm this, but my guess is that Marino has access to your email and phone numbers. He's screening who's in contact with you."

It was happening again. Everything she had tried to protect against.

"Despite everything you've been doing, he's been tracking you since before he walked out of prison. If not before."

Chapter Eleven

Grace wanted to hurry back to bed and hide from what had promised to be a glorious summer day. If what Callum had said was true, everything she'd done to hide had failed. She stared at her phone and willed his voicemail to pop up onscreen. Not even a missed call.

More than hiding under the covers, she needed to leave. She had put Alicia in a dangerous position, and another layer of guilt pancaked upon the ones she usually, hopefully stoically, carried.

Grace paced the living room and wondered if she should trust Callum's safe houses. Or she could go anywhere in her underground network. No, that would put others who had helped her over the years in the same position as Alicia.

Maybe she should update her parents, and there was a conversation with Hayden that had to be had. She stifled a groan. There were so many things she needed to do that very second that she couldn't move.

Grace shoved her phone into the pocket of her robe and walked toward the stairs. Her movements were too jerky. Her nerves trembled in her hands. "I have to leave. I'll write Alicia a note—"

"Hang on." Callum blocked her escape. "We're not running away."

He had said "we."

"I'm not running—"

"Yeah, Grace. It's what you do; you run. You hide. If you don't see that, then you need to take a minute to reflect."

She stepped around him, completely in agreement but having no idea what else to do. "It's all I know."

He grabbed her arms and recentered her in front of him. "We're not playing defense unless it's the right course of action, and I'm not convinced it is. Later, maybe. Right now? No."

"But—"

"And running before Alicia has even walked her dogs won't help anyone feel good about the situation."

"He could show up here. It doesn't matter that there weren't cameras and listening devices. Dominic has an agenda, and I don't understand it."

"We'll get there. We'll understand it."

He kept saying "we," and it knocked the panic out of her bit by bit.

"If he showed up right now?" Callum smirked. "Let him knock on the door right this fuckin' second. That would be the easiest way to solve this problem."

His confidence balanced her panic. "He's crazy—"

"I'm ready for him."

She shivered, and the last shreds of doubt were erased. Was Callum really what she needed to stop Dominic?

He stroked her arms. "If he gets near you, I will annihilate him."

She tipped her head back to meet his steadfast gaze. He would keep her safe. She hadn't remembered what safety felt like until right now. Her chin dipped, and Grace leaned into him. Her forehead pressed against his sternum. Callum wrapped his arms around her. "It will be okay. I promise."

All of these promises... She believed him. The warmth of his embrace melted her against his chest, and she let Callum cocoon her in his strength.

Argos and Toto pitter-pattered down the stairs. She inched back, pressing against his arms until he let go. The dogs reached the living room, and Alicia followed, adjusting her glasses to rub her eyes.

"Good morning, early birds. It sounded like you two were going to kill each other." Alicia tossed a sharp look at Callum. "Everything okay?"

"We're fine." Grace rubbed her arms. "We had to compare notes on an issue or two, but it's resolved."

Alicia eyed both of them.

"I took you for a morning person," Callum casually added.

She side-eyed him. "You'd better brush up on your people-reading skills. I'm only awake because you two had my boys up and ready for the day a full thirty minutes before my alarm. Want to tell me about the notes you loudly compared? I tried not to listen. Manners, and all."

Grace scratched behind Toto's ear. "People have been trying to call and email me, but I haven't heard from them."

"People, who?"

"Specific people," Callum said. "Important people. Attorneys."

Alicia cast her gaze between them. "Well, that sounds suspicious."

"Sure does." Callum let Sherlock nuzzle against his leg. "No telling who else has been reaching out."

"Callum had tried to reach me before he showed up at the library," Grace explained.

Alicia's gaze swung to Callum. "You did?"

He nodded.

"And you didn't mention that before?" She rested her hands on her hips.

The corners of his eyes tightened. His lips thinned as if he were trying to hide a smile, and something close to appreciation registered on his face. The more they interacted, the more they seemed to like one another.

"We got off to a rocky start," he conceded.

Alicia hummed and walked toward the dogs' leashes. "I suppose."

"I'll walk your dogs."

"Is Dominic outside?" Alicia asked.

His lips twitched. "Not that I know of."

"Is there a big baddie with a gun out there?"

"Nope. Haven't seen any sign of that, either."

"Then I'll walk my dogs, thank you very much." She clipped on the dogs' leashes. "How did Dominic mess with her phone calls?"

"What's the point in asking?" Grace slumped. "Unlimited resources. Dark web people. Sociopathic tendencies. That's the answer to almost every Dominic question."

"He's not infallible," Callum said, but raised his shoulders. "My office is working on how. When we know the how, we'll have a better handle on the why. But given who's not getting through, I'd say we have the basis for a good working theory." His phone chirped again. "Maybe we have answers already."

Callum answered the call, listened as they watched, and ended the call with hardly a word. Judging from his expression, that wasn't a great phone call. Nervous energy turned Grace's palms clammy. Sherlock threaded in and out of Callum's boots as if the cat had heard the phone call as well and understood that things weren't moving in the right direction.

Grace reached for her tepid coffee and wrapped her palms around the mug. "Don't look at us like that. Spit it out."

"As it turns out..." he cleared his throat and narrowed his gaze on her, like once again, another round of understanding had made itself clear, "it's the office of an assistant attorney general who would like to have a word with you."

Her stomach bottomed out. Grace mouthed, "Assistant attorney general, like, of the country?" She turned to Alicia. "What the hell is happening? I'm supposed to be dead."

Alicia blinked her eyes wide and then let out a low whistle. "Those would be quite the phone calls to miss."

Grace shook her head. "I'm not going through the Dominic Marino show again." She knew nothing that would warrant that many people reaching out to her. "I can't."

Or worse, the government was upset that she'd ditched witness protection years ago and faked her death. That was fraud. That was a valid reason for her attorneys to try to reach her. The attorney general's office probably wanted to throw her in jail. "They're going to arrest me."

"No. That's not it."

"Are you sure?" she pressed.

His lips flattened. "They wouldn't employ resources like that for this type of arrest."

"Then what do they want?"

"I don't know, but you have to meet with them." His halfhearted smile offered no support. "I'll take you there. We'll schedule the meeting and control as much as we can."

"No way in the world—"

"You do it this way, or they'll send federal marshals."

"So they *do* want to arrest me," she said as Alicia snapped, "*Marshals*? What for?"

Callum held up his hands, palms out in defense. "Don't shoot the messenger, ladies. I don't know what they want to meet about. Any guess is based on a whole lot of inference."

"So infer away," Grace demanded.

He stared at the ceiling and thought. "Given who Marino is and how he wriggled his way out of a conviction, I'd bet the DOJ would like another shot at him."

"Meaning?"

"Like I said—"

"You don't know," Alicia snapped. "Got it. But what is your guess?"

"No one will give us anything yet," he admitted. "So we have to ask why. There are specific reasons litigators keep their mouths shut."

"I don't know what those are," Grace said. "Extrapolate."

"Maybe they're convening a grand jury." He held up his hands again. "For what? No idea. But Marino burned the DOJ. They probably want to burn him right back."

"Can't we just ask about that?"

He shook his head. "No. I believe the process is confidential."

"For what?"

"What does it matter? Everyone probably has the same end goal: get Marino behind bars again. We won't know anything more until you talk to them."

"I can't handle another go-round with Dominic." Grace collapsed onto the couch. For a fleeting second, she considered hiding from the world by burying her face in Callum's pillow. Breathing him in might be the only thing to keep her from losing her mind.

As if knowing how close to the edge Grace was, Sherlock jumped onto her lap.

She dropped her chin onto the top of his soft head. "I haven't seen him in years. Haven't talked to him."

Callum remained quiet. Tension ticked in his jaw. She didn't like that an explanation wasn't immediately forthcoming.

"It doesn't make sense."

"It's not going to make sense to us." He rubbed the back of his neck. "What if Dominic didn't track you down to scare you—not to *repossess* you, for lack of a better word?" His lip curled in disgust before he shook it off. "Rather, he's making himself known to keep you from speaking with the DOJ."

That hadn't occurred to her. Then again, she hadn't known anyone was looking for her. The Department of Justice wasn't even a blip on her radar.

"He won't want you to talk to the AG's office, even if you don't think you know anything. It opens up a liability that he can't control."

The three of them stewed over his idea. It made sense, but something didn't sit right.

"If Dominic is doing that, why would he block you?" Alicia asked Callum. "You're an old family friend. Not involved with the attorneys or the DOJ."

"He isolated me from friends when we were married." She bit her lip. "Dominic's doing what he knows how to do."

"We'll know more once you sit down with the attorneys."

"No. I can't." She shook her head. "Someone in one of those offices is probably on his payroll. Maybe in all the offices. He covers his bases." But that didn't make complete sense either. Dominic had been clear. *Until death do us part.* She threaded her fingers through her hair. "Maybe it's both. He's warning and terrorizing me. Twice as much fun."

Tension flexed in Callum's jaw.

"That's it, isn't it? He's giving me options. I stay quiet, I stay his wife, or I'm dead like the world believes. And, bonus points for him, I don't speak with the attorneys." She'd bet he loved every second of this.

"Honestly? I don't know," Callum said. "The DOJ won't share details before it's ready for the world to know. Their investigations are confidential."

"Like that ever slowed down Dominic."

"My office is in contact with the attorneys you worked with during his trial. There will be some kind of amnesty or immunity that protects you."

"For the fake death issue?" Alicia asked.

Issue sounded as if Grace was late in paying her taxes. She had actually ensured that all of her finances were on the up and up.

Callum nodded. "That's the least of anyone's concerns."

Alicia led Argos and Toto toward the front door. "We should have called you years ago. All right. I'll be back in five. Go about your shouting or hugging or whatever you two are doing."

Chapter Twelve

Alicia left for work after she gave Callum a stern lecture to keep an eye on Grace. She and Callum were alone. She retreated to her bedroom. Sherlock paced along the edge of her bed until he found the perfect place to curl up and await the attention he deserved. Grace sidled next to him, absentmindedly stroking his coat. "I'm sorry Dominic knows where you live now."

He purred as if to soothe away her worries.

"What do you think about Callum?"

Sherlock continued to purr.

"I wish I knew what that meant. You've always got a good read on people."

Actually, Sherlock had made his opinion known. He never paid attention to new people unless he either hated them or trusted them. Rubbing his face on Callum's boots and kneading his thighs was a clear approval. That said a lot for Callum. Sherlock was a harsh judge of character.

She inhaled and held it until she decided to pack her belongings in preparation for their likely departure. At least choosing when to pack was within her control.

There weren't many items to shove into her backpack. Her belongings had been left at the rental cabin after she'd fled from the grocery store. Meaning she only had her computer, which was always with her, and a few days' worth of clothes and toiletries Alicia had recently purchased for Grace.

But an hour later, she still hadn't packed. Her body physically ached. The idea of shoving her belongings into her backpack—a task that she'd easily done dozens of times over the years—exhausted her to the point of tears. For the first time, Grace felt she couldn't keep up the lifestyle she'd committed to, and that made her tired and angry.

Callum knocked on her door.

She pinched her eyes closed. Fatigue weighed over her. The vulnerability was infuriating. And that made her eyes burn.

"Give me a second." She pulled herself together, opened the door, and returned to her bed. "How's it going? Any news?"

Callum leaned against the doorjamb. His gaze skimmed over the beautifully decorated room. Her hairbrush lay on the doily on top of the dresser that Grace barely used. She didn't have enough clothes to warrant more than the top drawer. "Everything okay?"

"Nothing's okay. That's why you're here, remember?"

He stepped inside her bedroom and walked to the bookshelf. This time, he ignored the books and focused on a porcelain figurine of a carousel. "My mom used to collect these when I was little. I don't know what happened to them. They probably disappeared in the divorce."

He hadn't been young when that happened, but she didn't recall the figurines. "You were in our house way more than I was in yours."

He meandered to the corner of her bed and sat down. "Do you remember that time you came over and the three of us were in the basement, lights out, playing with a Ouija board?"

She hadn't thought about that in years and laughed. "The things you two made it say. I was scared out of my mind for weeks."

His laughter rumbled. "Sorry about that."

"I think that was one of the last times I was in your basement with the lights off."

He tilted his head and gave her a funny look. "You were there the time everyone was playing spin the bottle. You took off like a bat out of hell."

A furious blush caught fire on her cheeks and flamed down her neck. Grace dangled her legs off the side of her bed and lay back so that she didn't have to look at him. "Well, yeah. You two were seniors. I was a freshman."

"Half of the hockey team was there. Definitely more than just seniors."

"You say that like it would have been a reason to stay." Their high school was on the smaller side. Everyone knew everyone. Most of her friends knew she worshipped the ground Callum walked on and would have done just about anything to make sure her bottle spin landed on him. "Well, I wasn't going to have my first kiss be from some random guy in your basement."

Callum scooted closer, dangled his legs, and lay back. "First kiss, huh?"

"I was shy." She elbowed him.

He jabbed back, softer than she had. "Ha. You are the farthest thing from shy."

Grace rolled her eyes. "Either way, Hayden probably didn't want his kid sister there."

"Bet he didn't," Callum muttered, then his lips quirked. "Guess you missed out. I could have been your first kiss."

"You would have made a puking, gagging noise if my bottle had landed on you. That's how that would have gone."

He laughed but didn't disagree. "I was young and dumb."

"I was younger." That had always been part of the problem in catching his attention.

"But," he said, voice lifting like a tease. "Do you remember the night you met up with us in New York City with your friends?"

Of course she did. They'd all been in college and met up for a long weekend. It had been fun...until it wasn't. The typical drama where she thought *maybe* Callum had noticed her, and then he had absolutely not. "Sure."

"I thought I was going to kiss you that night."

Her jaw fell open. "You absolutely did not. What are you talking about?"

"I mean, Hayden would've killed me—"

"You're making stuff up."

He crossed a hand over his chest. "Swear I'm not. I was a little drunk. You were mostly ignoring me."

"*Ignoring you?*" Was he out of his mind?

"Except, I think you chewed my ass out over something, and for a split second, I thought you were going to kiss me."

She knew the exact moment he was talking about. She also vividly remembered ending up in the bathroom, crying with her girlfriend, because she'd been so obvious, and he'd been the very definition of oblivious. Grace could have literally been holding up a sign that begged him to take her home, and he wouldn't have noticed.

Her heart hammered in her chest, and she whispered, "You wouldn't have kissed me."

He shook his head. "No. Because it felt like it was..." He held her eyes but lifted his shoulders. "A hate-kiss that would have turned into a hate-fuck, and we would have regretted it in the morning."

She couldn't breathe. He was the oblivious one. Why was he acting like that wasn't true? "I've never hated you in my life."

He searched her face, and she would have done anything if he just touched her. Not even a kiss if that wasn't meant to be. But she was so starved for him that her body ached.

He let out a long breath and pushed off her bed. "I need to—"

She followed him. "Callum—"

He turned around, and she was right there. So very close to his chest that she could feel his warmth.

"Fuck it." He yanked her to him and brought her mouth to his.

Every part of her went weak. He took her weight, holding her to his body, backing her until she fell onto the bed.

The warmth of his lips stole her breath, and the deep want she'd harbored for years ignited. Callum devoured her. He possessed her. The velvet slide of his tongue against hers lit a fire so deep and needy that her soul cried for more.

His hands threaded through her hair, and she couldn't hold him close enough. Grace melted under the strength of his embrace, losing her breath and tasting the sweet cinnamon of his kiss.

Kissing Callum Hale made her head swim. This was what she'd been waiting for her entire life.

His mouth slowed, nipping and sucking, taking his time as if he understood how desperately she needed his mouth on hers.

Callum inched back. His knuckles caressed her cheek. He smoothed her loose hair away from her face. For a moment, panic washed over her. But that wasn't regret in his golden-brown eyes. "That was the best bad decision of my life…"

She blinked, pressing against the mattress. "I don't know what that means."

He pulled her close and kissed her once more as if it would never happen again.

Grace knotted her hands in his shirt and demanded everything she'd always wanted. This could be it. A kiss not to be repeated. A moment they would never discuss.

Callum deepened the kiss, sliding his tongue past her lips, tangling with hers. His hand palmed her cheek and slid into her hair. Sizzling heat of arousal sparked in her blood, racing from her head to her toes, and spiraling deep in her core.

His immense strength enveloped her in thick muscles and a demanding hold. Her leg snaked up his thigh. Her pelvis tilted and her hips rocked, rubbing against him. He held her, and it surpassed every dream she'd had about this. Her fantasies had had nothing on reality as his rough hand moved under her shirt, up her back, and slid down to her ass, squeezing as if he'd needed to hold on to her forever.

His phone chirped.

They froze in her bed. His mouth stilled against hers. Their heavy breaths raced and teased their lips. She opened her eyes and fell into the deep desire burning in his. Callum wanted her. She could see it. She could *feel* it.

His phone chirped again. As though he hated to be interrupted, he brushed his thumb over her lip, then inched back to answer the call. "Yeah?"

He rolled onto his back. His fingers pinched the bridge of his nose, and his eyes stayed closed.

Grace pushed off the bed and smoothed her hands over her shirt and shorts. Her hard nipples pressed against her shirt, and, catching a quick glance in the mirror, her cheeks were painted pink with arousal. She needed to leave. She couldn't face him right now.

He moved to the window and peeked out the drapes like she'd seen him do in the living room. He didn't look out windows like a normal person, but always searched for lurking danger. That served as a reminder of why he was there. They had no business kissing. Even if it was the best kiss of her life.

She turned toward the door.

"Hey, I gotta go." He tossed the phone onto the bed and snagged her hand. "Where are you going?" Callum sat on the bed and pulled Grace between his legs, locking his thighs around her, and fastened his hands to her waist. "Don't run away from me."

"I'm not."

The corners of his lips tugged up. His fingers flexed into her side. "I should have done that a while ago."

She blinked like an idiot. That didn't make sense. Did he not know of the years she'd made a fool of herself trying to get his attention? "Why?"

"Then maybe we wouldn't have such a headache to deal with now."

Did he just suggest that if he had kissed her before Dominic, she wouldn't have married Dominic? "That's..." *Probably true.* "Pretty cocky."

"Yeah, well." He shrugged. "It is what it is." One of his hands cupped her cheek. His thumb teased her bottom lip again. "I just hung up on my boss and have to call her back. Do not run away. Do not leave this house when I'm not looking."

"I won't."

He laughed. "Yeah, babe. You totally would." Callum kissed her again, smacked her ass, and grabbed his phone. "I'll be back in twenty minutes."

Well, that wasn't planned.

There were countless reasons Callum should have considered kissing Grace a mistake.

He didn't agree with a single one of them. He had resisted kissing Grace for years, and look where that had gotten them. And what a kiss. Kissing her was better than anything his vivid imagination had conjured up, and some of those fantasies would melt a lesser man to the ground.

Callum dropped onto the couch in the living room. The floorboards creaked above him. Grace was pacing, probably freaking out, and his remaining on this couch took more willpower than he knew he had.

Fuck.

This would complicate the assignment. He struggled to find a reason to care. It was already complicated. What was one more strange development when Grace had returned from the dead?

He blew out a breath and returned Vivian's call. "Sorry about that."

"Everything okay?"

His attention was pulled toward the ceiling and the sound of Grace pacing. "Better than I expected."

"Good. We were on the right path," Vivian said. "The attorney general's office wants an informal chat before what is likely going to be an impaneled grand jury."

"That's what we thought."

"Yes. Though they won't confirm it. So, it's conjecture and confidential, and we're going to keep that to ourselves."

"I don't know who we would tell."

"We'll make arrangements for the meeting. It'll be someplace low-stakes. Maybe a field office or one of those corporate office rentals. If they hear what they like, then we'll move on to formalized discussions and the legal maneuvering."

"She'll need her attorney present."

"Everyone agrees with that, and our office will coordinate schedules. You just need to have her there when and where it's agreed upon."

"She'll have questions."

"Given what you and Dean figured out about her phone, and likely her email, we all have questions. Once we get a handle on the communication issues, we'll update you. She should act as though she's unaware. And stay put. If there's not a reason to leave, don't; otherwise, Marino will get wind of you."

"Stay put like a sitting duck?"

"If he had wanted to take her, he would have made his move. Thought we had agreed about that?"

He nodded to himself. "Yeah, yeah. You're right."

"Anything else I need to know, Hale?"

"Like what?"

"If I knew that, I would have asked you directly. Wouldn't I?"

"There's nothing else to share."

"We'll talk again after Dean finds better answers." Vivian sighed. "You know, I gotta tell you. I didn't think this would turn into the project that it's becoming."

"You and me both, Viv."

Callum ended the call and pushed off the couch. He'd update Grace, and maybe they could grab lunch. Alicia had told him to eat whatever he wanted from her fully stocked kitchen, but he needed to get out of the house. Fresh air and more space would do him good.

Grace hurried down the stairs, chin up and hand gesturing, ready to make a point. He knew that face and body language. He was about to hear her give him the riot act. That was the Grace he'd always known. He crossed his arms and almost hid his grin.

She opened with, "We need to get a couple of things straight."

"This have anything to do with upstairs?"

"I've known you too long for..." she flicked her wrist and eyed him from head to toe, "...whatever game you have going on."

"Trust me. I don't have a game."

"You know what I mean."

"I don't."

"Whatever it is you're doing. Trying to distract me. Or draw my attention from my ex—"

"Your ex-husband was the last thing on my mind."

She appeared to be in total disbelief. "Then why did you just do that?"

"Because I wanted to."

"That's a selfish reason." Her lips pursed, and she shook her head. "I will *never* let a man manipulate me again."

"Whoa. Hang on—"

"I won't be more pliable or listen better or follow your rules and directions just because you kissed me."

He strode forward.

She took a step back. "And I'm sure as hell not going to—" Her breath quickened. She pressed against the wall. "—not going to—"

Callum closed the distance. "Not going to what?"

Grace rolled her bottom lip into her mouth. "Pretend you were ever interested in me."

Her breathy whisper went straight to his dick. "I wasn't pretending."

"You were. Because I was *always* interested, and you never noticed."

He kissed her again. To shut her up. To prove her wrong. To take advantage of the moment when he could pin her to the wall and feel her go completely liquid in his arms.

Kissing Grace restored the sanity he didn't know he'd lost. There wasn't a moment of hesitation as her mouth opened to his. Her arms locked around his neck, and she tasted like everything he'd always needed.

But he needed to slow down. Callum pulled back. If she wanted to talk, then they should talk. Even if his mouth on hers was better than any words he could string together.

They breathed hard. Her eyes were just as wild and alive as he felt. "Why do you keep doing that?"

Too many reasons. Most of them were dangerous and the wrong answer. "Because it's fun."

Grace smacked her palms into his chest and pushed him away. "I don't want to play games with you."

"You don't think that was fun?" The only game he had in mind involved pinning her wrists over her head and starting this song-and-dance over again. But warning bells rang out in the back of his lust-fogged brain. Her ex-husband had put his hands on her in a way Callum didn't understand yet. He wouldn't do anything in the same universe as Marino. He let her smack his chest again and easily stepped back when she pushed.

"I think—" She threw her hands out. "I have complicated feelings about this."

"You think I don't? Grace, *I thought you died.*"

Her chin dropped.

"Okay," he said. "I shouldn't have said that."

She swallowed hard before lifting her chin. "Please don't make me apologize again."

"I won't. Promise."

Her eyes met his, and he appreciated how easily she now gave them to him compared to when they'd first collided. Callum lifted his hand between them, silently asking permission, then reached for her. He brushed loose strands of her hair behind her ear and cupped her cheek. Her eyelids slid shut. Grace tilted her chin and leaned her face against his palm for a long minute.

"I've always wanted to be with you," he admitted. "The situation didn't work."

The prettiest pink blush warmed her cheeks. "I never thought you even wanted to kiss me."

He wanted much more than that. "Now you know."

Chapter Thirteen

Grace didn't know what she expected would happen next, but Callum took her to lunch without kissing her again or revealing thoughts that were better left as a secret. There had been no indication he had melted her to the wall and left her gasping.

What had she expected? It wasn't as if he would hold her hand or something during a perfectly amicable lunch. But she also hadn't expected the way she was suddenly more comfortable around him. They acted as if this were their normal routine. One that was dripping with tension and chemistry. But incredibly, absurdly normal.

They ate lunch. They returned to Alicia's home. They did everything they would have done had this been years ago, before she had met Dominic.

After lunch, Grace went back to work, but this time her creative block was gone, and she lost herself in the book cover project. She wasn't sure how Callum spent the hours. They weren't avoiding each other exactly. They were simply ignoring what had happened.

Except, even with an epic level of focus on work, she could practically sense him walking throughout the house. She held her breath anytime his footsteps neared the stairs, wondering if he would make his way into her bedroom and kiss her again.

Seriously, was she twenty years old? *Stop thinking about him.*

Argos and Toto barked in unison downstairs, shouting doggy joy that Alicia had returned. They noisily scampered from the front window to the front door, seesawing back and forth in a way that Alicia would never believe her well-behaved fur babies would act.

Would she tell Alicia that she'd kissed Callum? Hmm.

That would most definitely change Alicia's opinion of him.

She had been impervious to Callum's charm, and Callum seemed to like that about Alicia. Almost as if he were the one who had been charmed.

Alicia's laughter boomed through the house, and Grace made her way to the kitchen filled with friendly banter. These two were so different from yesterday. She supposed that she and Callum were in a wildly different situation as well.

Callum was kicked back at the kitchen table with his long legs extended and his hands folded behind his head. A perfect picture of relaxation as he chatted with Alicia. "Hey, Grace."

No sign he'd had her pressed to the wall earlier. Absolutely none. How was that even possible? "Hey, yourself."

Alicia had her back toward them as she chopped chicken breast for Argos and Toto's dinner. Her shoulders shook as she laughed. "You never told me about wanting to be a magician."

Grace glared at Callum. "That's because I was eight."

"She'd do this disappearing act where she held up a sheet, would drop it, and duck into the hall."

"I was *eight*."

"Sometimes she'd get her dog in on the act. And no matter how bad, her stepmom would cheer and clap like Grace was Harry Houdini—wait, wasn't that the name of your dog?"

Alicia didn't stop laughing. "You've always been one for hiding."

Grace's heart squeezed. She would always miss Houdini. He was the best dog she ever had. "*I was eight*." But she could hear the laughter in her voice. "Houdini was an excellent magician's assistant." Grace padded to the refrigerator and poured herself a glass of lemonade. "How was the library?"

"Less exciting than it was yesterday."

Callum snorted.

Yesterday morning, Grace had eaten breakfast, having no idea how her life would turn on its axis. Especially having no idea that Callum would kiss her into another universe.

Sherlock threaded in and out of Alicia's legs, knowing that after the dogs were fed, she would top his food with the canned tuna.

Callum's gaze locked on Grace and followed her every move. With the kisses fresh in her memory, she shivered and spared him a quick glance, immediately regretting it. Counter to his usual cool nature, the sexy gleam in his expression made clear he was also thinking about their kisses.

Grace was cognizant of where she stood, how she stood, how she folded her arms, then how she uncrossed them. Awareness ticked in her pulse, as if she were a woman starved for attention.

Seriously, she shouldn't have kissed him.

Everything felt awkward and amplified, and she was as obvious as her eight-year-old self, showing off magic tricks of her disappearing act with her dog. Arousal flamed under her skin. Callum Hale was watching her. She wanted to scream.

Grace drank her lemonade and ignored him. Alicia put the dog bowls on their mats. Sherlock jumped onto the table and lifted his chin in an indignant show of impatience.

"You'd think there isn't food sitting in his bowl right now." Alicia swept Sherlock into her arms and ignored the dignified squirming as she walked to the refrigerator and pulled out the container of tuna.

Sherlock purred his approval.

"Are we eating in or out?" Alicia added the tuna flakes to Sherlock's bowl and petted the cat, who was devouring dinner like he hadn't been fed in months. "I'm not in the mood to cook. Either of you want to play chef for the evening?"

"We went out to lunch earlier." Grace never wanted to cook but would sous chef the hell out of whatever Alicia made. Not with Callum, though. They had enough heat to work with.

"Then you're cooking for us?" Alicia pressed.

Nerves jumped in her stomach. She wasn't good in the kitchen but had never cared if Alicia knew it. She shouldn't care if Callum knew it. But she didn't want him to see her fail at yet another thing, even if cooking dinner was low on the consequence scale.

"Yeah, I will," Callum volunteered.

Alicia narrowed her eyes. "You cook?"

"Sure." He shrugged. "Anyone can cook."

"That's not entirely true," Grace added, with no natural ability in the kitchen beyond microwaving or following Alicia's instructions.

Alicia scrutinized the oversized man in her cutesy kitchen. "Any good at it?"

His broad shoulders bunched again. "That's subjective."

Grace tore her focus from his form-hugging shirt and studied the pink KitchenAid mixer on the counter. It wasn't the right time to notice Callum's chest or the hard plane of his abdomen. Nor was it the right time to recall that was the same shirt she'd fisted a few hours ago.

"Wrong answer." Alicia shook her head. "I'm too hungry to wait for anyone who doesn't know how well they cook."

He laughed. "I'm a good cook."

"You can prove that to me later. What do we want for dinner, Grace?"

"I vote for ribs or tacos." Any kind of food that required her to concentrate on how she was eating so that she wouldn't fixate on Callum.

"Oh, same." Alicia tilted her head at Callum and smiled. "You can vote for anything, but you're automatically outvoted if you say something other than ribs or tacos."

"I'm good with either." His phone rang. Callum glanced at the screen. His smile flatlined. "Give me a minute to take this."

Grace's stomach bottomed out. His phone calls were never good news.

After Callum walked out the kitchen door to the backyard, Alicia whistled long and low. "Holy Mother Mary, what happened today?"

Grace sank onto the chair that Callum had abandoned. "What?"

"Don't 'what' me."

"I don't know why you're giving me that look." Except she totally did.

"So you and him…?" Alicia wriggled her eyebrows. "I thought you said there was no you-and-him. But obviously, you left some crucial details out."

"There's never been a me-and-him before. I told you that."

"Honey, the way that man looks at you." Alicia clucked her tongue. "You're leaving out important details."

"No way." But she was certain her blushing cheeks gave her away.

"I know what I see."

Grace pushed out of the chair but didn't have anywhere to escape. She opened the refrigerator and pulled out the lemonade again, topping off the glass that she'd barely sipped from. "Want some?"

"You're telling me you two never ever? *Never?*"

Never ever didn't mean kissing. "No. *Never.*"

"Well, what's stopping you?"

That was an excellent question.

"See? Right there. That look." Alicia hummed, nodding. "The way you want to protest but wouldn't be stupid enough to say no. Nothing's stopping you."

"*Alicia.*"

"You're not blind, so maybe just dense." She shrugged, took the lemonade carafe out of Grace's hand, and poured herself a glass. "I thought he noticed you at the library, but then I figured that was just the pepper spray."

"It probably was."

"But that growly, possessive way he watched you walk into the kitchen? Now *that time* I didn't have to think. I know. I saw, double-checked, and saw again."

"Can you really see that?" Grace could still feel his kiss on her lips. "No, whatever you saw was aggravation." But was it? Kissing him could have burned the house down. "That's not—"

Callum walked into the kitchen with his phone outstretched. "It's Hayden."

Hayden.

Talk about whiplash. From thinking about Callum like *that* to thinking about Hayden, who was one reason she shouldn't think about kissing Callum.

God, wait a minute. She was a grown woman. Her brother should have absolutely nothing to do with her thoughts about Callum and wouldn't keep her from kissing him again.

But that wasn't the reason she wasn't ready to talk to Hayden. She didn't know how much Callum had shared and didn't want to admit to bouncing from one alias-rented house to another. Now that Callum had forced her to slow down and talk about the decisions she had made, she saw how strange her life-after-fake-death looked.

"Grace?" Callum held out the phone.

She took it but didn't press the phone to her ear. She needed a game plan, or at the very least, to sound confident in her decisions. Just because Dominic had found her didn't mean she'd made the wrong choices.

"Callum and I will walk the dogs while you talk to your brother."

A different type of panic sparked. If Alicia so much as breathed their never-ever conversation to Callum, Grace would fall over dead. She flashed her friend a pleading glance.

"Don't worry." Alicia lifted her fingers to her lips and mimicked the twist of a key in a lock and reached for the dogs' leashes. "I might be right, but I will not rub it in anyone's face."

Callum tried to decipher Alicia's meaning, but he didn't ask for clarification and followed her out the back door that led out of the kitchen to the backyard patio that wrapped around the side of the house.

Alone with the phone call that weighed heavily on her conscience, Grace pressed the device to her ear. "Hey, Hayden."

She adored her brother. He was a hero. Her role model. She'd worshipped him as a kid and followed Hayden and Callum everywhere she could. Whatever he was about to say would come from a place of love.

Their connection crackled, coating his voice in static. "Gracie, what the fuck?"

Tough love. "I'm sorry, I—"

"Do you have any idea how scared I was?"

Her brother didn't get scared. "I—"

"No. You don't. Dad and Mari hadn't heard from you. They're a wreck."

"I'm sorry, Hayden. I didn't mean to freak you out."

"Freaking out? You fucking scared the shit out of me. Do you not get that? Do you not get that you've had a huge-ass problem, and you didn't loop me in?"

Her chin dipped, and once again her eyes burned—but these tears were the guilty kind, very different from the ones brought on by her frustration with Dominic. "I didn't know how to explain. I still don't know how to, to be honest. Did Callum tell you what's been going on with my phone? I didn't know about your missed calls and voicemails. I wasn't ignoring you."

He let out a heavy sigh. "Yeah. Yeah, he did. Which is why I'm not yelling."

"Could have fooled me."

"*Gracie.*"

"Okay, okay, I get it. I screwed up. I scared you. I didn't check in and explain when I should have." She twisted the black beads on her bracelet. "I didn't give you details because I was more worried about distracting you."

"Forget my job." Static crackled. "You're my family. My priority, and since I can't be there, Callum is. You get that?"

"I get that." She let out an unsteady breath and wiped at the corners of her eyes. She peeked out the living room window. Callum and Alicia walked down the street with both dogs sniffing from spot to spot. "Why is Cal here? Not why is he helping me—but why isn't he with you?"

"That's complicated. It's a conversation you have to have with him."

Callum mentioned betrayal. Now Hayden was punting the answer. For two guys who always called situations for what they were, they were more avoidant than she'd ever seen them. "Prying answers out of him doesn't seem to be that easy."

"The important thing is that he's with you. Do what he says."

"Obviously."

"*Obviously*. Since I can't be there, I'm relying on Callum. Can you promise me to do what he says?"

"I'm not going to promise unquestioning allegiance."

"*Grace.*"

"Fine, yes, I will listen to Callum." If Hayden had known what she'd already done with Callum, this would have been an entirely different conversation. "I've told him the same thing."

"Good. All right, I have to go."

The call disconnected. The connection had sucked, and when the line died, she suddenly missed her family more than usual. Grace sucked in a fortifying breath and used Callum's phone to call her parents.

Dad picked up on the first ring. "Callum—"

The worry in her father's voice cut deep. "Hey, Dad. It's me on Cal's phone."

"Oh, God. Gracie—Hey, Mari, Grace is on the phone. Hold on a second." A moment later, Dad announced, "We're both here. Wait—*is Callum with you?* How do you have his phone?"

"He stepped out." She swallowed hard. "But, yeah. He's here. Hayden sent him to help me, and, well, he knows everything."

"*Everything?*" Mari whispered.

"Yeah."

"How'd he take it? Is he okay?"

The memory of him with a face full of mace, bent over and cursing, popped into her mind. Explaining that wouldn't help this conversation along. "I think he was mad. Angry at Hayden, mostly."

"He thought he'd lost you." There was a strange softness in Mari's voice that Grace didn't understand. "Maybe we should talk to him."

A knot thickened in her throat. Grace couldn't explain why Mari's tone affected her. "I'll tell him, if he wants, to call you when he gets back."

Her parents were unnervingly quiet.

"Well," Grace broke the awkward tension. "Look, I know I fumbled and scared the hell out of everyone. I'm sorry."

"We just want to know you're doing okay," Mari said. "Is everything taken care of, honey?"

She bit her bottom lip and didn't want to lie. Apparently, she'd done too much of that lately, even if everyone had known she would not have been living a normal life. "It's more complicated than I expected, but Cal's helping me work it out."

"What about Dominic?" Dad demanded. "If he's giving you trouble, then Callum and I can sort that out."

"No, Dad. Dominic is..." *An unstable lunatic.* "...possibly in more legal trouble. I don't even know if I should have said that. Can we not talk about him right now?"

"Does he know where you are?"

Damn it, she didn't want to lie to them. "Callum is handling it."

"That wasn't a no," Mari said.

"No, it wasn't," Dad agreed.

"Look, I'm safe. I'm with Callum. He won't leave my side until everything is fixed."

"What does 'fixed' look like, Gracie?" Dad asked.

Callum's promise of a new life, of a little house with a vegetable garden and friendly neighbors, surfaced front and center in her mind. She didn't want to get her hopes up and certainly wouldn't want to do that to her parents. "I'm not sure, to be honest."

She stared out the window at Alicia and Callum making their way back to the house. "I have to go, but I love you and will let you know if I have any news."

Their phone call ended, and she continued to stare out the window. Argos and Toto contentedly walked along as Alicia and Callum chatted. If Grace had been forced to predict the future, she never would have guessed those two would have met, nor would she have imagined Callum kissing her. Twice.

They entered the back door and unclipped the dogs in the kitchen. They trotted off as Alicia and Callum washed their hands.

"Who's ready for tacos?" Alicia asked, drying her hands. "I'll drive myself. I have to run errands after we eat, and then I'm having drinks with friends. Callum, you drive Grace."

Callum crooked an eyebrow as Alicia ambled out of the kitchen, her purse in hand. "She likes to give orders, doesn't she?"

"I like to organize," Alicia called from the living room right before the front door shut.

They were all alone again, and now the house didn't seem to hold enough oxygen. "I'll grab my bag."

She got two steps in before he stepped close behind her and wrapped an arm around her waist, belting her to his hard body. Every nerve in her jumped to life, and Grace was acutely aware of how warm and solid his muscles were.

His hot breath teased against her ear. "You looked scared of me when I walked back into the kitchen."

The scent of his cinnamon gum and the warmth of his words twisted her insides. Maybe she was scared. A lifetime knowing each other, and suddenly now it was different. "I'm not scared of you, Callum."

His lips brushed against her ear, and fireworks sparkled up her spine. "I'm in a hell of a predicament right now. I'm supposed to be heading for dinner, but the only thing I want to eat is…"

"*Callum.*" She shivered.

He squeezed her closer. His lips drifted against her neck. "But I'm not doing anything if you look that wary around me. Are we on the same page?"

She nodded, breathless and squirming, wishing he would pull them into bed and *do* what he almost said, but she was completely terrified that he'd even thought it.

His powerful hands turned her around and held her still with a possessive squeeze. Looking up would only catapult her farther into this alternative reality where Callum Hale was actively pursuing her. She'd gone her entire life wondering what it would feel like to have his attention. Her best guess had been wrong. This couldn't be a tenth of his focus, and it was melting her into pieces.

"Grace."

She tipped her head back and met his smoldering gaze. "You caught me off guard."

He rolled his bottom lip into his mouth, staring at her as if it were *her* lip he wanted to suck. "I messed up before. I didn't say what needed to be said. I didn't do what needed to be done, and it fucked me over."

"I—*What?*" That didn't make sense.

"I should have told you." His lips quirked. "Or at the very least, kissed you years ago. Everything would have been different."

She tried to understand—then everything came crashing down. "You think we would have got together? Stayed together?" She blinked, trying to read his expression. *Be together, even now?*

"I would have chased you," he said. "You would have pretended to put up a fight. But we both know, if we'd admitted what was staring us in the face, if we'd gotten together, it would have been explosive. And that would have been it for both of us."

"I wouldn't have put up a fight," she whispered.

She thought she saw him flinch at the history they could have had and missed.

Callum backed up, pulling her along until he dropped onto the chair next to the kitchen table. His hands moved to her hips and lifted her up and onto his lap, straddling her over his thick bulge.

Unconsciously, she rocked her hips—then caught herself. A fiery blush burned her cheeks.

"Explosive," he growled against her neck.

A tornado of need spiraled in her core. Grace wrapped her arms around him.

"There you go," he whispered.

The uneven cadence of her breaths seesawed. He teased her closer. She shifted against the hard length of his erection, watching his reaction, needing more of him.

He exhaled a heavy breath that stoked her confidence, flaming her arousal. "You absolutely know what to do when we're together."

Grace kissed him.

Callum groaned against her lips. "Fuck, baby."

Her heart hammered. His hands clamped on her hips, rocking her against his cock. She swept her tongue over his lips, and their kiss ignited like she'd lit fireworks. Starved for him, she couldn't be close enough. His kiss was desperate, as if he hadn't touched a woman in years, and his hunger poured over her.

Arousal pooled between her legs. Her nipples beaded, tight and wanting. Adrenaline burned over her skin. He'd stolen her resistance and melted her restraint.

The rough skin of his palms smoothed under her shirt and up the bare skin of her back and down again, gliding over her sides, rocking her against him again.

Her phone blared.

His hands froze.

Their breaths raced, and she needed him to touch her more than she could understand.

It kept ringing.

She opened her eyes and met his.

"Fuck," he finally let out, snatching Grace back to reality.

She couldn't form words. Achy, heady need clouded every thought, but still she realized they couldn't do this right now.

The phone finally stopped ringing, but her text message chimed.

His lips quirked. "Fifty bucks says that's Alicia wondering where we are. I bet she'd leave us be if—"

"No." Grace inched back. "I'm not standing my friend up for tacos just because you're—" She gestured. "You."

"Me?" His grin hitched. "*You're* the reason we haven't left the house." He gripped her hips and rocked her again. "Distracting me."

Laughing, she rolled her eyes and pushed away.

Callum yanked her back into place. "You good?"

"Yes."

He cupped her chin and turned her face until she met his intense scrutiny. "Are we good?"

The warmth flooding through her was very different from the heat that had her willing to make out with Callum in Alicia's kitchen. She wasn't used to the gentle care that she heard in his voice. Not from Callum or any man. "We are."

Callum lifted her off his lap as though she weighed nothing and set her on her feet. "Let's go before we get in trouble with Alicia."

Chapter Fourteen

The next morning, Callum woke with a crick in his neck and a cat on his stomach. He squeezed his eyes shut and rubbed a hand over his face.

Sherlock kneaded his paws on Callum's stomach and stared directly into his soul. The cat might not have been the best home security system, but Callum would be lying if he didn't think Sherlock had an intuition and an ability to read people and problems. A security cat. Huh. Never thought he'd run into one of those.

"Come on, buddy. Let me have five more minutes to sleep." Callum had stayed up half the night holding himself back from crawling into Grace's bed, then spent the other half of the night imagining what would have happened if he had gone upstairs. He let out a frustrated breath and pushed the cat away. "Five more minutes."

Sherlock didn't budge.

Callum stretched. His neck and shoulder twinged after a long night of sleeping on a tiny couch. His stomach was still overstuffed after last night's questionable decision to eat his bodyweight in tacos. That was worth it. Mostly. Tacos were a fantastic distraction from Grace. Not to mention, who didn't love tacos? Totally worth it. At least until Sherlock used his abdomen as a launch pad and jumped onto the coffee table.

"Come on, cat."

The sun hadn't risen, but he was wide awake and directly below the bedroom where Grace slept. What he wouldn't do to be in that bed right now.

Sherlock glared at him from the coffee table and meowed as if demanding that Callum keep it professional. "That ship has sailed, my feline friend."

But that was where his mind should be. Fix the problems, and a world of possibilities opened to him and Grace.

What information would Dean have found overnight? Perhaps Vivian had an update from the DOJ. If so, he and Grace might have travel orders and a meeting with the attorneys lined up. Good. Then they could understand Dominic's behavior. His stalking her had to be more than wanting to repossess Grace like a lost belonging.

He scrubbed a hand over his face again and forced his shoulders to relax. His mind wandered from work to how this was different than the Army.

Did he enjoy working for Titan?

Yeah, even if he took his current assignment out of the mix, he did more than he realized he would. It was never boring. There wasn't much sit-around-and-wait.

Sunlight glowed through the gauzy drapes. The too-small couch didn't make lounging in bed appealing. He wasn't falling asleep again, especially when the possibility of coffee and breakfast was so close.

Alicia wouldn't kill him for poking around her kitchen. She'd almost let him cook last night, and he had something to prove after fumbling whether he believed he was a great cook. He absolutely was. A total master in the kitchen.

Twenty minutes later, the bacon sizzled in a cast-iron skillet and the coffee percolated. The scent had pulled him fully into the land of the living and, with the sounds of footsteps upstairs, possibly lured someone awake.

He poured himself a cup of coffee and waited. Anticipation tingled in his chest. He was too old to tie himself in knots over a woman, yet here he was, hoping like hell that Grace came downstairs.

She padded into the kitchen, and his heart double-tapped at the sight of her. Sleepy and soft and so damn appealing that he gripped the spatula harder. "Morning, gorgeous."

She stopped short, blushing, and then, with a surprisingly shy smile, beelined for the coffeepot. "Good morning to you, too."

Who knew flannel anything could catch his eye? Boy, had it. Everything about those pajamas was calling to him. "Did I wake you up?"

"The coffee and bacon did."

"It's almost done. Are you hungry?"

She leaned on the counter next to the stove and wrapped both hands around her coffee. Callum stepped away from the stove and pulled her close. "You doing okay this morning?"

She blew on her coffee, nodding with a sleepy grin.

He'd never been more aware of a woman in his life. He wanted his hands on her, unbuttoning the shirt, dragging down the pants, peeling away the layers until his palms ran over her smooth skin. That wasn't going to happen in this kitchen, but still, he gently took her mug from her and kissed her lips.

She sighed against him. The antsy energy that had itched in his arms since the moment he heard her footsteps upstairs calmed. Not that he didn't need so much more from Grace, but if she were in his arms, he was breathing easier.

Her kisses feathered against his mouth. "I'm doing better than I was sixty seconds ago."

Callum had never lived with a woman. Never made a woman breakfast, and sure as hell hadn't held someone in the kitchen for a good morning kiss, and he never wanted this to stop. Fuck, he was gone for her. Actually, that had been the case for years.

"What else are you making?" she asked.

Sherlock meowed from the living room as if he had input.

"What do you want?" He squeezed her hips.

"Pancakes? Toast? What do you want?"

Her.

He pulled the cast iron off the heat and shuffled the bacon onto a stack of paper towels. "Whichever is easier." Then he'd drag her upstairs, shut the door, and have what he really wanted. His heartbeat hammered.

"We could make that... later." Her eyelashes fluttered, and her tongue darted over her lips. "And go upstairs?"

"Great idea." He took her hand in his and crossed the kitchen. They needed to find themselves behind a locked door. "We should—"

The click, click, click of Argos and Toto trotting down the stairs slowed Callum and Grace in the living room. Alicia stood behind her dogs. Her gaze dropped to their joined hands, then she acted as if she had seen nothing. "I can't believe I'm up this early for a second day in a row." She eyed Callum as she walked toward the kitchen. "This didn't happen before you showed up."

"There's bacon on the counter," Grace said, like it was a peace offering.

He didn't let go of her hand and couldn't get her up the stairs fast enough.

The dogs whimpered and trotted back into the living room.

"Come on, boys. Give them privacy," Alicia called from the kitchen.

Grace faltered on the stairs. He faced her; her jaw fell open, embarrassed and guilty. His lips parted, ready to coax her the remaining few steps, but spotted Argos and Toto, attentive and watching... the front door? Their heads tilted as if hearing what he couldn't.

Their low growls rumbled. Their fur stood up. His blood ran cold as their barks sounded in a way he'd never heard from them before. Callum jerked Grace behind him—and the front window exploded.

Chapter Fifteen

Grace screamed as Callum tossed her behind him.

The dogs and cat erupted, barking and growling and hissing as the animals charged into the living room. Alicia called her pets, and none obeyed.

Fire climbed the drapes. Fuel and fire burned. Grace watched in horror. Fire skimmed over the shining accelerant glistening on the hardwood floors with a whoosh, eating into the pink rug where glass and a shattered bottle lay.

"Get the leashes." Callum remained calm amid the spreading fire. "Where's the cat carrier?"

Alicia returned with the leashes. "In the shed."

He snatched a screeching Sherlock and handed him to Grace.

A fire alarm blared.

The drapes fell away and exposed the broken window. Callum inspected the front yard as best he could, then stalked to the kitchen door that opened to the backyard, scanning for threats as the fire crawled across the pink rug, consuming the beautiful little details Alicia had obsessively pulled together.

Grace couldn't move. Why would Dominic want to set Alicia's house on fire?

"You two, get out. Where's your fire extinguisher?" he demanded, then realized she wasn't right behind them. "Grace. Now."

"Dominic's out there!" she cried, then she saw the gun in Callum's hand.

"Wish he were," he growled. "Let's go."

But Dominic never did his dirty work. "Callum, it's a trap."

The kitchen fire alarm screeched. Alicia struggled to pull Argos and Toto out the back door. Sherlock clawed Grace's arms and hands. Grace refused to loosen her hold, but she couldn't move her feet.

Callum registered her panic, that she might rather die in a fire than face him again, and hustled to her. She braced for him to yell.

"I promise you, baby." He wrapped an arm around her back and half-carried her and Sherlock toward the door. "I won't let anything happen to you."

That kickstarted her brain. Her legs moved. She and Callum moved into the fresh morning air. Sherlock demanded freedom. Argos and Toto barked and yanked at their leashes. Grace searched for her ex-husband or his goons. Callum swept around the house as though he was in the movies, gun sweeping, and then returned to herd her and Alicia from the backyard toward the driveway.

"I don't understand." Sherlock tore at Grace's chest. "He's not here."

"Get in the car," Callum demanded. He lowered his gun and pulled Alicia's keys from his pocket. How did he have the wherewithal to grab her keys on the way out? Just as calmly, he dialed 911 while ordering, "Get in the car, pull onto the street, and lock the door."

Alicia forced Argos and Toto in the backseat. Callum succinctly reported the pertinent details to the emergency dispatch. Black smoke poured from the broken window. She was looking for Dominic.

"Grace," Alicia called. "Get in."

Sherlock hissed and clawed. Tears pricked her eyes. She had brought this to Alicia's picture-perfect house. Callum yanked open the passenger door of Alicia's car. "Trust me."

Grace toppled inside and released Sherlock, who sprang from her arms into the back-seat with the dogs.

"Go over there. Keep the engine running. If anyone that you don't like shows up, drive away. I'll find you." Callum shut the door and turned toward the house.

Alicia backed out of the driveway and parked where he had directed.

Black smoke billowed and wheezed from the broken window. She couldn't see the fire but imagined the way it would eat through Alicia's books and belongings. Tears spilled down Grace's cheeks again. "Alicia, I'm so sorry."

Unflappable Alicia let her bottom lip tremble. "We're safe."

Grace reached over and gripped her hand. After all the times that Alicia had held hers, this didn't feel like nearly enough. She didn't know what more to do. "I'm so sorry. I will make this right."

"We're safe," Alicia repeated, voice cracking.

Grace would do anything to rewind time and never cross the doorstep to the beautiful house and break her friend's heart. They watched Callum retrace their path into the backyard.

"I never should have brought this to your home."

"*You* didn't do this. I know that." Alicia squeezed Grace's hand and shook it.

Finally, they heard sirens. An eternity passed before the fire engines roared down the street and people in gear jumped out. Callum exited the front door with a fire extinguisher in his hand.

"Every day, I hate my ex-husband more."

"What if it wasn't him?" Alicia muttered.

"Who else could it possibly be?"

Alicia shrugged.

Callum and the newcomers met in the middle of the yard. Grace wished she could read lips. The gestures and head nods were all they had to understand the conversation. The group walked into the house, Callum leading the way, as two additional county vehicles pulled up.

One man inside poked his head out the front door, gave a signal, and returned inside.

"No one's running around like my house is burning to the ground."

Grace sniffled. "Maybe he put it out."

"Maybe. Oh, God. Grace."

She followed Alicia's gaze. Blood trickled over her knuckles.

"You're bleeding."

She rolled up the sleeves of her flannel pajama shirt.

Alicia's jaw hinged. "Sherlock destroyed you."

Now that Alicia mentioned it, Grace's arms and chest burned. She opened the visor and inspected her neck and chest. Dozens of claw marks crisscrossed her skin. "Don't worry about me. I'm fine. I'm worried about you—"

"Callum's coming out," Alicia said.

She glanced up as Callum and a fireman headed toward the car. He gestured to them.

"Guess he'll let us out of the car now." Alicia glanced at Grace's hands. "We need to clean you up first." She held up a finger. "There are tissues in the glove box."

The two men waited. Argos and Toto pressed their faces against the window. Sherlock jumped onto the center console.

"No tissues." Grace shut the compartment. "Callum doesn't look happy."

Alicia let out an exhausted breath. "I'm not happy."

Guilt rolled over her again. "I'm so sorry."

"You didn't break my window and burn my house. I'm sending Dominic the bill, and that asshole, with all of his money, can pay to redecorate my entire place."

"You have a more positive attitude than I would have." Grace mopped the back of her wrists on her pajama pants.

"I haven't seen the inside. Maybe with everything charred and covered in fire retardant foam, I'm going to sing a new tune. But for now, your ex-husband will redecorate my house with all of his fuck-you money. The bastard."

Grace didn't know how, but she laughed. "A fuck-you redo."

"More like a fuck-him, but yeah. Oh, boy. That man of yours wants us to get out of the car."

"He's not my man."

"Whatever he is, he has a glower that's hard to ignore."

All of him was hard to ignore.

They left the car running for the pets to stay in the air conditioning and joined them. Grace didn't know what to do with her arms and neck. Now that her adrenaline had slowed, the cat scratches burned and stung. Trickles and dribbles of blood smeared over her skin.

Callum made introductions, and both men noted her scratches. The fireman whistled. "There must be an unhappy cat in the car."

"Unhappy would be an understatement," Alicia said. "The fire is out?"

"Believe so. My people are inspecting, but it seems like your friend contained the situation."

Two police cruisers pulled up behind the county vehicles. Neighbors poked heads out of doors. A few stood outside watching in various shades of dress for the day. Pajamas. Casual summer clothes. Business suits. This would be the talk around the water cooler.

The fireman tilted his head to the police officers ambling toward them. "We should go speak with them."

Alicia nodded.

An ambulance parked behind the line of emergency vehicles. He eyed Grace's injuries and then Callum. "Perhaps you want to take her to be cleaned up."

She agreed and went in one direction with Callum, while Alicia met the police officers as they walked into her house.

"Sherlock tried to kill you," he said.

"Apparently, he's not the only one who tried this morning." She fell into step with him. "Why would Dominic do that? Smoke us out and just disappear."

Callum's silence didn't sit well.

"Really. I don't get it. If he wanted to send another message, he could have used FedEx again. Maybe spice things up with UPS or DHL or go all-American with USPS."

His silence unnerved her.

The EMTs took one look at Grace and set to work.

Twenty minutes later, the cat scratches stung worse than before, but she'd been swabbed and smeared with antibiotic cream, covered in bandages, and ordered to see a doctor if signs of infection surfaced.

Callum had been on the phone, pacing as he kept an eye on her. He was more agitated than when the front window had shattered.

The fire trucks left. More police cars arrived, with men and women who had a decidedly more detective feel than those who initially arrived.

Callum ended his phone call and returned to her side. He took her hand, inspected one arm, then the next, gently placed her hand by her side, and then tipped her chin up to inspect her neck and chest. "Sherlock beat the hell out of you."

"All for saving his little furry life." She fell into step alongside him as they walked into the backyard. "What's going to happen?"

"If it's Dominic's people, a police investigation that will probably turn up a whole lot of nothing." He shrugged.

She faltered. "*If*? Who else would it be?"

They settled onto the chairs on the patio outside the kitchen. "No idea. This feels messy."

"Alicia and I already decided that Dominic can pay to redecorate her entire house."

Callum's lips twitched. "Did you?"

She nodded. "I don't know how we'll ask him to do that, but I never doubt Alicia."

"After what I've seen, I wouldn't either." He leaned back and stretched. "What a way to start the day."

Grace stared at him. Other than demanding she get in the car, he was the epitome of calmness.

His head tilted. "What's that look for?"

"You're incredibly cool under pressure."

The corner of his grin hitched. "It's not like a missile hit us during breakfast. Speaking of which, I'm starving." He stood up and offered a hand. "Let's get changed and grab some grub. We'll pick up something for Alicia, too."

"Cal, you're acting like this is not a big deal."

"No, I'm acting like we need to fuel our bodies, because today is going to be a fuckin' headache."

Okay, well, that made sense. "It's not normal, how calm you are."

"Just another day at the office."

They changed out of their pajamas, and he drove them to a diner that served breakfast, lunch, and dinner twenty-four hours a day. The packed parking lot promised good food and strong coffee. Exactly what they needed.

They slid into a booth, and a minute later, a waitress popped over, pulled a pen from behind her ear, and, without missing a beat, tossed out oversized menus. "I'm Mauve. What can I get you?"

"Coffee," they said simultaneously.

"That kind of morning, huh? Got it. What else?"

"Bacon, hash browns, two eggs over easy, and a side of sausage." Callum flipped the menu over. "Are the desserts any good?"

"The pie's better than the brownies. Get the potapple."

"What's potapple?" she asked.

"Potapple pie. Think if sweet potato pie and apple pie had a baby pie. *Potapple*. It started as an experiment when Eddie, back in the kitchen, had a little bit of filling left from each but not enough to make a whole pie. Bam. Potapple. Bestseller."

"I'll have that too. But first..." She stared at all the choices and ran smack into decision paralysis. "How about..."

"Don't want what your man's having?"

Did they really look like they belonged together? "He's not my man."

"Matter of time." Mauve shrugged. "I'd fall over dead from clogged arteries if I ate that at once, but he looks like he can handle it."

"I'll have the whole-wheat pancakes and fruit salad."

Mauve snickered. "Gotta balance him out. Got it. All right. Give me a minute, and I'll bring over a fresh pot of coffee."

"Awfully quick to say I'm not your man," he said when they were alone.

Grace's chin shot up. "You're not."

"Didn't say I was. Just noting your light-speed-like clarification. Especially considering what we were on our way to do before we were interrupted."

She could already feel her cheeks heating. "Interrupted? We were attacked." Though it astounded her how casually he could discuss them when she couldn't even wrap her head around him wanting to kiss her. "Besides, sex doesn't make you *my man*."

He looked like she'd issued him a challenge. "Doesn't it?" He winked. "It sure as fuck would make you my woman."

A full-body shiver ran from her head to her toes and left her speechless.

Mauve returned with their coffees.

Grace shut her jaw after realizing it was hanging open. She needed coffee before replaying what he had just said. Callum was offering everything she ever wanted, and she simply couldn't process it.

Mauve brought the syrup and broke the trance Callum had on Grace.

She took a sobering breath and tried to pivot the conversation. "Why don't you think Dominic did it?"

He flicked a sugar packet back and forth between his fingers without opening it. "I didn't say that."

"You said *if* it was his people. Who else would it be?"

"That's one hell of a question. Got any ideas?"

"No." She tugged on the long-sleeved shirt that covered her cat scratches. "Do you?"

He slowly shook his head as if someone else might actually be behind the fire. "Vivian found Alicia a nice rental house that will take the dogs and Sherlock."

"That's what you were doing on the phone?"

He nodded. "Amongst other things, but yeah. She needed something better than the local pet-friendly motel. Something to take the edge off of what's going to be a huge pain in the ass to fix, but not too far from her job and community."

He'd thought of all that? Her heart squeezed. "You didn't have to do that."

"I know."

"I'll pick up the cost," she insisted.

He flicked the packet again. "It's already taken care of."

"I have a bunch of Dominic's money sitting in a trust. I can use—"

"It's taken care of."

His expression showed no willingness to negotiate. Appreciation swelled in her chest. She reached across the table and grabbed his hand. "Thank you."

"We need to go to my office to debrief. After we get Alicia squared away, we can hit the road."

"What happens after we talk at your office?"

"They'll have a safehouse ready for us by then."

A glimmer of excitement and nerves spun in her belly. "Who will be there with us?"

His eyes narrowed. "Is there someone you want to bring along?"

She shook her head. Alone in a house with Callum? With nothing to do except wait for a meeting. "No one else."

Mauve arrived with their food, and they thanked her. Callum dug into his overflowing plate. The quiet didn't keep her mind from sprinting through what was to come. No distractions. No roommates. No reason to ignore what they'd started. She couldn't wait until they were alone.

Except... he terrified her.

She did not know where his supposed long-term interest had come from. He might not realize this was nothing more than a curiosity or an itch that needed scratching. He'd been the one sharing. She was the one who had always wanted him, and when—if?—this all came crashing down, he'd walk away unscathed, and she'd be more shattered than from anything Dominic had put her through.

But Callum wouldn't hurt her. And if he said they had a future, even if she couldn't see how it would work, then she should trust him enough to give them a chance.

Wait.

He hadn't said they had a future *now*, only that they *would have* if the past were different. Her subconscious was making promises when none had been given. They didn't live in the same places, though she didn't actually live in any one place. And her brother would go ballistic if he thought about them together.

But again, she was an adult. He'd get over it. Still, Grace didn't even understand why Callum had left the Army. There were so many unknowns that idealizing the future was unrealistic.

She cut her pancakes. "Hayden will freak out about the fire."

"He'll be fine." Callum pushed hash browns onto his fork. "Out of everything he can get upset over, a broken window won't—"

"It was a Molotov cocktail."

"You're not hurt. He'll be interested in why it happened, but he won't freak out."

"You know him better than I do, I guess." Maybe she could ease Callum into the discussion about the Army. "Did you think you'd both get into West Point?"

His eyes narrowed. He chewed the hash browns for a long time. "We didn't compare stats."

"What does that mean? You both wanted to join the Army. That was a great way to—"

"Why are you asking?"

She shrugged and stuffed a pancake in her mouth so she couldn't answer.

"We were both strong candidates. West Point was right to take both of us."

It took forever to swallow. "What'd you major in?"

"Why?"

"I'm curious."

"Philosophy."

Her fork froze mid-bite. "Really?"

"Yeah. Really."

"I thought West Point would only offer majors like war studies or global law or cyberterrorism."

"What are you getting at? You don't care what I majored in. Spit it out."

Now that he'd said philosophy, she was incredibly interested and wanted to know everything else he might surprise her with. But for now, she had to get down to business. "Why did you leave the Army?"

His expression hardened. "I'm done with the twenty questions."

"You know everything about me. You've asked *a thousand* questions—"

"First, trust me, I don't know everything, and second, you're the one in a situation. Not me."

Sleeping together was a sort of situation, but she wasn't ready to point that out. What if he changed his mind because she was too nosy?

His jaw ticked again, but this time, frustration had the muscles twitching. "We should place Alicia's order."

Callum caught Mauve's attention for the to-go order.

Grace crossed her scratched-up arms and ignored the bites of pain. "You're not going to tell me."

"I'm not going to talk about it. At all. Got it?"

"Fine." She saluted him. "Aye, aye, captain."

"Give me a break."

Her questions hadn't been that intrusive. The more he wanted to avoid it, the more she needed to know.

They finished breakfast in an uncomfortable silence. Mauve placed Alicia's food on the table with their bill. They settled up and returned to his truck. Every minute felt more awkward than the last.

She fastened her seatbelt. "Why don't you want to talk about the Army?"

Callum tossed her an aggravated look and turned the engine over. "Why didn't you tell anyone that your ex-husband hit you?"

"Screw you, Callum."

He backed out of the parking space, threw it in drive, but jerked the wheel into a parking space before he pulled onto the road. He dropped his head back, stared at the ceiling, and then rubbed a hand over his face. "I'm not ready yet. Can you give me that?"

It wasn't the same thing, but their silence was for the same reason. It hurt too much to admit. She nodded.

His head dropped. He pinched the bridge of his nose. "I won't throw Marino in your face again. I'm sorry."

She pulled his hand from his face and linked their fingers together. With her other hand, she unfastened her seatbelt. Grace leaned toward him, wanting to wrap her arms around him and ease whatever ugly scars the Army had left, but Callum gathered her first.

Falling harder and harder for him, maybe he needed her just as much.

Chapter Sixteen

Callum drove through Granite Creek, with its wide brick sidewalks and welcoming mom-and-pop shops. Flower baskets hung from lampposts. Sandwich boards and signs peppered the storefronts, enticing the end-of-summer foot traffic inside for ice cream, a new book, or handcrafted decor.

"This is where you live?" Grace pressed against the window, wishing they didn't have a meeting at his office and that she could hop in and out of stores for the rest of the day. "It's out of a storybook."

"Probably why Vivian headquartered us here. She needed something nice to put up with the lot of us."

Grace tried to imagine Callum's boss. She was someone who could handle a gaggle of men who likely tipped the scale toward alpha with characteristics like Callum. Trained military or law enforcement. More than capable. Probably gruff and used to getting their own way. The Vivian who Grace imagined wasn't the type to locate a headquarters in a heartwarming small town.

"The office is actually an estate all the way through town," he explained.

Light traffic and a lack of stoplights helped move the drive along. They'd been in his truck for hours. The main thoroughfare transitioned from cutesy stores to residential. Callum turned from one road to the next, winding up a hill, and then bypassed a private gate.

They summited the hill, turned through a horseshoe driveway in front of a massive Victorian manor, and parked in the small lot adjacent to an expansive entrance. "This cannot be your office."

He glanced out the windshield and admitted, "It'll really blow you away once you go inside."

Grace had to rewrite Vivian in her head as she drank in the large house's turrets and gables and a wraparound porch. Vivian had to be more like a strict schoolmarm capable of ordering a group of bullheaded men around with a stern look. "I don't think I'm dressed nicely enough to walk in."

He laughed, but she gave a serious once-over of her casual shorts and lightweight long-sleeve T-shirt that covered her bandages.

Callum gestured to his pants, which had too many pockets, and the T-shirt stretched over his chest. "There's no dress code. Don't let all those windows and spindles fool you."

And by windows, did he mean the stained-glass ones or the ones at the top of the towering spires?

They crossed the parking lot and walked to the overstated entrance. Callum rested his hand on her lower back as he swung open the grand door. She was stunned. "This place is..." The polished floors gleamed. The tall ceilings towered. "Amazing. It should be in an architectural magazine."

"It probably has been."

"I believe it." The foyer opened on both sides to what had once been mirrored living rooms. Or rather, drawing rooms? Parlor rooms? First of what had to be many living rooms? Grace didn't have words to describe this house. But the central staircase had stolen her thoughts. It was almost as wide as the entry hall and reached toward a floor-to-ceiling stained-glass window.

In one of the living rooms converted to office space, three men, similar in height and stature to Callum, huddled in front of a large flat-screen monitor displaying a blueprint. One man swiped his hand over the screen, and the blueprint switched to a satellite view. He swiped his hand over the screen again, and the blueprint reappeared.

"Come on, I'll introduce you to some folks." Callum led her in.

"It looks like they're busy." She hung back. "I can wait over here." She realized the blueprint was of Alicia's house and caught up. "What are they doing?"

"We're installing a security system for Alicia." He glanced over. "To supplement the dogs and cat."

The three men turned, and Callum introduced her to Decker, Rhys, and Wes. They were all-business but nice. Decker had an edgy look. Rhys hid under his hoodie jacket despite the temperature outside reaching the nineties. Wes was the most talkative. All were exceedingly professional and focused on Alicia's house.

"Alicia agreed to a security system?" Grace calculated an estimate of what their hourly rate was and the cost of the hardware. No matter what number she came up with, it would be out of Alicia's budget. Grace would make sure she picked up the bill. She was the reason

Alicia needed it, after all. "Why didn't you tell me? I'll pay for it. Make sure she doesn't spend a dime."

Wes laughed. "I believe she told Vivian that your ex-husband was paying out of something she called the fuck-him budget."

"Wait. When did Alicia and Vivian connect?" Grace shifted, uncomfortable that she'd been left out of the discussion.

High heels clicked down the grand staircase, and Grace turned. The woman coming down the stairs was definitely the boss. She walked the walk, strutting actually, and Grace was immediately in awe.

"Vivian Maddox." With red lipstick that matched her nail polish, black leather pants tucked into fuck-me high-heel boots that deserved their own fashion shoot, the woman held out her hand and assessed Grace with eyes darting over her like a mental X-ray machine. "Sorry to meet you under these circumstances."

Vivian wasn't a schoolmarm. She wasn't the enforcer of a strict dress code or the manager of these men. She was the queen bee.

"Dean and Scar need to talk to you, then we'll debrief," Vivian told Callum before returning her laser focus to Grace. "Come with me. I'll stash you somewhere comfortable while you wait."

Grace followed the semi-scary lady and her kickass boots as they ascended the scene-stealing staircase.

"You've known Hale for a while," Vivian said over her shoulder.

They rounded the landing and headed down a wood-paneled corridor. "For as long as I can remember."

Vivian opened the door and gestured for Grace to step inside. "You have the advantage. I've only known him for a few months."

The large room was appointed similarly to the space downstairs, except this room didn't include any modern accents, such as screens and communication equipment.

Grace ran her hand over her forearms and to the bracelets on her wrist. Soreness and pain bit against the bandages. "I was surprised to learn he'd left the Army."

"He was surprised to learn about you."

Ouch. "We've covered that a time or two."

"It is what it is." Vivian crossed the space. "Do you want anything to drink? I can promise the coffee isn't that military mud most of those men like to brew."

The large room was appointed in Queen Anne decor. The couches were reminiscent of Alicia's living room with their claw feet and carved wood but not as whimsical. Bright light poured in through towering windows. It was formal yet inviting. Vivian's leather contrasted like a modern sore thumb in the delicate space.

"I'm fine." Grace walked deeper into the room. "I could draw in here for hours."

Vivian dragged a high-back armchair next to the couch. "Sit."

She dropped her backpack on the floor and obeyed. It wasn't her fault that Dominic firebombed Alicia's house, but she felt as though Vivian might disagree. "I didn't know my ex would do that to Alicia."

"The Molotov cocktail?" She crossed a leather-clad leg over the other. Her boot bounced. "Who else could have?"

"Who else?" This was the third time someone had implied Dominic might not be the culprit. "I don't know. The people who work for him. I never got to know them. He kept me separate from everything." Like life.

Vivian drummed a quick beat on her leg. "I actually wanted to talk to you about Callum."

Grace flushed. "What do you want to know?"

She lifted a shoulder. "Why did he stay at Alicia Jackson's house?"

"As opposed to where else?"

"Taking you someplace safe."

"We didn't think we were in danger, and I guess I didn't want to leave my friend."

Vivian pursed her lips.

"Was he supposed to do something different?" Grace asked.

"No, I'm just parsing his actions. Understanding him as an operator."

"Oh, well, I'm no help on that."

"Doubtful."

Was Grace missing something? "I mean, I know what you already know. Actually, you probably know more than me, because he won't explain to me why he left the military—he'll tell me when he's ready." She couldn't read Vivian's face. "He's a good guy."

"I've gathered. What else?"

No one could dispute that Callum was a good guy. Not necessarily warm and friendly, but his moral character was on the straight and narrow. What else could Vivian want to know? "He's smart. Not always nice. At least not to me." Though that wasn't the case lately. Visions of him trapping her against the wall sent a shiver down her spine. "He's always been protective of me."

"How?"

"In the way that comes with having an overbearing older brother and Callum always being there. Both of our parents were divorced. Our house was... calmer. He spent a lot of time with Hayden, and as circumstances go, with me."

"You were never romantically involved?" Her eyebrows lifted.

Grace's lips parted. That was far more personal than she had expected. But she wasn't an idiot and understood why his boss might ask. Emotions clouded judgment. Getting physical opened up a Pandora's box. "No, we never were."

Vivian crossed her arms, tapping her fingers, assessing her.

Grace twisted the beads on her bracelet. Part of living in hiding for years meant she never interacted with anyone she didn't want to. She was out of practice at having uncomfortable conversations.

Someone knocked on the door.

Her relief was instantaneous. Short of Callum arriving with a plan to tell Vivian about kissing Grace, she celebrated the interruption.

A woman with a laptop in her arms and a tall man filed into the room.

"Sorry to barge in." Her dark hair transitioned to deep turquoise tips. That blue was the same shade as the fairy wings she'd recently colored on a book cover. "But if I don't help Dean, he's going to be pulling at strings and driving everyone to the edge." She smiled at Grace. "I'm Scarlett; this is Dean." She gestured to the man. "And if we don't nail down a couple more things, it will take all day, and I might kill him."

Dean scowled. "It wouldn't take all day."

Based on what Callum had explained, Grace would have thought Dean would be the one carrying a computer. "You're security analysts?"

Scarlett snorted. "I am absolutely not. Think of me like a social media maven. A tracker of online gossip and a sleuth of the slippery no-names internet forums where villains of all sorts cavort without worrying someone like me can track them down to their day job." Her firecracker grin sparkled. "Which I can do. Little hobby of mine. Taking on anonymous keyboard warriors."

Grace loved Scarlett already. "That sounds like more fun than it should be."

"It is, and from what I've heard about your internet skills, you could jump into the murky, dark deep end with me and have some fun."

Dean, far more buttoned up than Scarlett with his faded taper and sharp jaw line, gave Scarlett a harsh look. "Maybe not right now." He shook Grace's hand. "I'm an analyst and, although I'd rather neither of you troll people on the dark web, I'm impressed with the way you covered your tracks online. You could have set up an online camp for drug lords, and no one would have noticed."

The compliments caught her off guard. "A lot of good that did."

Vivian relinquished her spot and gestured to Dean. "Grace and I are finished. More or less."

Were they? Had Vivian culled her from the pack to ask about what kind of person Callum was?

"One more thing." She paused at the door as if suddenly not ready to release Grace to Scarlett and Dean. "Have you decided what's next?"

"For what?"

"When the legal wrangling is done, and you're a full-fledged member of society again. What's your next move?"

"Oh…" Callum's promise of a house with a yard and neighbors who knew her real name jumped to mind. And Callum. He was there with the cute house as well. "Not really."

Vivian gave her a funny look. "Maybe you should."

Scarlett scrunched her nose, brow furrowing, as Vivian strode out. "Was that weird? That seemed off."

Dean took the laptop from Scarlett and sat in Vivian's vacated chair. "Don't look for problems where they don't exist, Scar. We have enough real ones to decipher."

Chapter Seventeen

Callum had been summoned into the war room and found it empty. He didn't know what most of the rooms in their headquarters had been before Titan had repurposed the space, but now he couldn't imagine this bright room with its enormous solid wood table as anything other than his team's assignment and debrief zone.

His team...

With every day that passed, Callum became more enmeshed with Titan.

His team. It worked. He liked it.

Vivian strode into the war room with a glare.

That didn't bode well. "What's wrong?"

She circled the war room in stewing silence before planting herself at the head of the table. She dropped into the leather chair and tapped her fingernails on the smooth wood. "You have dug yourself into quite the shithole, haven't you, Hale?"

He rocked onto his heels and shoved his hands into his pants pockets. "The Molotov cocktail was messy. I didn't see it coming. Chew my ass out for that. Fine. But Dominic's not messy, and it doesn't make sense. So, I don't think I'm in a hole. I think we have a different angle to consider."

"Agreed, but that's not what I'm talking about." Her sharp look could have cut glass. "And you know it."

"I don't know—"

"Do not fucking lie to me." She pointed vaguely behind her as if he were supposed to read her mind.

Grace.

Well, hell. That surfaced faster than he had anticipated. Callum moved to the window, ordering every muscle in his body to stand down and at least pretend that Vivian's scrutiny didn't have him on high alert.

The window overlooked the large driveway and smooth asphalt where they parked. The gang was all here. He hadn't thought twice about why they had all been called in. Unease knotted in his gut. Had they been brought in because of Grace? Or worse, because of *him* and Grace. Dean was always in, but the whole team? Vivian couldn't possibly know the lines Callum had already crossed and was desperate to cross again.

He turned to face Vivian. "What are you getting at?"

"You told me there's nothing between you and Grace Willoughby."

"There wasn't."

"*Wasn't*, Hale, or *isn't*?"

He threaded his fingers into his hair, then ran a hand over his face. "To be honest—"

"Jesus fuck. Yeah. Do that. Be honest."

"I don't know."

Vivian slapped the table. "It has not even been a week, and you somehow managed to sweet talk that poor woman into bed? I thought better of you."

He couldn't form thoughts. Finally, he shook himself out of the disbelief. "It's been a wild few days, and I didn't *sweet talk her*." He tossed out his hands. "Grace isn't some poor helpless woman that I've conned into my bed, not that it's any of your business."

"You're wrong there."

"It's more complicated than I realized, but you can take your fuckboy accusations and shove 'em."

"More complicated than you realized? Yeah, me too. Me fuckin' too." She leaned back in her chair and concentrated on him as though calculating quantum physics. She pinched the bridge of her nose, gave a frustrated shake of her head, and straightened. "I gotta believe you're doing what you think is right. Hell, you threw your entire career away *because* you only do what you believe is right."

Just the mention of him refusing orders reverberated in his head like she'd smacked a goddamn gong. Without even closing his eyes, he saw that woman and child through the crosshairs of his scope. He could hear the barking orders in his earpiece. *Take the shot. Take the goddamn shot. Finish the job.*

Those orders would replay for the rest of his life, no matter if he was wide awake or reliving hell in his nightmares. His fists balled again. Vivian might know, but she didn't understand. He wanted to shout that he hadn't thrown away his career. *It* abandoned him. Hell, he wanted to tell Vivian never to mention it again, but all he could do was stand there.

"That's why we hired you, and that's why I'm putting my blind faith in you. You do the right thing."

Did he? He didn't pull the trigger, but that didn't save the woman and child. As quickly as he refused, he was relieved of duty, and someone else carried out what he still believed were illegal and immoral orders. Doing the right thing meant more than refusing. Didn't it? He didn't know what else he would have done, but it still fuckin' haunted him.

Vivian tapped her nails on the table again—one, two, three taps. Never more. Never less.

"Grace is in a precarious position," Vivian lowered her voice, "and you're the save-the-day hero."

"I'm not—"

She held up a hand. "Anything that she thinks or feels, or *thinks* she thinks or feels, is compromised. Hell, you're not special, Hale. I could probably say the same thing for any of her..." Vivian pursed her lips. "...liaisons that she's had since she assumed a new life."

His jaw clenched. The casual comparison of his situation with Grace to anything she had in the past rubbed him the wrong way, not to mention that she hadn't dated while she'd been hiding. "Grace and I have a history that goes back decades."

"A history you failed to mention, huh?"

"A platonic history," he clarified.

Vivian tapped her nails again. "That doesn't mean she's not in a vulnerable position, and hell, that vulnerability may even be what you find attractive. You made your move. Never have before? Right? So why now? You're the hero. She's the damsel."

"Absolutely fucking not."

Her bright lips quirked. "You're awfully quick to disagree without giving it thought."

"You're wrong." Though, was she? The burn of uncertainty churned in his gut. He'd kissed Grace out of nowhere. He'd been pulled toward her like steel to a magnet and had held her when he'd never touched her after years of wanting her. Why now...?

He stopped overthinking. Vivian had to be wrong.

"This is different from any assignment you've had," she said. "Falling for our clients is always a concern. That's the nature of the beast. Be aware of it. You need to understand what part of your psyche this job speaks to and how others see you."

She was wrong.

Vivian continued, "Then you'll realize there's a reason for the white-knight-and-damsel-in-distress storyline. It happens all too often. But what you don't see in those stories is that it never ends the way you think it will. *Or should.*"

He wanted her lecture to roll off his back. Instead, it nailed him in the gut.

No amount of explaining how he was different, how she was different, how this entire situation was not exactly what Vivian had just explained came to him. He'd royally screwed up.

"Don't look like I shot your damn dog," Vivian added. "You would have come to this realization on your own. I'm just seeing it for what it is without the rose-tinted glasses of adrenaline and hormones."

A heavy numbness blanketed him. It was the same suffocating weight that had arrived after he officially became a civilian again. Since that point, everything in his life had been temporary and devoid of life. But it had disappeared the moment Grace maced him. He hadn't realized it until now, and hearing what Vivian said, that darkness was coming for him again.

Chapter Eighteen

The road noise was the only soundtrack to the drive that felt like it had lasted eons. They had only been in Callum's truck for five minutes. Something was off. Grace had expected Callum to interrogate her after the meeting with Scarlett and Dean had turned into a working lunch, but he hadn't said much.

"Scarlett dug up things that I bet Dominic thought were buried."

"Yeah," he mumbled. "Like what?"

"Questionable crypto promos. More like gambling for his investors than anything close to legit. She's going to send that information to their contact at the FBI, maybe to butter up the feds and find out what the Attorney General's office wants—Earth to Callum?"

"Hmm?"

"What's the matter?" She studied his profile and had never seen him concentrate more on driving. The twenty-five-mile-per-hour speed limit and the stop signs every block didn't warrant his level of attention. "You learned something while I was with Scarlett?"

"Not really."

"Well, something's wrong. You've been quiet and broody since we left."

He lifted a shoulder, checked his mirrors. "Just thinking through our next moves. Do you care if we swing by my apartment? I could use clean clothes."

Her curiosity piqued. "Sure. Of course."

"Great," he said in that same monotonous tone.

Had time in the office reminded him she was just his job?

"Could I use your laundry?" She'd been meaning to wash clothes before they had to leave Alicia's.

He glanced over. "I didn't plan to stay there that long, but there will be a washer and dryer where we're going."

His five o'clock shadow had thickened. She wanted to touch the scruff on his face. That was clearly not in the cards anytime soon. "Okay."

"It'll have everything you need." At the stop sign, he turned off the main street. "We could literally bunk there for weeks without having to leave."

Playing house with Callum sounded like fun, so long as the moody, broody man driving the truck transformed back into the man who made her stomach flip.

After a series of turns, they found themselves in front of a small two-story brick apartment building that couldn't have held more than a dozen units. Air conditioners hung in the windows of the bland building. The flower planters were the only sign of personality.

"Home sweet home." He shifted into park. "It's nothing fancy and is barely furnished."

"I can wait in the truck if you prefer."

His eyebrow arched. "Why?"

"You don't seem happy I'm around, to be honest."

"I'm happy." He opened the door. "Come on. Let's go."

"I don't believe you," she muttered under her breath, but joined him.

They crossed the parking lot together, and Callum took her hand. Alrighty then. Grumpy. Moody. But willing to hold hands. She could work with that and glanced up. He didn't look down, but he squeezed her hand.

Butterflies stormed her stomach. The handhold made her float. She pinched her lips together to hide how over the moon his touch made her. She didn't know what was bothering him, but his taking her hand said more in the last two seconds than he had since they'd left his office.

They reached the front of the boring brick building, and Callum released her hand after another squeeze. He unlocked the glass door and led her to the second-floor hallway that was broom-swept and spot-cleaned. Clean but bare, this place wasn't where she imagined he would live.

His unit was at the back of the apartment building. A corner unit. The apartment door opened to... not much. Grace stifled her reaction as they walked into a space devoid of anything.

"Like I said, home sweet home." Callum tossed his keys onto the counter. "Furniture came with the place, and I've never spent more than a couple of nights in a row here. I travel a lot, and whenever I'm off the clock..." His shoulders lifted. "...I ask for more work."

She tapped her teeth. "It's good to stay busy."

He followed her gaze to the closed blinds on all the windows.

"If you open the blinds," she suggested, "you'd get a little light in here. Maybe liven the place up."

"I've never thought twice about the lighting. This is where I sleep and shower and store my clothes."

"That's a little sad, Cal."

He dropped his duffel bag onto a pathetic couch. "When my housing becomes a priority, I'll find a place I care about."

Was that his time in the Army rubbing off on him? No, she didn't think so. Callum and Hayden had always lived together and never given the impression that they lived in bare-bones apartments. Their housing assignments and rentals leaned more toward bachelor pads.

"Give me ten minutes to pack a bag, and we'll hit the road again."

She wanted to ask more about his empty apartment and his quiet mood in the truck, but thought of the way he held her hand in the parking lot instead. Grace stepped between him and his bedroom. "Wait." Before she lost her courage, she pushed onto her tiptoes and pressed her lips to his.

He didn't kiss her back.

Her heart sank. Callum didn't move away. He searched her face as if he needed answers. She didn't know the questions. After wanting him for so long, she refused to let whatever had happened break the connection heating up between them. She steeled herself for rejection and kissed him again.

Callum Hale didn't kiss her back, and she thought she might die.

Until he did.

Whatever had fouled his mood and kept him at bay disappeared, and growling into the kiss, wrapped one hand around her waist and threaded his hand into her hair with the other, holding her to him as if he planned to devour her in the hall.

She knotted her arms around his neck, needing to be closer. His tongue delved past her lips, hot and needy and driving her wild—Callum pulled back, leaving her too exposed. Too raw. Too much in need of this man. "*What*?"

His chest heaved. An awful expression darkened his face. She saw regret and wanted to be sick.

Grace spun. She didn't know where she'd run to, but she had to get out of his apartment.

"Wait." His hands clamped on her shoulders.

"I'd rather not." Pain cracked in her throat. "Let me go."

His fingers squeezed into her flesh, and he held her at arm's length, turning her to face him. "Give me a second."

"For what?" Was this the same man from the morning? She heard the pleading in her voice. Embarrassment burned up her neck, but she had to know how he could hold her hand in the parking lot but now pry her off of him when they kissed. Tears welled in her eyes. "What did I do wrong?"

"Nothing." He held her still when she tried to pull back. "This is complicated, Grace."

"*Since when?*"

"Since I thought more about it and realized that maybe we needed to talk—"

"I have talked and talked and talked. So have you, I thought. What more is there to say? You either want me or you don't. I don't have it in me to play games."

"I *would never* play games with you." His jaw ticked. "It's not that simple."

"It is—" Screw it. She pulled her shirt over her head—and forgot she had those ugly bandages all over her arms and neck. Not exactly the sexy move she'd been aiming for. But her point was the same. "Do you want me? Yes or no?"

"You are proving my damn point."

"That's impossible. You haven't explained a single thing."

"Put your shirt on, Grace."

She shimmied her shorts down her legs. "No."

"What the fuck are you doing?"

"Trying to find the man who almost took me to my bedroom this morning. You were just holding my hand. You're in there somewhere. You *just kissed* me like you wanted to. So I'm not grossing you out or something."

"You," he stepped back, "are in a position—"

"I'm halfway naked. I can see my position. You can too. I'm being as completely upfront as I can be. What's going on?"

"You're vulnerable."

"Yeah, I am. I've stripped nearly naked in front of the guy I've wanted my entire life, and he's rejecting me."

His lips parted, but nothing came out.

Angry tears burned the back of her throat. "I don't know why you left the Army. I don't know why you won't kiss me. I don't know anything, and I'm in my bra and underwear, begging. God." She turned around, snatched her clothes off the floor. "If you'll excuse me, I'm going to redress in the bathroom and maybe search for my dignity before I drop dead of embarrassment."

His warm hands covered her stomach and folded her close to the solid muscles of his torso and thighs. She gave a half-hearted elbow to his gut. He held her still and close enough that she could feel his thickening erection. She wanted to scream and didn't know what to do.

"Listen." He dropped his lips against the back of her head. "I am going to fuck this up, and I can't. It would kill me."

"You're doing that right now. I'm throwing myself at you, and you're saying no."

He turned her in his arms. "I don't want to exploit whatever—"

"Exploit me, Callum. Take advantage of me. Take my mind off everything that has happened. For God's sake, make me forget the world."

"I want to." Frustration ticked in his jaw. "But we shouldn't. *I can't.*"

"I don't believe you. You said we were honest, and I don't believe a word coming out of your mouth right now. You never should have kissed me, you liar—"

He hooked his arms under hers and lifted Grace to his chest. In one swift move, he strode into the bedroom and lay over her on his bed. His hand covered her hand, and he pressed her palm against his cock. "Call me a liar again, babe. Tell me I don't want you again."

"Then why won't you kiss me?" she whispered hoarsely.

"Because you're a damsel in fuckin' distress, and I'm the goddamn big bad wolf. I'm what you will regret."

She froze, unable to believe what he had just said.

Callum released her hand and cupped her cheek. "I have wanted you too long to blow it because I'm an impatient asshole."

The heavy air in her lungs wisped away, and she couldn't take a deep enough breath. "I promise you're not."

His thumb smoothed over her skin. "You are going to regret me."

Her eyelids sank shut. "I could never regret what I've always wanted."

He brushed his lips over hers.

She opened her eyes, and those stormy eyes she never knew how to read were now an open book. Worry mixed with hunger. Arousal warred with apprehension. "I need you, Callum. More than anything you're worried about."

He kissed her again. Sweet and soft yet shimmery bursts of electricity sparked from the touch. Her tongue tested his resolve, running over his full bottom lip. His breath shook. She made Callum Hale quake. Absolutely impossible, but it was true.

His forehead dropped to hers, and his chest expanded as if he were sucking in all the oxygen in the room. Callum eased his body against her, his hips pressed to Grace, weight settling between her bare legs.

"I'm not fucking you right now." His fingertips skimmed from her cheek down her neck. He traced the line of her collarbone and followed the thin strap of her bra, following the fabric until he teased along the cup. "Not because I don't want to."

She trembled under the pads of his fingers. "Because you're cruel and awful."

His lips quirked. "Because I want to take my time." He dragged his knuckles gently over the spilling mound of her breast, then over her bra again.

She whimpered. *Touch me. Tease me. Take me. God, please, be inside me.*

"Because it's not the right time." Callum eased to her side. He trailed his fingers down the valley of her breasts and over her soft stomach. A trail of goosebumps followed. He teased over the waist of her underwear and slowly slid his palm lower and lower until he cupped her pussy. Dark hunger flared in his eyes.

His eyes locked on hers as he slipped his fingers under the fabric and caressed her slick skin. There was no hiding her need.

Callum dragged in a strangled breath. "Are you okay?"

"I swear," her voice shook, "I will hate you if you stop."

His smile crooked with a silent rumble of laughter, but he whispered, "The things I will do to you with just my hand."

"Callum..."

He dragged the fabric down her legs and pressed his cinnamon kiss to her mouth. Sweet and slow, his tongue slid against hers as his fingers dipped and danced, coating the digits in her arousal.

"Spread your legs for me." His deft fingers teased her seam, easing her open to his touch. "All mine."

She nodded into his kiss.

He pressed into her, testing her body and giving her more until his thick fingers filled her. Her hips writhed. In and out, bending his fingers just enough, letting her ride his hand as she drowned in the onslaught of kisses. Like he knew how badly she needed this orgasm, his hand never stopped moving, teasing, bringing her closer and closer to the edge. "Callum…"

She reached for him and palmed the erection straining against his pants.

"Not yet." He smoothed his thumb over her clit, circling until she could cry. Her ragged breath quickened. His fingers thrust into her again and matched the way her body moved. The hungry lift of her hips begged for more.

"I need…" She couldn't think. The buildup of this orgasm was too much. "Callum."

"Give me your hand," he said against her lips. "Touch yourself."

Her fingers dropped to her clit.

His tongue speared her mouth. She rubbed herself as his fingers fucked her, driving her to the edge of a detonation she would never recover from.

"Fuck, baby. Come for me."

Bright white lightning rolled over her. Heated bliss tore through her, and she bucked on his hand, crying out his name, riding the explosion until it became too much.

Her back arched, panting and boneless, he didn't stop. Heaven started building again before she caught her breath.

"One more," he whispered against her ear.

Another orgasm rolled through before the first one finished. Every part of her flew high.

This was better than she could fathom, and he let her bask in that pleasure.

Carefully Callum wrapped her trembling, gasping body to his chest and held her until she was limp and loose and thoroughly melted in his arms.

Chapter Nineteen

With a duffel bag of fresh clothes and Grace at his side, Callum revved his truck onto the highway and left behind Granite Creek. Tension hung heavy between them, but this was unlike the concerns bothering him earlier as he had driven to his apartment. Before, he had questions, and, to be honest, he still had them, but now, he was fuckin' horny.

Was there any validity to what Vivian had said? Did Grace see him as her white knight? So long as Grace didn't regret the way they spent their time together, he didn't care.

Actually, he did care, and if they had stayed in that bed any longer, he would've talked himself into stripping off his clothes and burying himself in her needy, hot body.

She would not have said no.

It was better this way. At least, that's what he kept telling himself. Getting Grace off was the only way he knew to blow off steam without losing his mind.

In a few short hours, they would be in a safe house, all alone in the middle of nowhere, where his resolve would be tested again. Callum needed to understand exactly how Grace viewed him and their dynamic. His willpower was only so strong.

"You called me a damsel in distress," Grace said, interrupting his thoughts. Their minds were in the same place. "Is that why you bundled me up and got us out the door before you changed your mind?"

His grip tightened on the steering wheel.

"I'm not a damsel in distress, if that's what you're most worried about. Don't forget I threw myself at you."

"You didn't throw yourself at me. You just…" He gestured to her. "Reminded me of what was in front of me. Very directly." He cleared his throat. "Did you and Vivian talk about…" He lifted his shoulders. "Us?"

"Absolutely not, though she asked questions about you."

He glanced over. "Like what?"

"Like how well I knew you. What kind of person you are. That kind of stuff."

Ding, ding, ding. There was his answer. Vivian could read body language like she read a book and had cornered Grace with questions. He and Grace had enough electricity to power a small town. No wonder Vivian thought they'd slept together.

"I asked Vivian why you left the Army."

His molars clamped.

"I know I shouldn't have. I'm sorry. But she said the same thing Hayden did."

"You asked Hayden?"

"They said it's your story to tell. I'm ready to listen when you're ready to share."

It was his turn to be cornered. He didn't want to talk about it, but at a certain point, avoiding the explanation was disingenuous. She needed more from him, and apparently, an orgasm, holding her hand, and bodyguard duty wouldn't cut it for the long haul. *The long haul...* That was what he wanted with her. Still, he struggled to explain. "Something happened."

"I got that," she said quietly. "Part of me is aggravated that you won't explain. Another part of me realizes it's probably hard to talk about."

He swallowed against the knot in his throat. She wasn't wrong.

"I'm even a little embarrassed to say this," she continued, "but I'm jealous that everyone knows that about you except for me."

"It's not that I'm hiding something from you." But retelling the story triggered the mental hell all over again.

"I'm not trying to coerce you into sharing. I just thought I should tell you I asked Vivian. It wasn't fair to you."

He let out a long breath. "We'll talk about it at the safe house."

"Really?"

"Yeah. Sure. I don't want to talk about it. It's hard. It sucks. It's a goddamn nightmare."

"Callum—"

"Trust me, there's nothing to feel jealous about. Just a story of something that happened. It won't change who you think I am as a person. At least, I don't think it will."

"I don't think you're harboring an awful secret like you shot up a village of civilians or something."

He grimaced inwardly. She was closer than she realized. He had to change subjects, or the stress that was pounding at his temples would turn into a headache. He checked his mirrors and changed lanes. "I'll tell you. It's fine. But not now." He focused on the road and thought about the seeds Vivian had planted in his head. "Back to this whole damsel situation. Can I ask you something?"

"Would I say no to my knight in shining armor?"

He groaned. "When I asked you about who you'd dated, you said no one."

"Yeah," she whispered.

"But you had friends on your list. Male friends..."

"I didn't."

He frowned. "Didn't what?"

"Get physical. I said I didn't date. I didn't...do anything in that department."

He looked over quickly, dragged his eyes back to the road, then looked at her again. "What do you mean?"

"*What do I mean? What do you think I mean?* I was in a horrible marriage, and after that, I abandoned my life. Dating or hooking up with a friend or whatever else you're thinking about didn't come up."

"So you didn't—you haven't—"

"Oh my God, Callum. You're such a guy."

"Yeah. I am a human, Grace. With human needs. Last time I checked, which was very recently, you had those too."

"Human needs," she muttered, half-embarrassed. "That's one way to describe me ripping my clothes off." She drew in a shaky breath and let it out slowly. "Those needs were long buried until recently. Do with that what you will."

"No one?" he asked.

"I told you. *No one.*"

No one had touched Grace in years. Grace hadn't touched anyone either. Callum wasn't sure which he liked better. Both, he decided with every possessive fiber of his body.

But that was a problem for the damsel-in-distress concern. If she hadn't been with anyone since her ex-husband, Vivian's theory took on a whole lot more credence.

As for him, did he have a savior complex? Vivian thought it was an automatic part of the job that he had to manage. But she hadn't taken into account their past. This was his second chance, and he wasn't fucking it up.

He reached over and took Grace's hand. He could feel her uncertainty in the stiff way she unfolded her arm. She wasn't making it easy, but that had been their entire existence. He threaded his fingers through hers. "My boss brought up a legitimate concern, and as much as I don't wanna believe it, you need to hear it."

"Let's hear it then."

"It really holds water, considering you haven't been with anybody since your ex-husband."

"Quit stalling and tell me."

"Everything you're feeling about me is because you're in danger, and I'm the guy that can save you." Silence ticked by long enough that he looked over, gut churning and not thrilled with how long it was taking her to refute that point. "Grace?"

She pulled her hand into her lap. "Do you want honesty?"

Fuck. "Yeah, babe. Rip off the Band-Aid just like you did your shirt."

"Somehow the shirt was easier."

"Woman, you are killing me right now."

"You were the first boy who ever made my stomach flutter."

Every part of his body tingled. He wanted to grin, but didn't trust what she might say next.

"Then those flutters turned to much more. The older I got, God, I wanted your attention so badly. Especially in high school."

"Eh, high school," he admitted with a sheepish nod.

"You were so much older than me, and it was never gonna happen."

He was a senior when she was a freshman. Even if he looked—and he wouldn't admit if he did or not—their age difference had been too much. Now that they were adults, a couple of years didn't matter.

"When you came back from West Point, I literally didn't think I could want you any more." She ducked her face into her hands, half-laughing. "I was wrong."

Why hadn't he opened his goddamn mouth? He probably would have screwed it up, but God, he had killed himself when it came to her during college. "I could be saying the same thing."

"I'm still not convinced of that, because I was hopelessly, obsessively, head over heels for a man who didn't notice I existed as a woman."

Every part of him ached to rewrite the past. He spent years tamping down the pull he felt for her because of the unwritten bro code and his rule-following moral compass. Regret bubbled in his lungs. "Trust me. I noticed you."

Just days ago, he'd told Grace their lives would have been different if they'd gotten together before she met Dominic. He'd said it like a cocky line, but in his gut, he knew it was true.

Everything would have been different if he had said something and crossed that stupid imaginary boundary. He had no doubt she wouldn't have married Dominic, and he hated himself for not saying a thing. Hindsight was going to be the death of him.

But that was then. He needed to be damn sure about now and hear their connection wasn't just a damsel waiting to be saved and bedded. "You haven't been with anyone in years. All of a sudden, I'm here, and your rules have changed."

She twisted her bracelet and pulled the beads until they clicked. The silence dragged on. "It's not that they changed."

"Then what?"

"You're different, Callum. You always have been."

Every doubt he had about them was officially gone. He loved this woman. Maybe he always had.

Chapter Twenty

Callum double-checked the GPS and turned onto a nondescript driveway curving off the side of a mountain. The term driveway was a bit of a stretch. This was more like tire tracks, partially marked with crushed rocks. Tall grass and brush reached the truck's side mirrors. Weeds ran down the center. They had been cut back, but not within a week or two.

Grace twisted her bracelet around two fingers. "You know that Dominic's people were able to get to a guy in witness protection."

She hadn't said much since their bare-all discussion. In the last few hours, their conversation revolved around whether the air conditioning was too cool or if she needed a pit stop. "I agree, though Viv said the feds don't."

"Right, as if people hiding in witness protection randomly decide to recant their testimony."

"I didn't say you're wrong. Though I wonder if Marino had that kind of reach, why didn't he use it during the trial?"

"I don't know."

"Maybe that's what the DOJ wants to talk to you about."

"I didn't even know he was out of prison. How would I know if he scared people into changing their testimony?" She focused on the grass slapping the sides of his truck. "Have you been here before?"

"Nope." A doe hopped across the driveway. He eased off the gas. When there was one, there were probably more. He scanned the grass and saw another lurking in the brush, waiting to bound across the driveway. "But like I said, it has everything we need. Space. A stocked pantry." A security system that could probably track the difference between a deer and a sniper crossing through the woods they were about to enter.

They rumbled up the driveway. Tall grass and brush gave way to trees with a thick green canopy that blocked the sun. "It's safe. That's all that matters."

"No more Molotov cocktails or FedEx deliveries."

"None." The truck threaded up a hill on the side of a wooded mountain. Bits of sunshine blinked through the shadows. The terrain became rougher. That was by design, he was sure. Everything about this location would have been expertly calculated.

The house came into view at the end of a horseshoe driveway.

"It looks like a regular house," she said.

"Exactly the point." It blended in. Not fancy nor dripping in visible security. Titan had probably purchased this house and retrofitted it surreptitiously. He parked and leaned forward to get a good look out the windshield. "It's our new digs. At least temporarily."

Grace popped out. Callum studied her for a second too long before he joined her. He wasn't sure how long ago he'd actually fallen in love with her, but now that he saw it, he couldn't unsee the blaring obviousness.

He unloaded their bags. Pitiful, actually. They both had duffels, and she had her backpack. They both lived on so little. Clothes and necessities. What did her rental cabin have? She had continually moved. It was the first time he really thought about how few possessions she must keep.

Loneliness struck him in the chest. *Her* loneliness. He could relate to a minimalist life. His time in the Army hadn't been conducive to settling down. He didn't collect things. He hadn't set up deep roots. That was apparent even in his current bare-bones, drab, undecorated apartment, but at least he always had a home base. Grace didn't.

Callum unlocked the front door.

Her gaze swept through the open layout of the living room, dining room, and small kitchen. Deer mounts lined the wall above the couches. A trophy fish hung over a soot-stained fireplace. Well-read fishing and hunting magazines were piled haphazardly on the scuffed coffee table.

"It looks like we walked into someone's home," she whispered. "It's like someone lives here."

"That's the idea." He meandered down the short hallway lined with faded pictures from hunting and fishing expeditions. Most were action shots with faces artfully obscured. A man's back faced the camera as he reeled in a monster with the fishing rod bent under the weight of the catch. Another focused on a net with large trout, leaving the person behind it unfocused and unrecognizable. Still another showed the back of a man in blaze orange, rifle slung over his shoulder, walking into the sunset.

The floorboards creaked underfoot. The air conditioning hummed. He noted the sounds, eyeballed what he thought were the well-hidden cameras that fed into a state-of-the-art security system, and searched for covert weapons caches.

The hallway off the living room-kitchen area was short with four doors. One bathroom, two bedrooms, and a linen closet. He opened the closet and mentally cataloged the boxes of ammo placed above towels and washcloths. The bottom shelf was dedicated to first aid supplies. Useful and expected, given the established hunting motif of the house.

He closed the linen closet and opened the bathroom door. Nothing special unless the 1980s were having a moment again.

Callum moved on to the two bedrooms. One was larger than the other, but both had large closets and dresser drawers filled with generic clothes in several sizes, along with more weapons.

This place really looked like they'd stepped into a hunter-and-fisherman's home, and strategically, the layout was a winner. He could see their surroundings from almost every angle.

Grace waltzed into the bedroom and pulled the drapes open. "That's a huge backyard." The windows had a fantastic view of the back and side of the house. A two-person swing faced the tree line. Chairs surrounded a well-used fire pit. "Very pretty, and very quiet."

He nodded. "No neighbors are the best neighbors."

"Will we have to keep all the drapes and blinds closed?"

Callum lifted a shoulder. "No. We're not going to make ourselves into sitting ducks, but we're not going to hide in the dark. *Safe* house, remember?"

Her lips were pinched together as she nodded. Her gaze locked on the trees as if she were expecting an offensive line to infiltrate the backyard.

"Hey, you okay?"

She didn't look away from the window. "Sure."

Callum squeezed her shoulder and found knots of tension under his hand. He flexed his fingers into the muscle and wished his will alone could relax her. "You're safe here. Whether or not we have the drapes open. No one knows where we are."

"The people you work with do."

"Well, yeah. But they're not your problem."

"This is the first time I'm staying somewhere I didn't choose."

"So?"

"Anyone can be bought. Dominic has a way of flipping people to join his team. Threats and money do wonders."

Grace didn't trust a soul on earth, and that had included him until recently. If he or Hayden had fixed her problems years ago, she wouldn't see every new place as a threat. "Not everyone," he reminded her. "Not me."

He would keep reminding her until it stuck.

She released an exhausted sigh and turned from staring at the backyard. "I trust you."

Good. "Are you okay with this room?" It was bigger. The bed had decorative pillows, albeit with stitched scenes of ducks and bears. He dropped their bags on the bed, ensuring she was okay with sharing a room.

"Sure."

That didn't sound like the same woman who had admitted wanting him her entire life. "Are you hungry?"

She rested her hand over her stomach as if just remembering she should eat. "I'm starved."

Nothing good came from a worried woman with a calorie deficit or low blood sugar. "Let's raid the kitchen. These places come stocked with an all-you-can-eat shelf-stable buffet."

"Oh, yum."

"Give me a chance. I'll surprise you."

They checked the kitchen cabinets and found more food than they could need. A deep freezer in the attached garage and shelves lined with provisions confirmed they wouldn't have to leave to eat well. He grabbed a frozen pie crust from the deep freeze and collected cans from the garage, pantry, and kitchen.

She eyed everything on the counter and picked up the pie crust box. "What are you making?"

"Chicken pot pie. It's not really a summer food, but it is a comfort food, and that seems like a hell of a good idea." This was step one in reaffirming her trust in the world. Creamy, savory carbohydrates. He opened drawers until he found a can opener among the various self-defense options. A taser. Pepper spray. More knives than would ever be in a typical kitchen. "Can you preheat the oven?"

She checked inside the oven door before turning it on. Maybe she'd noticed the various weapons stashes throughout the house. "What temperature?"

He was winging it and didn't know. The pie crust box offered recipes for cherry and pumpkin pies. Meat and veggies were the same-ish, he guessed. He washed his hands and dried them on a hand towel with screen-printed fish. "Three-fifty."

"You know your way around a kitchen."

"I thought I showed that this morning making bacon."

"Oh my God, that was this morning. I'm so tired that it feels like decades ago."

"Go sit down."

"No, I want to help."

He assessed whether it was an empty offer, then handed her a colander and opened two cans of vegetables: one of corn and the other of mixed peas and carrots. "Drain these."

She stared as if he'd sprouted a third eye but did as requested.

Callum set a pot of water on the stove and cranked the dial to high, filled a bowl with ice cubes and water, and set it next to the sink. "We'll flash-boil them for a minute, drain 'em, throw them into an ice bath, drain 'em again, and voila, the canned taste disappears."

"Really?"

He raised his shoulders. "I mean, I haven't run a taste test or anything, but yeah. It's what Hayden and I do, and we lived on canned crap like kings."

A curious smile curved on her lips. "Alicia would be impressed."

Alicia wasn't the woman he wanted to impress.

The stove slowly heated the water, but eventually it boiled. Callum turned down the dial so the pot wouldn't boil over, and Grace dumped in the vegetables. He opened a can of condensed cream of chicken soup and cracked the cap on a small carton of milk, mixing them with a can of chicken.

After a minute, she strained the flash-boiled vegetables, dunked them in the ice bath, and drained them, giving the colander a couple of shakes. He took them from her, dumped them into his bowl, and scoured through the spice containers.

"What are you looking for?"

"No idea. A bit of everything." Callum added dashes and shakes of whatever sounded good as she mixed.

Grace tapped the spatula on the bowl. "I should take pictures for Alicia. Really, she would be applauding at this point."

They unrolled the pie crusts and pressed one into a tin. He dumped in the soupy vegetables and slapped the second crust on top. To be honest, the whole thing looked bland, but if he had to bet, Grace would like it. He stabbed the crust all over with a steak knife. "Alicia's high opinion isn't the one I'm after."

The way Grace's smile curved until it made her eyes shine was going to get him in trouble before they'd had dinner. He tossed the pie into the oven.

"How long?" she asked.

He picked up the pie-crust box. "It says forty-five minutes to an hour."

Grace flipped the oven light on and peeked at the pot pie. "That's a long time. Thirty-five? Forty?"

"I've never made a pie." He laughed as he cleared their trash. "I have no idea. Sure. That'll give me time to check in with my office."

"I'll go work on a book cover."

"Do you need to be on the internet for that?"

She shook her head. "Nope. Just a program on my computer. My client had just approved the concept, and now I'm playing with the proportions of the image in the background before I go much further."

She settled on the well-worn couch, pulled a crocheted blanket over her legs, and booted up her device. Years of remote work in a constantly changing setting had given her the ease to simply slide into a job. She flipped the laptop screen so that it functioned like a tablet, removed a stylus from her bag, and dove into her work, completely relaxed.

Callum lingered. Her stylus swiped over the screen over and over again like she was shading a tiny spot. The book cover had her complete attention, and the way her hair fell over her face had his. If he didn't call Vivian right that moment, he wouldn't be able to let Grace work.

He pivoted from the living room and dialed Viv. Surely he'd given her enough time to handle the police and hunt down the motivation behind the firebomb through Alicia's window.

Vivian answered on the first ring and got down to business. "It wasn't Marino."

He shut the bedroom door behind him and agreed. The MOs were different. Marino's note was clear, if not creepy. The Molotov cocktail was messy and pointless. "How do you know?"

"Because Dominic Marino is furious someone is messing with his woman."

His molars ground together. "She's not his woman."

"I know this. You know this. But a certain billionaire does not, and he and his people are blowing up every line of communication we've got a read on, demanding to know who put his wife in danger."

"Ex-wife."

"Again, Hale, I know. You know. He doesn't seem to care, and he's pissed. Want the good news?"

He paced. "Yeah, Viv. I want some good news."

"He doesn't know about you."

Callum froze. "How's that possible?"

"Maybe he's not keeping as close an eye on her as we thought. Maybe he's not putting the full weight of his resources on tracking her."

"You sound like Dean with all of your ideas and no answers. Speaking of ideas," he grumbled. "Grace and I talked, and I'm giving you an official heads-up: we don't have a damsel situation. And you don't have to butt into my personal life again."

Vivian snorted. "Think you have that all sorted out, do ya, Prince Charming? It doesn't work that way."

"It's different."

"That's what they all say."

"Never mind." He shouldn't have brought it up. "If not Marino, then who firebombed Alicia?"

"And *why* did they firebomb her place?" Vivian mused aloud. "I have the same questions, and nothing yet. Before you jump down my throat. We're working on it while you two stay low."

"Staying low as we can. Don't worry."

"And make good decisions. Smart, level-headed, fully clothed decisions."

He blew out his cheeks. "Gotta go, Boss."

"Don't blame me when this all comes crashing down," she muttered and hung up.

The phone rang again. This time it was Dean, who proceeded to give Callum a more technical explanation of what Vivian reported. Interesting, but he didn't walk away from the conversation feeling as though he knew more.

Callum opened the bedroom door. The hallway opened to the living room, where Grace remained on the couch, studiously sucked into her work. Her anxious energy had all but disappeared as if she were content so long as she wasn't thinking about the fire at Alicia's or her ex-husband.

Callum itched to do something. He didn't have a mission objective—well, other than keeping Grace safe, and if he interrupted her now, she might bring up what he'd pushed off until they arrived: the reason he was no longer in the Army. He wasn't ready for that conversation yet. Soon. The right time would come to him.

Instead of bothering her, Callum checked on the chicken pot pie. The scent of baking dough warmed the air, but it needed far more than the thirty-five minutes they'd set the timer for. He reset it.

"It smells delicious." Grace stretched her arms over her head. "How long until it's done?"

"Maybe fifteen more minutes."

"We're going to starve to death." Her smile warmed her eyes. "Want to see my cover so far?"

His body jumped at the chance to sit next to her, and if he hadn't realized he was already gone for this woman, that would've been a bright sign.

He joined her on the couch. Grace scooted closer, brushing her hair off her shoulder as she removed the crucial inches between them. The crocheted blanket still covered her legs; her hands were on her computer, arms covered by the long sleeves.

"How are the cat scratches?"

She glanced at them. "Not bothering me since you gave me a couple of orgasms."

His jaw fell before he caught it. Callum tipped his head back and laughed. She didn't tiptoe around *anything*. That had been how they had been years ago. She always told him what was on her mind—except for that crucial part that he'd also been hiding—and he loved to see it again. More and more of her shone through. "Good to know that's a cure for pain."

She snuggled next to him. "Look. This is the cover. I love it."

He put his arm around her.

"It's a fantasy novel with fairies and wood nymphs. Lush greenery and stars that are visible during the day." She zoomed the screen into the sky where she'd painted the tiniest details. A constellation reflected the vivid green trees. The minutiae wouldn't be apparent when she zoomed out again.

Grace scrolled down and tapped the screen with her stylus. "This is my favorite fairy. I haven't read the story, obviously, but I've named her Evangelina. That sounds like a fairy's name, doesn't it?" She tipped her chin up and offered a gentle expression that held more of his attention than her book cover.

Callum nodded. His chest tightened as if invisible hands pressed against his lungs. The way she looked up made him ache to be closer. He wasn't sure he could wait until after dinner to undress her. The next time he made her come, it would be with his tongue and then his cock.

Her attention returned to the screen, unaware that she was screaming his name in his mind, and zoomed in on the screen again. "I gave Evangelina a flower bracelet that no one will ever notice, but that I'm obsessed with."

He tried to focus. Honest to God, he did. The idea that he couldn't sit next to her without dirty fucking thoughts was ludicrous. "You're really talented."

She repositioned the illustration. "If you zoom below this tree, you can see a little kid fairy trying out their wings for the first time. Honestly, no one will ever see it, but I'll know it's there."

She shifted against him. Her loose hair tickled his skin, and his cock twitched for more. The air between them was too warm. She didn't seem to notice as she continued to point out invisible details.

Callum locked his attention on the illustration's complexity. If he looked up, he'd kiss her. The timer beeped for the pot pie, and he jumped.

With a tilt of her head and a lift of her eyebrows, she laughed. "Wow, I really sucked you into the fairy's world." She swiped the screen, smiling and proud of her work. "It really is one of my favorites."

He still had a lot to learn about her. Tech savvy. A talented artist. As he put physical distance between them, he wondered what else. Peeling back her layers gave him a new perspective on a woman he thought he already knew.

Callum checked their dinner. Smelled good, but he would have thought it should have been bubbling through the steam vents in the pie crust. He shoved it back into the oven. "Not ready."

"How much longer?" Grace walked into the kitchen as she stretched. Her fitted shirt lifted and exposed the soft stomach that his hands had been all over. She was trying to kill him.

He punched another round on the timer again. "Not too much longer."

She leaned against the counter. "Did your office have an update?"

"Kinda."

"Well?" she prompted, assessing him. "Any news on Dominic?"

He hated Marino's name on her lips. "Dean tapped into Marino's communication channels, and he's upset that someone put you in danger."

Lines tightened at the corners of her eyes. Her arms crossed, and her lips pursed as though she'd sucked on a lemon. Gone was the relaxed woman on the couch. Her walls were going up before his very eyes. "I don't understand."

"I don't either, but they'll figure it out."

She pressed her fingers to her temples as if fighting off a headache. "I just want to be rid of him."

Empathizing could only go so far. She needed a distraction. Hell, he did too. They couldn't sit around with nothing to do while waiting for dinner, or Grace would work herself up when all Callum wanted was for her to completely let go.

Should he ask her about the book cover again? He scanned the well-lived-in house. Board games and puzzles were stacked on the lower layer of the coffee table. A flat-screen television hung on the wall between the mounted bass and trout. Come nightfall, there was a fire pit to sit around, though he wasn't sure how much fun she would find in poking a fire with a stick.

Or he could just take her to bed.

Callum wrapped her in his arms and let her meld to his chest. Everything about holding her felt right. Apprehensions evaporated. Vivian's disproven theory disappeared. This was the woman he was meant to hold. He dropped his lips to the top of her head.

"I need this," she whispered against his chest. "You."

He lowered his mouth to hers, and like a balm to a burn, she soothed parts of him that vibrated. Her lips fit on his as though they'd been born to kiss. Every part of him needed to be with her.

Callum swept her into his arms and returned to the couch, cradling her in his lap, his hand sliding up her thigh. Her mouth moved to his neck and set the world on fire—and he froze.

Her languid body tightened. "What?"

He focused on a stuffed fish on the wall, its head facing the living room, watching, and he remembered exactly why they were there in the first place. "Give me a second."

"*No.*"

"Trust me." There was a not-small chance of a live feed streaming into Dean's office that very moment. Fucking Wes and Rhys would have popcorn by now. "There are security cameras."

Her eyes went wide.

"It was just a kiss." He brushed her hair off her cheeks. "We didn't put on a show."

Grace straightened and stared about the room. "Who's watching?"

"I'm not sure, but Dean probably has a live feed he could pull up at any moment."

Her jaw set, and he could see the tension simmering, but then she laughed. Grace tipped her head back and cried, "Come on. Do you know how long I've wanted this guy?"

Wanting to pull his hair out, he had to laugh, too.

"I'm being serious," she managed.

"Believe me, you're not alone in that frustration."

"The cameras can't be *everywhere*, can they? The bathroom?"

He liked the way her mind worked. "I'll find out."

The oven timer beeped.

"Okay, come on, universe," she called.

"Sit still a minute." He pulled the pot pie out of the oven so they wouldn't forget and burn the safe house down, then turned toward the garage. There had to be tools in there.

"What are you doing?"

"Getting what I need to clear the security cameras from inside this house."

Chapter Twenty-One

A shiver of expectation rolled over Grace. She wasn't hungry for dinner and watched Callum work his way through the living room like a predator stalking his prey. His eyes swept the corners and shelves; he inspected the knickknacks and the stuffed fish that were hung on the wall. He unscrewed air vents and electrical outlet covers. Every now and then, he tossed a dish towel over a fish head, a bookend, and what had to be a security camera.

"Can they hear us?" she asked.

"Maybe. They're probably watching right now and having a hell of a good laugh."

"Are you going to get in trouble?"

"I didn't permanently dismantle anything." He checked the base of a bear-shaped lamp, crouched low to feel along the underside of a mounted deer's head, and then pulled a knife out of his pocket to pry loose a vent cover painted to the wall.

He moved with practiced efficiency, as if he were actually at work, searching for trouble. Every move was calculated. Controlled. Sexy as hell. And raising her level of anticipation by a mile. "Why are there so many cameras?"

"In case of a breach. Different angles give different intel."

Her stomach dropped. He's sworn the safe house was the best place for them and that his work associates wouldn't turn her over to Dominic. But the cameras supported her hypothesis. Anyone could be bought. Dominic could easily find her just as he had flipped witnesses.

"Don't overthink the cameras," Callum called.

"You don't know what I'm thinking."

He shot her a look over his shoulder. "Think about what I was going to do to you on that couch instead."

Her stomach flipped. Oh. Hell. She twisted the bracelet on her wrist. "I'll put dinner in the fridge."

He stopped and stared at her.

Grace pretended not to notice her heart tripping. "I mean, if *that* is what we're doing instead of eating. God, don't look at me like that, Callum. If you can tear the house apart, I can put dinner up."

But she suddenly understood the difference. Clearing the cameras meant they could get naked whenever. Putting the food up meant *now*. *Now* was written all over his face. The air squeezed out of her lungs. She was drowning, and he was the oxygen that could save her.

"One more minute." He charged toward the bedroom like a man on a mission to save humanity. Callum Hale wasn't trying to seduce her with sweet talk or touches. He was giving her privacy, offering her safety, and being up front and clear on what he wanted. *Her.*

She put the food they'd worked hard on into the refrigerator. Her heart galloped at the sound of his footsteps returning toward the kitchen—and he didn't stop until she was backed against the wall. His forearm pressed over her head, and his body caged her in place.

She tipped her head back and fell into his stormy eyes. His free hand cupped her cheek, running his thumb over her parted lips. Her soft breathing stuttered.

"Not a damn soul can see you." His jaw tensed. "Grace—"

She kissed him.

No hesitation. No room for second-guessing. She lived for the touch of his lips against hers. Just like every time before, need flared, flamed, and exploded as if the unspoken years of missed opportunity could burn.

The hand on her cheek dropped to her waist, and with a hard, hungry yank, Callum belted her against him. She arched to him, sweeping her tongue and deepening the kiss until her knees turned liquid.

He tore away, chest heaving. His gaze darted to her kiss-swollen lips, then Callum leaned closer, locking his eyes on her as if he could read her soul. "I'm not fucking you against the wall."

The corners of her lips lifted. "What if I say please?"

"You're going to be the death of me," he rasped.

"Please—"

Callum swept her into his arms again. "Not yet."

His lips claimed hers again. The yearning for him pulsed between her legs. Arousal ached in her pussy. Callum carried her into the bedroom, kicked the door shut, and lay her down as though she might break.

She burned so hot, she shivered. Years of wanting him, fantasizing over how he might look at her, was nothing compared to the way he stood before her now, memorizing her in bed.

His erection strained against his pants, and stripping off his shirt, he fell onto the bed beside her, pulling her mouth to his. Hot, wet strokes of his tongue delved past her lips. He sucked and teased and pushed her to the edge.

She inched away and tossed off her shirt. He didn't miss a beat and snagged her shorts away. In her bra and underwear, she couldn't be close enough. "You have on more clothes than me."

Callum stripped, and she'd never seen a man more perfect. Hard muscles cut over harder muscles. His intensity was too much as he stroked his thick length, watching her, waiting with a ravenous need.

"God, you're perfect." His strong hands unfastened her bra. He dragged his hands over her skin until he hooked her panties and dropped them to her knees. Callum cradled her in his arms again as he had when he carried her into the bedroom. Then again, carefully as though she might break, he laid her out and slid the fabric free of her legs. "Perfect."

She'd never have agreed, but in his eyes, she believed it.

He lifted her foot into his hand and kissed her ankle. The velvet hot slide of his tongue worked up her calf and teased the indentation at the back of her knee.

Grace wriggled her hips. Anticipation coursed through her blood as he kissed higher, shouldering her thighs apart. She couldn't catch her breath. "Callum."

His lips hovered near the sensitive place at the top of her leg, breathing against where she wanted him the most.

She bit her lip. "Please," she cried out, back arching with the stroke of his fingers.

His fingers and tongue parted her open, sliding against her. His approving growl reverberated through her pussy. The tip of his tongue circled the tight bud of needy nerves. Grace lifted her hips, begging for more.

His chin dropped, and Callum pressed his tongue into her. She died at the intrusion. Sensation after sensation exploded. He alternated his tongue and fingers, and she cried his name. He sucked. His fingers plunged. The back and forth, the building pressure, brought her closer to the razor-sharp edge of heaven. "Please."

He gave her what she needed.

Harder and faster and more, until she was bucking on his face, riding against his hand. Grace orgasmed like she'd never come in her life.

Her fingers threaded into his hair. "I need you inside me."

He repositioned, flexing his rigid length against her wetness, meeting her eye as though he had so much to say. Instead, he reached for his pants, extracted a condom, and sheathed himself.

She reached for him. He covered her. The head of his cock pressed into her. So much. So good. He stretched her, splitting her apart as her legs wrapped around his powerful thighs and her teeth bit his shoulder. Her eyes rolled shut. Every part of her relaxed and tightened in a seesawing war of need and pleasure.

He worked in and out until fully inside her, and this intoxicating fullness had never seemed so possible. "*Grace.*"

"Please fuck me."

The corners of his lips lifted—then he pulled away and plunged in. Over and over, Callum thrust and flexed and pushed her to the precipice of a blistering orgasm.

She clung to him and fell into rippling, spasming bliss. His name rang from her lips as she called to him, burying her face into his neck as he drove into her, building an orgasm again.

The climax exploded within her. Her body tightened around his, and Callum groaned, needing the release he'd given to her. He pumped harder, stretching her orgasm until he strained, hoarsely gasping, face buried in her neck, and came.

Goosebumps erupted down his back. His breathing hammered until he collapsed, pulling her to his side.

They stared at each other.

"Holy hell." Callum rolled on his back and intertwined his fingers with hers. "What was that?"

"That was..." She tried to think of an all-encompassing word for the way he'd blown her mind. "Awesome."

Chapter Twenty-Two

With every second that ticked by, Grace fell harder for him. Years of wishing and wanting had come to fruition, and now her mind raced to catch up with the jumping jacks of awareness her heart was doing. He'd always been in her orbit. A family friend. A man she'd lusted after. But he was more than all that. He made her heart ache for another chance at life.

Callum tugged his shirt over his head and leaned down to kiss her. "I'll reheat dinner."

The quick kiss turned into a lazy one. "Or we can forget about it and stay here all night." Her stomach growled, and she covered it with her hands.

He grinned against her lips. "Maybe dinner first. You need sustenance." He smacked another kiss on her lips and left.

After he shut the door, she covered her dopey grin with her hands. Callum Hale fucked like a god. She squeezed her eyes shut and relished the soreness in her body and the emotion caught in her throat. They needed *sustenance*. She sighed like a happy, dopey, lovestruck woman.

Callum could cook.

He could sweep her into a safe house and then into bed.

And, oh, the orgasms he delivered.

Stupidly blissful, she curled into the sheets. They even smelled like him, and like a fiend for more, she inhaled deeply. Had she fallen for him? This was so much more than she understood.

After a few minutes of pulling herself together, she padded into the living room. Callum had the pot pie in the oven to reheat and was on his cell phone, amusement dancing across his expression as he listened to whatever the other person was saying. He saw her, pointed to the trophy fish on the wall covered by a dish towel, and mouthed, "Not happy."

"Tell Dean it was for his own good."

Callum repeated her words and snorted at what Dean said.

Her cell phone buzzed on the coffee table next to her abandoned laptop. Grace hurried over. She wanted to catch up with Alicia, but saw her stepmother's name on the display. "I'll be two minutes," she said to Callum and headed toward her bedroom to answer.

"Hey, Mari." Grace shut her door. "Sorry. I meant to give you a call. But one thing led to another, and time has—"

"Oh, my darling. I've missed your voice."

Every muscle in her body froze as the bile in her stomach threatened to launch itself from her body.

"Grace? Come on now," Dominic purred.

She stood like a statue, her limbs stuck with the phone against her ear, as disbelief pounded in her chest. She needed to wrench the phone from her ear and double-check the screen. It had been Mari's phone number, hadn't it? But the man speaking to her was Dominic.

"Don't go silent on me now. We've got so much to discuss."

She shook her head. Words still wouldn't form. Was Dominic with Mari and her dad? Where? Their house? Had he... she didn't know, caught them? Taken them?

"It's confusing," Dominic cooed like the slick sociopath he was. "I understand, but I wasn't sure if you'd pick up the phone if you weren't sure who was calling." He chortled as if this were charming small talk. "Have a seat, Grace."

Could he see her? Her gaze darted around the bedroom. Callum had dismantled the security cameras. They had been hidden everywhere. It was possible Callum had missed one, and Dominic had watched everything unfold between them in bed.

Nausea hit her like a Mack truck. Her ex-husband could get eyes anywhere. Everywhere. Even the place Callum had promised was safe. Dominic could have turned someone at Titan.

"Take a deep breath. It's time we caught up."

His voice made her blood boil. God, fuck this guy. Would he ever be gone from her life? "Where are my parents?" She hated the shaking of her words. "What did you do to them?"

"There's that voice I missed so much. You didn't visit. You never wrote—"

"I want nothing to do with you."

Dominic chortled. She could picture his head tossed back as he rocked in an expensive leather office chair, behind a desk the size of Manhattan, cocky and conceited—except he couldn't be in one of his offices if he had Mari's phone. "Where are my parents?"

"The years and distance have given you quite the mouth. I didn't expect that after seeing you at the grocery store."

"You didn't see me." But he confirmed exactly what she already knew. He had been there, had tracked her down, and wanted to mess with her. "Though I got your letter. I threw it in the garbage because I don't care about you."

"We never had pets like Alicia does. Did you enjoy her dogs and cat? Or were they just a mess of pet hair and—"

"*Stop.*" She wanted to throw up. Dominic was somehow with her parents and could get to her friends. "You don't get to know anything about me. Let me talk to Mari."

"Darling, you don't want me to list the things I know about you. You'll have nightmares for the rest of your life."

Furious tears burned at the back of her eyes. "Leave me alone. Leave my parents alone. Give Mari back her phone and go away. I don't have anything to say to you. I don't have anything I want from you. *I don't want you.* That's why we're divorced, Dominic. Don't you get that? I want *nothing* to do with you."

"I don't know if that's true, but that's not why I called. Wait, wait, darling. Don't hang up. You know you want to know why I called."

She only wanted to know Mari and Dad were safe. "I want to talk to my parents."

"I can't do that right now. Listen, you're going to meet some friends in the next few days."

"We don't have any mutual friends—"

"Shut up, Grace, and listen."

Her hands trembled. Trepidation rolled through her limbs, and she couldn't produce a single word. She hated who she became when he was near. Weak and unable to fight. She couldn't even hang up on him.

"When you meet with our *friends,*" he said with such cool detachment that slivers of ice pricked her skin, "you'll be the woman I married. The woman who knows her place. Who knows what to say, and most importantly, *what not to say.*"

"We are *not* married anymore," she said, voice shaking.

"Marriage isn't something you can walk away from. I chose you. You're mine. That's the bottom line."

"No." Fear had a stranglehold on her.

Dominic's laughter poured through the phone again. "You're stuck with me. That's simply the way it works." He clicked his tongue against his teeth. "This little game you've been playing of hide-and-seek has been fun. We'll keep it up until it's time for you to come home."

He sighed like he was disappointed in a petulant child. "In the meantime, focus on the business at hand. When you meet with our friends, you'll do, say, and behave as I would expect of you. Understood?"

She didn't speak.

"I'll take that as a yes. We'll chat after the meeting. Nothing too formal. Just to check in and see how the conversation went."

The line went dead.

Her heart hammered. Grace fumbled the phone. Her fingers danced over the keys and dialed her dad. He answered on the second ring.

"Dad?" she cried.

"Gracie, honey?" Worry dripped in his voice, but not the fear or anger that would come from sitting next to Dominic. "What's wrong?"

"Where's Mari?"

"She's reading in the living room. Gracie, what's going on? What's the matter?"

"Do you see her? Tell me if you see her. Dad, go look for her. Now."

"Hang on. Honey, everything's okay. All right. I'm looking at Mari and putting you on speakerphone. Gracie? Can you hear us?"

"Hi, Grace," Mari said. "What's going on?"

Tears crashed down her cheeks. "Oh, thank God." She dropped onto the bed and folded over. She couldn't catch her breath. "You're okay?"

"Sure, yes," they both said.

"Everything's fine," Dad said with a harder edge. "Where are you? What's going on? Is Callum with you?"

She ignored her dad. "Mari, do you have your phone?"

"Yes. Right here," Mari laid on her stern-mom voice. "What is going on?"

"I don't know. Dominic called, but it was Mari's number that he called from."

"I promise, sweetheart. I have my phone in my hand."

"She's dancing it in front of my face," Dad confirmed. "What the hell did Dominic want?"

There were so many things Grace hadn't told them over the years. She didn't know where to start and wasn't ready to discuss the meeting with the attorneys. It would needlessly worry them when they'd worried so much about her already. "I don't really know. To mess with my head."

"What did he say?" Mari demanded.

She bit her lip. Was she allowed to mention the attorney's meeting? Even if she was, she didn't know the details. Dominic obviously knew about the meeting and wanted her to keep her mouth shut. There was no need to involve her parents in anything he was involved in. The man was a black hole and sucked the life out of everything. "That he missed me."

"He's an abuser. That's what they say and do. You need to stay away from him," Mari ordered.

"I know. I'm staying away."

"People get sucked back into bad situations. There's no shame in asking for help—"

"Callum is helping me with Dominic. He will deal with him. He'll fix everything."

Dad and Mari paused two long beats before Dad added, "What does that mean?"

"We have to meet with investigators."

"Why?"

"It's sort of hard to explain." After telling them time and time again that she would explain later, Grace could tell that her dad and stepmom were reaching their threshold.

She was their grown daughter but was skating dangerously close to the brink where one of them—probably Mari—would put their foot down and demand Grace be more forthcoming with details. "I have to go. I need to tell Callum about Dominic's call. I'll call you later. I promise."

She ended the call and tried not to fall apart.

Callum knocked on the bedroom door and walked in. "Hey, do you—" His scrutiny tightened on her face. "What's wrong?"

Grace tossed the phone onto the bed and wanted to curl into a ball and hide.

He moved closer. "What's up?"

"Dominic called."

"Just now? That's who you were talking to?"

"I called Dad and Mari. I had to make sure they were safe."

"What are you talking about?"

"My phone rang while you were on the phone with Dean. It was Mari's phone number, but Dominic spoke. I couldn't wrap my head around why they were together or how he had Mari's phone. But they're safe. She has her phone."

"He spoofed her phone number."

She nodded. That made sense. "I get that now. But when it was his voice…" The bile that had coated the back of her throat was just now going away. "I freaked."

"Why did he call?"

"He knows about the attorney meeting."

Callum frowned. "You're sure?"

"I'm positive."

"Those plans were made under lock and key."

"I promise you. He knows, and he doesn't want me to say anything."

Callum scrubbed a hand into his hair. "How the hell does he know?"

"Not only does he know about the meeting, he knows what it's about."

He paced between the bed and the window. The lines on his forehead deepened, then he shook his head, like her, not understanding how this was possible. "Then what's it about?"

Defeated, exhausted, she shrugged. "He didn't say."

"Then he doesn't know." He continued to pace. "Tell me his exact words."

"He didn't specify a meeting with the attorneys. He called them 'our friends' and said that I should behave like we're still married. He was…" She rolled the bracelet beads between her fingers, wishing that black tourmaline would protect her from Dominic's energy-sucking venom. "Amused. He acted as if I'd been off on an adventure and would eventually go home to him."

Fury ticked in Callum's jaw. "How does he know about any of this?"

"How? I keep telling everyone how. He uses money and resources to get what he wants. He's tapping into your network. Or the attorney general's office. Just like he did with the witness protection people."

Callum ran a hand over his face. "I have to talk to Viv—"

"Wait. Don't you understand? Dominic knows who we're meeting with. You can't call your office."

He cut her a sharp look. "The leak's not my people."

Grace folded her arms across her chest, almost scared to say aloud what had to be true. "Someone's working with him."

Callum inched closer, ready to argue his point, but his rebuttal died, and his pupils became pinpricks of sudden apprehension.

"The attorneys. The DOJ. Your people. We only have a few options to choose from." One of their resources had failed them. "Dominic told me to sit down." She scanned the bedroom. "Can he see me?"

"No. I tore this room apart. No cameras." Callum rubbed his forehead, thinking over what she had shared. After a long moment, he looked over. "Did he know about me?"

She thought it over. "No. He would have had lots to say if he could have seen in this bedroom."

"Come on."

"Where?"

"We're going to eat. We're going to think. Sitting here, getting aggravated does nothing but help him out. He wants you off-kilter. Why else would he show his hand?" Callum pulled her off the bed. "Either way, we won't figure it out in here."

Chapter Twenty-Three

They didn't figure it out, but Grace was eventually convinced that Callum should update Dean and Vivian about Dominic's phone call. They were tracking her phone calls already, and if they didn't report his call in, they'd wonder why she had gone radio silent.

Other than that, Grace didn't know what to make of dinner. Talking out Dominic's motives had zapped the energy from her, and worse, Callum had turned to stone after she had accused his teammates of treachery.

She did what she knew best. Run and hide. That was what she was good at. At least when she ran away this time, she figured he understood she needed space. Grace hadn't exactly been smooth with her claim of the sudden onset of a headache.

And he had let her go.

Grace showered and slipped under the covers. Falling asleep would be impossible. New houses always had their own sounds to get used to. It was one of the things she realized while moving often. She cataloged what she heard. The house settled. The air conditioning clicked. Callum's footsteps paced the living room and kitchen. He went outside. His truck door opened and closed, and the pacing returned in the living room, then tracked down the hall.

He stopped outside the bedroom door and knocked quietly as he entered, whispering, "Are you asleep?"

"Trying." Facing the wall, she imagined what he looked like at the threshold of the bedroom door. Large. Powerful. Decisive. That would have been her best guess until she heard Callum let out a long breath.

He stepped in. The door clicked shut behind him, and she heard him pull his shirt over his head. Her pulse picked up. His zipper slid down, and the sound of fabric falling to the floor jump-started her heart.

"You sleep in more clothes than I do." He eased the comforter back and climbed into her bed without a moment of hesitation, a big spoon to her little one. "How's your headache?"

"I didn't really have one. Just... a mess of thoughts. What are you doing?" It was far too early for bed, and he wasn't making a move on her.

Callum snuggled close as though he'd lain in bed with her time and time again. His hand rested on her hip. His fingers flexed. "What kind of thoughts?"

She should face him, but every muscle protested turning in his arms. If she turned around and saw an expiration date on them, the fantasy would be over. Just another second to savor his warmth and strength. God, she'd gone her whole life wondering what this might feel like.

Just another second...

Grace memorized the feel of his arms, the weight of his hand on her hip. She committed all of it to memory and pulled away from his hold, forcing herself to face Callum and reality. She turned in his arms. Their eyes locked. "I thought you were mad at me."

"Why would I be mad at you? The world, yeah. It never stops. But you? I won't make you guess, Grace. If I have something to say, I'll say it. I expect the same from you."

Her stomach flipped. His stormy eyes didn't blink, and in the most unnerving, soul-baring way, he searched her face, gaze wandering from her eyes to her mouth and drifting back again in the laziest sweep she'd ever seen. She was sure a man had never ever studied her before, just as she was certain no man could make her feel like she was drowning in him with a simple look. "I'll try."

Two fingers caressed her cheek and tucked her hair back. "Okay for the time being."

He always seemed to look into the future, when she had no practice with anything except what was immediately in front of her. "Are you going to tell Hayden about us?"

A crackle and spark danced in his stormy eyes. "Why wouldn't I?"

"You didn't before."

He skimmed fingertips along her jawline. "I had to get my head out of my ass. Didn't I?"

She laughed.

"There's that beautiful grin." He rested his heavy-muscled arm over her and cupped the back of her head. "We have a lot going on, but you and me? Don't worry about that." He smoothed his hand over her arm, killing the downward spiral of uncertainty, and tucked her head to his. "There you go." Their foreheads touched. "Just like that."

"You worried," she whispered, "that I fell for you because I'm the damsel. But what if you're only here because you like to save the day?"

"I do like to save the day." He grinned. "But you're more than that."

She nodded.

"Grace." His fingers threaded into her hair and softly stroked the back of her head. "Are you okay?"

"I haven't been in years."

His lips flattened. His cheeks ticked.

"Until you," she admitted. "And I'm scared this will go away."

"It won't."

They lay in the darkening silence. He stroked her hair. He was so much more than she could comprehend. She was in love with him. Admitting that to herself was scary, and realizing that was surreal. She'd thought of the years she ached from what was just puppy love. But this was different. It was real and returned.

"I was dishonorably discharged," he whispered. "They kicked my ass off the team that I would give my life for, for my country that I bled for."

"Why?"

"I didn't follow an order."

That wasn't possible. Callum Hale was the king of doing the right thing.

"It's a nightmare that plays in my head almost constantly," he admitted. "The order was illegal. I'll stand by that for the rest of my life. But that didn't matter."

"What was it?"

He stroked her hair. Minutes ticked by. "It doesn't matter. It was carried out anyway."

"By Hayden?"

"No. Never. But I said no, and someone else said yes. Maybe I could have done more. I keep trying to see how I could have changed what happened…"

"What was it?"

He pinched his eyes closed. "Someone at the wrong place. The wrong time." He shook his head. "They weren't armed. They posed no threat. I couldn't stop it." He released an unsteady breath. "They're dead. Nothing I could do except go home and report it to anyone who would listen. I don't know what will come of it. I know what should… But what will?"

Grace didn't know what to say. "I'm so sorry."

"I'm mourning the person who needlessly died. Compound that with former team-mates spinning a narrative to cover their asses. They irreparably ruined my belief in...everything, and during dinner, I kept thinking what it would mean if someone on my new team did that again. I don't know how I'd handle that."

"What if they did?" Dominic's reach into law enforcement had left people dead before. It wouldn't be a stretch to believe he could turn people again.

His chest expanded with a breath so deep she wasn't sure he would take another. The corners of his eyes tightened, and he let it out slowly, not answering with a slight shrug.

"We'll cross that bridge when we come to it."

She tried to remember the moment during her marriage to Dominic when she realized she was completely on her own, that no one would truly be loyal to her, that she would never be safe. "I've spent years not trusting anyone. I don't want that feeling for you."

"Don't take on that worry for me," he said. "I'm fine."

"I'll try."

His dark eyes intensified. Seconds ticked by. "Try harder."

"I don't want you to feel the way I do—did," she amended.

"I trust my team. I do... I don't have any reason not to. Except Dominic knows more than we do. That threw me for a loop."

"He's always one step ahead."

Tension flickered in the chiseled indentation of his cheek. "That's what you keep saying." He stroked the back of her head again. Callum skimmed his fingers over her skin before brushing his lips over the spot he'd just touched. "I want to know about Dominic."

"You know everything—"

"No, I don't," he whispered under his breath. "You didn't tell me everything from before."

"Do you mean when I was married to him?"

His chin barely lifted.

"You know he hurt me." She'd pushed down the bitter memories so far that it was almost like they had happened to someone else.

"I read the summary of the court filings from your divorce."

She remembered him saying that. But she also knew that paperwork from well-paid negotiations didn't paint the truth. "There are a lot of reasons a man hurts a woman. Power. Inferiority. Stupidity. Dominic liked control. Anything he did to me physically paled compared to what he did mentally. I lived in constant fear."

"I would never hurt you. You know that, right?"

"You don't have to say that. I know."

"Maybe you know. But now you've heard it."

She loved Callum and had fallen so deeply for him that keeping her mouth shut was nearly impossible. He wouldn't hurt her, but she couldn't handle the risk yet. She kissed him instead of chancing the words would inadvertently fall from her lips, and then took off her pajamas.

He stripped and rolled on protection.

"I hate the years I missed with you." His hand ran over her. "But if there's a fuckin' god up there pulling the strings, and all that brought me to you? I have to be okay with it."

Grace straddled him. He palmed her ass and ran his hands up and down her back. She lowered herself onto him, and his hands locked on her hips, moving her, giving her everything she needed.

He gripped her hips, thrusting into her as she rode him, and as his climax neared, she waited, wanting, *needing*, to fall with him. She drew tighter, begging for his orgasm. He flipped her over and drove into her. He fell, and she tumbled with him, knowing this would be theirs for the rest of their lives.

Callum woke with Grace in his arms and believed everything would be all right. He wasn't a look into the future kind of guy. More like look into next week. But that had changed, and if he could count on this type of morning every day, he would die a happy guy.

Carefully he checked the time without waking her. God, he'd slept like the dead, yet the urge to get up and jump into the day didn't surface. His muscles were loose. His mind was clear. And he was happy.

Legitimately, categorically happy when he had never noticed that he had not been. Grace Willoughby had rewired his brain, and he was here for it.

She stirred against his side, easing into the day with that same sleepy smile that had made him lose his mind only a few days ago. "Good morning."

Yeah, this was what he wanted. "Morning, beautiful."

His phone rang, interrupting the quiet peace.

"So it begins." She dropped an arm over her eyes. "Tell Viv and Dean good morning, too."

Callum groaned and reached for it on the nightstand. It was Dean. "Got good news?"

"Yeah, hello to you, too."

He ran a hand over his face and pulled himself out of bed, mouthing, "Give me a minute," as he tugged on his clothes piled next to the bed.

"Are you just waking up?" Dean asked.

"Just haven't had my coffee yet."

"Man, it's almost eight. Sounds like you're on vacation."

"Give me a break. It's a lack of caffeine, not my stay at the fisherman's getaway in the forest." He beelined for the coffeemaker and fiddled with the filters.

"Well, I don't have much to update you on," Dean admitted.

Few issues slowed Dean down. An ugly shadow of doubt crept into Callum's thoughts. His trust in his new teammates had never wavered until Dominic called. Doubting Dean wasn't fair. He'd given zero reasons for Callum to be concerned.

But there *was* an issue, and Dean was the lifeline of information. If that had been corrupted, Callum had bigger problems than Dominic Marino. He cleared his throat. "Not a lot?"

"A lot less than I wanted by this point. I can't backtrack how Dominic spoofed Mari Willoughby's phone number, only that it was spoofed."

The shadows of doubt jumped for more attention. "How's that possible?"

"I only have one answer, and it fucking sucks: I don't know."

A heavy weight pressed against his shoulders. "Where does that leave us?"

"Nowhere good yet. Hey, I have another call coming in that I have to take." Dean ended the call as abruptly as he had started it.

When was the last time Dean hadn't been able to trace a simple phone number or track down a location? In the few months Callum had been with Titan? Never. He tried to remind himself that this wasn't the Army with unlimited government resources. The private sector didn't have the same rules in play though, with more leeway and less bureaucracy.

His ears perked. Callum turned as Grace paused at the mouth of the hall.

"Hey." Her hair hung loose on her shoulders. She rested against the wall and let it take her weight as though her body was too heavy to hold upright. "I couldn't fall back asleep and decided to get dressed."

She walked to him like a woman on a mission and wrapped her hands behind his neck. His heart stuttered. Her warm softness pressed against him, and every part of him hardened. Grace pushed onto her tiptoes. Her lips grazed his neck, and prickles of awareness burst over his skin. "I like waking up next to you."

Fuck... so did he.

Callum curved his arms around her back and belted her body to his. She smelled like sweet summer, and breathing her in was enough to make him forget what they were doing. He needed to pull away and update her on Dean's phone call. But he didn't want to.

"I like sleeping next to you." He tightened his grip on her. "And everything that leads to sleeping next to you."

A stain of color warmed her cheeks as his hands ran over her hips.

"Everything to do with being with you." She was his. Did she get that? He said it, showed it, and wanted to figure out more ways to prove it.

Grace peered up at him.

"You're mine. All mine." Such simple words. They still didn't convey what he meant.

He kissed her. A tiny moan purred from deep within her. They had years to make up for the time they missed.

Chapter Twenty-Four

Several days had passed since they arrived at the safe house, and Callum still had no actionable intelligence on Dominic. Grace's meeting with the attorney had been delayed until today, and he couldn't believe they would go in blind.

He felt her tracking him. He dropped their duffel bags by the front door. He didn't know where they would be tonight, but it was finally time to say goodbye to their fisherman's lodge. "What's wrong?"

"For all the time we've spent in bed, or you have talked with your people and planned for today, we haven't talked about *after*."

He smiled. Callum had a plan.

He'd had it for days and had tried his damnedest to give her the answers in every possible way without talking about specifics. That would come tonight, wherever they ended up, and involved something like a celebratory dinner, giving her that requested fuck-against-the-wall, then again in bed until he had told her everything.

That he loved her.

That he'd follow her to the ends of the earth.

That she could call the shots with how and when and where they would live their lives, because his only answer would be abso-fuckin'-lutely.

All she needed to do was wait five hours for a meeting to learn what needed learning, so they could start their future without uncertainties. "Let's get through today, and then we will talk until you're sick of hearing my voice."

Her eyebrows lifted. "Yeah?"

"Yeah, babe." He sidled close to her and laid his hands on her hips, bringing her close. "I don't want your ex-husband hanging over our heads. I want to hear from the AG's office. I want to know what we're dealing with. I want everything on the table. With that, and with you and me. Does that make sense?" He pulled her close—

The kitchen window cracked. The glass shattered. The whiz of a bullet split the air and tore into the wall behind where Grace had just been standing. He tackled her to the ground as his cell phone rang.

Smashed between his body and the floor, she covered her head. "What's happening?"

"Stay." He tucked her against the couch and grabbed the Glock attached to the underside of the coffee table. "Move with me." He directed her into the windowless hallway. "Do not move from this spot." He checked the mag in the Glock and pressed it into her palm. "Do you know how to use this?"

"Callum—"

"Grace. Yes or no?"

"I think so." She kept her chin high even as fear trembled in her eyes.

His phone kept ringing. "Six bullets in the magazine. One in the chamber. It'll automatically rechamber. Pull the trigger if anyone but me comes toward you." He turned before she could protest.

Callum remained low and moved near another window overlooking the backyard. *Nothing.* His phone continued to ring, and he pulled it from his pocket. Headquarters lit up the screen. "Yeah," he answered.

"One shooter. Coming from the northwest. No visual ID," Dean relayed. "Correction. Two heat signatures. One on each side."

Callum opened the gun safe and removed a twelve-gauge and an assault rifle. He walked by Grace. "Doing great. Stay put."

"Good thing you didn't disable the exterior cameras as well," Dean grumbled. "They're closing in on the perimeter. Smart use of the tree line. Closing ground quickly."

"That was a hell of a shot," Callum muttered, pressing against the living room wall. He skirted the shelves and the flat screen. "How the fuck didn't we know someone breached the property?"

"If I had eyes on you right now, I could tell you where to position."

That wasn't an explanation. Callum snagged the dish towels off the cameras around the room. "Update."

"Move to the window left of the kitchen table. Rear shooter's moving fast. Got eyes on him?"

He spotted the man armed with an MP7. "Yeah. Who are they?"

"Fuck if I know. I patched Gage in. Viv will be on in a moment."

"You got eyes on the target?" Gage demanded.

"Affirmative."

"You're green to take the shot, Hale."

The man slowed and scanned the house, lifted his weapon, and—

Callum pulled the trigger first.

Grace screamed.

The tango dropped.

"Shooter one. Down. Update on man two?" Callum demanded.

"Drop down and to your right."

Callum dove. Bullets sprayed through the front door and shattered the windows.

"Callum!" Grace yelled.

"Stay down!" He moved into position and zeroed in on his target. "We're halfway over with this, Grace. Doing great." The operative moved like special forces, smooth and efficient, and posted behind the bed of Callum's pickup. "Any intel on these fuckers?"

Behind the tailgate, the target didn't give Callum or Dean anything to work with. Still, he wanted answers.

"You'll know soon as I know," Dean said.

The tango repositioned, submachine gun trained on their safe house. For all Callum knew, the other man had called in the cavalry and was awaiting his backup to smoke out Callum and Grace. They needed to get the hell out before the guy's buddies showed up.

"He's waiting you out for a reason," Gage said what Callum was thinking. "Do something about it."

Callum had crap on a good angle. He blasted the front door with the twelve-gauge to entice his target to move. No dice. Only a spray of bullets responded. He was holed up and waiting Callum out. That meant problems.

"He's using a comm system," Dean reported. "Not able to patch in yet. Give me a minute."

"He doesn't have a minute," Gage growled. "Hale, get out of there. No telling who he's calling in."

"I'm in their transmissions—" Dean cursed. "You've got less than two minutes. They're bringing in air support."

Fucking air support? What was this? A goddamn cartel hit?

"Take down the shooter," Gage commanded.

Callum caressed the trigger. "Got shit for angles." He chewed the inside of his cheek. "What the fuck does air support mean?" They might be in the mountains, but this was Virginia, not a war zone.

"Got the helo. AH-6 Little Bird."

"Fuck." Those bad boys were equipped with Hellfire missiles.

"Sixty seconds and closing."

Callum checked his pockets for the truck keys, then he lined up his shot. "Cover your ears."

His index finger caressed the trigger, needing another moment.

"Go, goddamn it," Gage barked.

Callum took the shot and turned to Grace. "Get on your feet, babe. Let's roll."

Tears streaked her face. He snagged their bags and his woman and hauled ass toward the truck. "Head down."

She stumbled but kept up and didn't complain when he tossed her into the cab of his truck. He threw their bags and weapons into the backseat, then Callum wasted half a second and snapped a picture of the man on the ground by his tire, pulled the balaclava back, snapped another picture, and jumped behind the wheel. As soon as Dean identified the shooter, they'd have more information.

He turned the key in the ignition and roared off. Gravel spit. Brush smacked the undercarriage.

"Five seconds," Dean reported.

Callum mashed the gas pedal. They flew toward the tree line—and the house exploded. Grace screamed. The reverb rolled over them. The truck skittered into the brush. Callum fought for control.

"Keep your head down." They rumbled over the grass. Ascending the driveway hadn't been smooth, but this was rough.

Callum made a sharp overcorrection, righted it, and gunned down the driveway. They bumped and jostled and jerked. Branches and brush scraped the truck. The high-pitch scratch of brush and sticks tore over the truck's finish. He didn't take his foot off the gas.

They came out of the woods. Tall grass whipped against their sides and undercarriage as they rolled down the mountain. No shots sounded. No aerial assault. Nothing hit them. The main road waited for them dead ahead. Callum didn't bother with anything more than a cursory look before he blasted out of the driveway, fishtailing onto the paved road, and righted himself behind the steering wheel. His adrenaline pumped. Heart racing, he double-checked his mirrors, saw nothing, and took a deep breath. "You okay?"

"Do I look okay?" she screamed.

"You look alive. That was my goal."

"Oh, my God. Why is this happening?"

He checked her over again. "We're okay. Everything is okay."

"*Okay?*" Grace threw her hands out and gaped. "Define okay. Because this is not my okay."

"Are you bleeding?"

"No."

"Then you're okay." He drew a deep breath and let the punch of adrenaline retreat. He eased off the gas pedal. The truck slowed to the speed limit.

Panting, she twisted in her seat to check behind them.

"No one's following us. Put your seatbelt on."

"They *blew up* the house."

"Yeah. Yeah, they did." He pulled at his hair, then fished his phone out of his pocket and swiped the screen. Vivian picked up Dean's line. "Is Grace okay?"

"We're fine. I have pics for Dean."

"I don't know about fine, but alive," Grace muttered.

"I'm here," Dean announced. "Send them to me."

"Why would Dominic do this?" Grace demanded. "What—"

"It's not him," Dean interrupted.

Callum handed Grace his phone. "Don't look at them, but I need you to send pictures to Dean." After instructing her on how to securely send them, he waited. "Got them?"

"Yeah. Running him through our systems now."

"The sooner I meet with the attorneys, the sooner this ends," Grace said. "Right?"

"Maybe." Callum checked his mirrors and the windows. No tails. No fucking helicopters. "What do you know about the bird?"

"Not much yet," Dean admitted.

Callum tried to understand all the angles. How could Dean, of all people, not have every detail on that helicopter? His molars ground. "How's that possible?"

"They stealth masked the transponder. They had to have been skimming the treetops. They're so low they're off the grid."

"*That's not good enough.*"

"He's working on it," Gage growled, having joined the conversation. "No one likes what's going on."

"Why would someone else be trying to kill me?" Grace wanted to know.

"Someone doesn't want you meeting with those attorneys."

Vivian, Gage, and Dean discussed sending a cleanup team and managing the burning house. The last thing they needed in the August heat was a forest fire.

He glanced at Grace. Anger poured out of him. None of this felt right. "The question no one is asking is how the hell the safe house was targeted."

"Yeah, we're asking it all right," Vivian muttered. "If I had an answer, you'd know it already."

"Somewhere, there's a leak," Dean added. "I'm being outmaneuvered. Trust me, I'll find it."

Trust Dean? At this point, Callum wasn't sure he even trusted Gage and Viv. But there weren't many options, and he needed to stop second-guessing.

He checked on Grace again. Someone had tried to blow her up. Any minute now, that was going to kick in, surpass her anger and confusion, and she was going to freak out. "You know I won't let anyone hurt you."

"You could have been hurt back there as well."

He lifted a shoulder. "I'm not concerned—"

"You're not bulletproof. You're not bombproof—"

"I'm as close as you're going to get, babe." He returned his attention to the phone call. "Call me when you have actionable intel."

"Where are you going?" Dean asked.

His jaw set. He didn't know yet but didn't plan to share. "Gotta figure that out."

Callum ended the call and tossed the device into the cup holder.

"I liked things better when I hung out at libraries, and no one bothered me." She pressed her fingers to her temples. "I can't figure out why anyone would want to kill me."

"They're trying to keep you from that meeting. Which means we need to get you there in one piece for this to end."

She nodded.

He ran a hand over the back of his neck. Who else would be interested in what Grace had to say to the federal attorneys? "What can you tell me about Marino that I don't already know?"

"I'm not sure."

"Think. What haven't you said?"

"He probably has piles of money stored in offshore accounts. He doesn't like animals. No pets. No real friends. Just associates. His fingers are in so many types of businesses. I'll always be convinced he's somehow associated with the Mafia or something. You know all this."

He did.

His phone rang. That was awfully fast for actionable intelligence.

She checked the screen. "Oh, no. It's Hayden."

He let out a breath. Talk about bad timing. Callum needed to give him answers, and all he had were more problems. "We might as well get this over with." He answered on speakerphone. "Your timing is on point. You're on speaker. Grace is here."

Hayden laughed. "One of my many talents. Gracie, how are you?"

She almost whimpered. "Never a dull moment lately. I'll let Callum explain."

Callum gave Hayden a quick and dirty rundown that left his closest friend speechless for long enough that Callum worried Hayden had stopped what he was doing and was trying to come home to kill him. "We've got it under control."

"The fuck you do."

"Actually, we do," Grace snapped. "Don't act like you could have done anything for me that Callum hasn't."

"Easy," Callum whispered under his breath. "Hayden's worried."

"Yeah, well, I'm... I don't know what I am. But the sentiment stands."

"Cal—"

"Hayden Gregory, do not ignore what I just said."

"I'm not ignoring you, but don't tell me it's under control if you just left a situation where *the goddamn house blew up*."

Callum checked the mirrors and didn't know how long brother and sister would battle it out. He'd let them exchange a few more jabs.

"You don't know what you're talking about. I'm going to hang up if you don't hear me: Callum saved my life. End of story. The only thing you need to say is thanks."

After an awkward pause, Hayden added, "All right. You're heard loud and clear, little sis."

"You didn't say thanks."

"Grace," Callum said under his breath again. "Give him a break."

"You've got my eternal fuckin' gratitude for protecting Grace."

"Not a problem." Telling Hayden about everything else with Grace was going to be as much fun as a colonoscopy. Callum checked the rearview mirror and squinted. "All right, man. We gotta go."

He hung up the call before Hayden could respond.

"What's wrong?"

There had been no oncoming traffic driving off the mountain. They'd had no one behind them. But a big ass SUV had just barreled by them going the opposite direction. Now there was a second one on his tail. It didn't sit right in his gut.

Grace twisted in her seat.

"Turn back around. Don't do anything that you normally wouldn't." He kept an eye on his rearview more than the road.

"Callum—look out!"

Chapter Twenty-Five

The truck blasted over the spikes. Grace screamed as the truck shook and rumbled. The tires blew out. Panic flooded her system. Callum gripped the steering wheel and fought for control. Their shredded tires thundered around them like angry highway gods. The truck wanted to stop. He pushed it along the isolated road, and she understood that pulling over would be a death trap.

Grace checked her side-view mirror. The SUV behind them had crawled up so close that she could barely see it behind them.

"Listen to me carefully," he said with a calmness that made her focus. "Keep your head down. Reach into the backseat. Grab the rifle."

"I can't."

"I won't ask you to do anything you can't handle."

She wanted to believe him. Her heart slammed in her chest. "Callum…"

The truck roared in protest as he pushed it beyond its limits. "You can, babe. Head down. Do it now."

Her teeth chattered as she ducked down and reached into the second row for the rifle. Its cool metal was heavier than she expected. She eased toward the front seat, scared of doing something wrong, and—the back windshield exploded. She screamed again. All she could do was scream. The heavy gun almost dropped. Grace hung onto it as Callum covered her head and slammed her down. He jerked the truck from side to side. "*Grace?*"

"I'm not hurt." Her lungs screamed in her chest. Panic punched in her temples. Every part of her shook.

Another bullet blasted into the truck and tore off its side-view mirror. Callum zigzagged their dying vehicle. He would have to pull over, and whoever was behind them would shoot before he even sighted the gun in their direction.

"Gotta listen to me, babe."

She could hear it in his voice and already knew what he would say. Tears caught in her throat. "I can't do it."

"You don't even have to aim. Just point and keep your head down."

Why was this happening? She listened to his instructions, moved her hands the way he told her to.

"Do you feel that? It's like a switch."

She nodded.

"Flip it. Brace yourself and hold the trigger down."

She did. The gun roared. She couldn't hear. The air burned. She could taste the gunpowder, but refused to let it stop her. It just fired and fired and kept firing.

Callum pulled over. Her ears rang. Her eyes burned. Steam and smoke billowed from the engine behind them as it lost forward momentum. "They're stopping."

God, did she kill someone?

They wanted to kill her, so why not?

Except she couldn't handle it if she did. That was why the world needed people like Callum and Hayden.

"Stay down." He took the gun and twisted in his seat. "You blew their engine up." He reached into the backseat and handed her a handgun, taking the rifle from her hands. "Anyone comes at you, pull the trigger. I'll be back."

The gun shook in her trembling hands. It had to be more dangerous to hold it than not. She set it down and peered out the space where their back windshield had been.

Callum had the gun up and was yelling. Her ears rang, yet still she heard the pop, pop, pop of guns. The car she had seen on the side of the road with the tire spikes raced toward them. Callum jumped onto the smoking hood of the SUV she'd shot and crouched down.

Two people from the car that had just arrived rushed toward the disabled SUV. Grace didn't know how Callum could see them, but they definitely couldn't see Callum.

As one drew even with him, he swung the back of his gun like a baseball bat. The person dropped and didn't move. Callum jumped on top of the other, and they crashed to the asphalt, wrestling.

She didn't know what would happen if someone pulled over and tried to help. She hadn't seen any vehicles, and wouldn't know if they were their enemy or a Good Samaritan.

Callum landed another punch, and the attacker fell back. He strode up to their truck. "Get our bags. Phone." He reloaded his weapons and pulled zip ties from a compartment. "Let's go."

A minute later, he tied up the two men and took pictures of their faces. She followed him to the car, barely able to feel her legs. Hell, she couldn't feel any part of her body. Only the sensation of every muscle jittering under the flood of adrenaline.

Callum snapped pictures of the truck and the SUV, and their plates and the plates on the car they were about to take. "Let's go."

"We're leaving them here?" she asked.

"A cleanup team will handle them and extract intel." He quickly inspected the new vehicle. "Get in."

"We're taking their car?"

"Got a better idea?"

She didn't and shook her head. Callum placed his weapons in the backseat and gestured for her to do the same with their bags.

"What are we going to do now?" she asked.

"Be anywhere but here." He nodded toward the car. "Kinda like that joyride you and your friends went on in my car your senior year."

Laughter bubbled in her chest when every part of her wanted to curl into a ball and cry. "But without anyone shooting at us."

That night seemed so long ago and like it was just yesterday, both when she would have done anything for his attention, including taking his car from the neighborhood pool and driving around the block. "You were mad enough that you might have if you'd had a weapon."

Callum pulled onto the quiet road and left the wreckage of the run-in behind them. Their new ride had an impersonal scent of pine and plastic. Its clean carpets and console reminded Grace of a rental car, which reminded her that everything in her life over the last few years had been temporary. A rental cabin. A loaner vehicle. A friend's house. It had all been temporary and left her untethered to anything that was actually hers—like Callum. He was hers, wasn't he?

He swiped his thumb across the screen of his cell phone, opened his phone app, and called his office.

Vivian answered, "Have a game plan?"

"No, but I need a cleanup team. Who's with you?"

"Gage and Dean."

Callum explained the last five minutes and handed over his phone again. "Send the pics in the same way you did before."

Grace selected the pictures and uploaded them through the secure portal she had used for the first person who had shot at them. She returned the phone to Callum as he waited for his office to receive them.

"Look," Callum grumbled. "We need a plan, but you need to get a handle on whoever's tracking us and how. Any idea who's behind this?"

"Not yet."

"They're moving faster than we are—"

"Which is why," Vivian said, "we want to move the attorney meeting up as soon as you can get there. No more messing around. Find out what's going on. Deal with it and move on."

"Now?" She wasn't in the right headspace. Her clothes were dirty, and she'd been sweating through the hot August heat while shooting a gun and probably smelled as bad as she looked. Grace glanced over and could tell that Callum's scowl was less about his clothes and more about the change in plans.

"The more we know," Vivian continued, "the more we can anticipate the problems. Since no one will tell us a damn thing, this is our best option."

"I need five minutes." He ended the call without waiting for their response.

Tension flexed in his jaw.

"You don't think we should go."

"I think... if I trusted them, then yeah, we should. Their logic is sound."

"But you don't."

"At this point, Grace. I don't trust anyone but you."

The air conditioning cooled as the car devoured the miles. They drove in silence, and she thought about his distrust and hers. They distrusted his headquarters for different reasons. Dominic could buy anyone, though they didn't think he was involved. She didn't see how he wasn't.

Her stomach knotted. What had he said about after all this was over? Grace dropped her focus to her hands in her lap. The after would never come if they didn't get rid of her ex.

"I want to call Dominic."

He tore his gaze from the road. "What? Why?"

"I won't tell him you're with me. Just that someone is chasing me, and I want to know what he wants."

"Screw him and whatever he wants. I'm so sick of his name."

"Then call Vivian back and say we're on our way."

"Why?"

"I want to get it done because I want *the after*. After this crazy day from hell, I want to know if this is real between us, and I don't want to wait to figure it out." She stared at the road. For as bold and outspoken as she had been with what she wanted, this was too scary, and she didn't have the guts to look at him. "I want to start my life over, and I can't until this is done."

Callum pulled off the road onto the shallow gravel shoulder. He shifted into park and reached for her face, turning her chin to face him. "This is real."

"I know that..." She felt horrible for needing to hear it again and again.

"You don't have to wait to clear things up with your ex. I had thought that too. You know that? I was waiting, but when I hear you questioning us?" He shook his head. "No. You need to know exactly what I think."

"I already know you want to be with me. I can't explain what I mean."

"I'm in love with you. I've been in love with you."

Her heart stopped.

"I didn't want to tell you this now. If this could all be behind us, and I could fucking hold on to you while I make you understand... But now's the time you need to hear it. I'm here for everything you need. Hear me like you've never listened in your life. This feels fast, but it's a lifetime in the making."

Her eyelashes fluttered. Emotion choked away her words.

"You know that," he whispered, "and I know that."

Tears sprang into her eyes. His thumb smoothed over her cheek. She should say something, but she couldn't talk.

"You're not ready to hear that, baby," he said softly but with unwavering confidence. He believed in her. *In them.* "You're about to panic. About to run." His smile wasn't hurt. It was more like understanding, and that scared her even more. "And we can't have that."

"Callum—"

"I'm not worried. I can predict the future when it comes to us. Not this mess of today. Not with your ex. Not the attorney general's office or the leak with my team. But I know you and I work out."

"Everything had moved so fast with Dominic, and this is faster than that." Comparing the two men made her stomach turn. Callum was nothing like Dominic. He wasn't taking away her independence or folding her into another person like some kind of make-a-wife origami.

He didn't flinch at the comparison. "*We* are a long time coming."

Callum wasn't talking about moving in together or marriage like Dominic had. Grace had thought she'd fallen for Dominic when he hadn't given her a chance to breathe. That wasn't what Callum was doing. Still, the slamming staccato of her heart screamed for her to slow down. They needed speed bumps.

His phone rang.

How about that for a speed bump? Not what she wanted, but she needed the interruption to catch her breath. Grace read the display on his screen. It was his office calling back. "It's been five minutes."

Callum tipped her head to his and casually kissed her as if she weren't panicking. He answered the call. "We're taking the meeting."

"Sending a location and directions to you now. I'll have someone meet you there and take care of whatever car you're driving."

Chapter Twenty-Six

The rest of the drive was quiet, but as the miles passed, Grace's adrenaline high crashed. Her hands shook, and a tremor moved through her that she couldn't control. She flexed her muscles, balled her hands, then shook out her fists. "I feel sick."

Callum glanced around their new car. "Do you have any candy in your bag?"

"No."

"Gum?"

"No." A headache thumped at the back of her head. "Why? Are you hungry?"

"Your system could use a hit of sugar."

"Maybe I could use an iced coffee." That would wake her up but wouldn't stop the shakes she could barely hide. Now that they were driving through a populated area, there had to be places they could stop. "Do you think we could find a coffee shop soon?"

"Eventually."

It didn't take long before they spotted an exit with fast food and coffee options. Maybe she was hungrier than she realized.

Her legs shook when they got out. Callum took her hand as they crossed the parking lot and walked into a coffee shop with a full bistro menu.

Grace leaned against him in line, her back to his stomach. His hands locked around her waist as they waited. This was sweet. It was real. It was entirely too cutesy for a man who looked like he was better suited for an action movie than suburbia.

They stayed locked together until they ordered, and he paid for their order in cash.

"I'll be back in a minute." She needed to wash the smell of gunpowder off her hands. It was probably in her hair and all over her skin as well. She'd have to see what could be done in the restroom.

His gaze skirted around the coffee shop, and she realized he was searching for a threat. Had he held her that way in line to keep her safe? Or because he wanted to? Doubts that hadn't been there before were sprouting, and her jittery stomach turned upside down.

"Give me a second." Callum knocked on the bathroom door and, not hearing anyone respond, opened it. His hand perched precariously close to his concealed gun.

"No one's in the bathroom waiting for us. You don't have to do that."

He ignored her and checked the stalls. "Now we know for sure."

"Please don't do that, Callum. It makes me feel like a crazy person. No one knew we would stop here."

He shrugged and semi-agreed, but left her alone in the bathroom. She stood in front of the mirror and—whoa, she looked worse for wear. Her disheveled hair was tangled on one side. Dark circles formed half-moons under her eyes that looked like they'd been crying. She actually hadn't been crying. Maybe she'd teared up a few times. But not *crying* crying.

Grace scrubbed her hands in the soap that had little scent, then splashed her face with water. A little under-eye cream, concealer, and a hairbrush would go a long way in changing her appearance. She could do that in the car.

Grace returned to find Callum holding their coffees and food. She pointed to her hair. "You didn't tell me I look like roadkill."

He bent over and kissed her. "The hair thing makes me want to mess it up on my own."

That put a little bounce in her step, and she took her coffee.

He snagged her around the waist, and laughing, she couldn't remember ever feeling content and safe, despite every reason she should be jumping at shadows like he was. Callum was right. They were a long time coming. None of the awkward get-to-know-you moments had to play out. They had already done so over the years.

They returned to their newly acquired—stolen?—rental car and, as Callum accelerated onto the highway, they polished off their sandwiches and sipped coffee like they hadn't been in a gunfight hours before.

Then, she was suddenly more tired than she thought possible. Her eyelids were too heavy to hold open. "I'm exhausted."

"Take a nap."

"You're not tired?"

"I'm used to adrenaline crashes. The caffeine's probably done more for calming your system than you realized."

That made little sense. Then again, Grace had a hyper friend who would always fall asleep after an espresso. The road noise lulled her toward sleep.

She woke up and didn't know how much time had passed. They had pulled into an office parking lot. Grace rubbed her eyes as Callum pulled to the curb and parked behind a large SUV that was similar to the one she had shot.

"Ready to do this?" he asked.

Big black SUVs made her uncomfortable. She smoothed her hands over her legs. Of course, she was ready, but her nerves pitted deep inside her gut. She noted the two men in uniform by the front door. "Who are they?"

He pursed his lips. "Someone arranged for security. Not sure if it was Titan or the AG's office or what, but we've had a shit day. Once you get inside, everything will be okay. We'll learn what we need to know. They'll get what they need from you, and it will all be over soon."

She chewed on her bottom lip. "Then what?"

His grin hitched into a beautiful smile that snapped her out of her nervous spiral. "A cute house. Flowers in the front. A little vegetable garden in the back. Someplace safe."

Her heart climbed into her throat.

"You know the kind," he continued, "like where we grew up. Friendly. Not too big. Not too small." Callum tilted his head. "What'd you say? With lots of happiness and laughter."

The nerves transformed into bits of sunshine warming her from the inside out. Grace nodded, words clogging in her throat. "That's what I said."

He nodded toward the building. "Come on. Let's go."

A person she hadn't met before exited the SUV in front of them. Callum left their car running and got out. He gathered their belongings and met Grace on the sidewalk. The other person got into their car without saying a word to Callum. Their temporary car followed the big black SUV out of the parking lot.

"Where are they going?" she asked as they walked toward the tinted-glass office doors.

He shrugged. "Wherever cleanup teams go to clean up. Probably best we don't know."

The generic building reminded her of an office park with doctors' and dentists' offices. Dated but practical, with big windows like those in old schools and mature landscaping skirting the building.

Once inside, she eyed the directory of offices corresponding to the suite numbers. Accountants and tax services. Consultants. Lots of businesses that appeared to be last names with "and associates" tacked on. She didn't have a good idea of which office they might need to go to.

Callum bypassed two more agents standing near the elevators and led them up a flight of stairs to the second floor. The overhead light illuminated a clean but worn carpet. This wasn't anything like the meetings she'd had with investigators and prosecutors after Dominic had been arrested. "I thought we'd be in some flashy government building."

"I always picture government buildings more like the DMV. Fluorescent lights and two-hour-long lines." He shrugged. They stopped in front of a door with a Bastamonti and Associates nameplate. "Ready?"

They entered a generic office suite with large windows. An empty reception desk greeted them. Callum frowned. "Guess we have a seat."

She folded onto the couch. He paced in front of the desk, typing on his phone. Despite the bright windows, the small space closed in on her. The stuffy air hung heavy. She needed to calm down. "You're making me nervous. Or maybe it's all the guys with guns waiting downstairs."

Callum shifted his weight and shoved his hands in his pockets. Finally, he perched on the edge of a chair in the corner. "They were only making sure you got in safe."

She was. They'd made it. As soon as she got that through her head, her anxiety would calm down.

A tall woman in flats, dark pants, and a blazer rushed out, smoothing her dark hair back. "Have you been waiting long?"

Grace stood, her stomach tying into knots.

Callum approached. "We have an appointment."

"We're expecting you. Follow me." The receptionist walked briskly and gestured them into a conference room with more gusto than manners.

Grace took in the space with its plain walls and oversized windows. A generic table with a platter of catered sandwiches was surrounded by chairs. Folders and paperwork were piled at the head of the table. "The sandwiches are fresh. Mr. Bastamonti will be with you shortly. He and the others had to take a quick conference call in his office. Is there anything you need?"

"I'm fine—" She wanted to splash water on her face and clear the apprehension from her mind. She couldn't be worked up before the attorneys walked in. "Actually, could you tell me where the restroom is?"

Just as briskly as the receptionist had walked them into the meeting room, she stepped into the hallway, towering over Grace, and pointed the opposite way they had come, directing her to the far side of the office suite.

Grace walked away but turned, lifting her eyebrows as Callum trailed her. "You're not seriously going to follow me into this bathroom, too."

"Yeah—"

Several voices reached them as though a gaggle were approaching. The lawyers were coming. Her palms became sweaty. Nerves prickled down her spine. She needed to pull herself together. Callum's phone rang. She rushed to take advantage of the distraction. "I'll be back in a second."

Grace didn't give Callum time to respond and left.

She pressed her clammy hands on her shorts and wished she had more appropriate clothes. Did she even brush her hair? Yes, before she'd slept in the car. Quickly, she finger-combed it as her heart rate climbed. *Calm down. This is okay. Nothing bad will happen here.*

She followed the meandering directions. There had to be a more direct route to the restroom. This place was nothing like the posh office space she remembered from meeting her attorney during Dominic's trial. That law firm had required a retainer that could have paid her lawyer's child's first year of tuition in college. The hourly fee was just as exorbitant. She wondered how much she would pay for that office to send her former attorney here.

What if the attorney general's office brought any of the agents she'd met with about the witness protection program? That would be uncomfortable. But they had to admit there had been huge missteps in protecting the witnesses who testified against Dominic.

Grace entered the bathroom and faced the mirror. With her palms on the counter, she braced herself for whatever conversation would come. She glanced at her reflection. "You can do this. You've survived worse."

Today's meeting would finally extricate Dominic from her life.

Then she would have *the after* with Callum.

She splashed water on her face as the bathroom door opened. The receptionist entered as Grace reached for a paper towel. "Are they ready for me?"

The receptionist turned the lock on the door.

"What are you—"

In a fluid motion, she slapped her hand over Grace's mouth, stifling her scream. The woman yanked her with far more strength than Grace expected.

She struggled to get free. She kicked and screamed. With every ounce of her panic and fury, her legs thrashed. Her teeth snapped. Grace bucked and bit. She jabbed her elbows and stomped until she caught sight of their reflection.

The other woman had complete control. Stronger and certain of the way she held Grace, she was waiting for that moment of clarity when Grace realized she couldn't escape. It happened in a flash.

Grace couldn't get free. Her limbs gave up the fight, and the receptionist dragged her across the bathroom like she was a rag doll.

What are you doing? Fight.

She'd survived too much to go down this easily. Grace fought all over again. Her kicks and swings were still as fruitless as before. Her smothered cries for help went nowhere. It didn't take the woman much effort to cross the bathroom, releasing Grace long enough to open the frosted bathroom window.

Grace screamed, hurtling toward the door.

The receptionist clamped a hand over Grace again, dragging her the two measly feet she'd run. Far stronger than her, the woman lifted and shoved her out the window.

The free fall of freedom was short-lived. Grace smacked onto the mulch bed on the backside of the building. Air was crushed from her lungs.

She blinked.

Couldn't breathe.

Couldn't gasp.

Time moved slowly, but the will to survive reinflated her lungs. Grace pressed onto her hands and knees, gasping for oxygen. Pain radiated through her body. She crawled through the bushes, choking for air, blindly scuttling away from the building.

Grace heard the receptionist land behind her. She heard words she didn't understand in a language she didn't know. She had to get away and fought to get to her feet, stumbling and staggering toward the sidewalk. How long had it taken to get her out of the bathroom? Thirty seconds? A minute? Not long enough for Callum to notice she was gone.

A man appeared ahead of her.

"Help."

He eclipsed the summer sky, looming over her like a mountain.

"Help—"

He grabbed her. The receptionist hadn't been gentle, but this man was rough. He tossed her over his shoulder as though she were nothing more than a garbage bag—limp and loose, barely able to yell for help.

Grace screamed again. She kicked. It didn't matter. He tossed her into the trunk of a car and shut it.

Chapter Twenty-Seven

Don't panic.

But Grace was panicking. White-hot hysteria threatened to steal the last shreds of her composure. *Stop. Think.*

Road noise drowned out her thoughts. Which meant they were driving at a high rate of speed without many turns. This had to be a highway.

She tried to kick through the rear panel but found that impossible. The trunk had been reinforced. They had been expecting her. Prepared for her, even when she hadn't known she would be there. How was that possible? They had sneaked past law enforcement and infiltrated one of the law firms.

The trunk was so hot. She was losing track of how long she'd been in there. It was hard to breathe.

Think. Concentrate. Do not pass out.

Callum would know she was gone by now. He would be looking for her. Until then, what was she sure of?

The man and woman spoke another language. Mandarin? She wasn't sure, but didn't recall Dominic working in Asia. Then again, Grace hadn't really understood his full reach until it was too late.

Dominic didn't know they had her. She was certain. He was many things—a narcissist, probably a psychopath or sociopath. Conceited and egotistical. He was an abuser. The times when the emotional abuse had crossed into physical abuse still haunted her. But he saw her as a possession. Something that was part of his collection or that he used to prop up like a trophy on a shelf. He would never let another person shove her into a trunk.

She didn't know how that helped her right now. What else did she know?

These two didn't want her dead. They could have killed her in the bathroom. She was still breathing. Why? Knowing that was almost as important as escaping.

Sweat trickled down her temple. Her clothes stuck to her.

The vehicle decelerated. She tracked the traffic pattern in her head, deciding they were on a main road with occasional stoplights until they turned and rolled over a speed bump. The car crept slowly, and her anticipation inched up. They would stop soon, and she would attack whoever opened the trunk.

Finally, the car stopped. The car doors opened and closed, but she didn't hear voices. No other sounds either. What was happening? Maybe they had brought her somewhere nobody could hear her scream. Or maybe they needed a pit stop at a gas station restroom. Either way, eventually the trunk would open.

The beep-beep of the trunk unlocking threw her heart into overdrive. It pounded against her chest. Her fists curled, ready to fight. She expected sunlight to blind her as the trunk opened, but only a dim orange light, like from a storage facility, crept over her.

Just like in the bathroom, Grace kicked and screamed and punched. She wriggled and fought against the hands that grabbed her. "Get off me!" As if that would help, but it fell from her lips as she screamed and kicked. "Get off—"

The man wrapped a cloth over her face. Chemicals burned her nose and throat. Grace fought against it, yanking her head left and right, but with every jerk of her muscles, a haze descended. It was as if she were drifting farther and farther from her body until she lay there like a rag doll, unable to open her eyes.

Callum ended his phone call with Vivian and impatiently waited for the approaching gaggle of attorneys to meander down the hall in their well-dressed suits and their spit-shined shoes. He didn't do well with people like this. Dean, Wes, or Rhys were better suited to deal with the people who held more power than they deserved simply because someone had appointed them to do a job.

He worked his jaw. Some were probably qualified. Some were definitely political kiss-asses. Some had an agenda. Some simply wanted to uphold the law. The agenda-wielding, political kiss-asses were the ones he blamed for leaving the Army. Vivian and Gage should be the ones to handle that type. Callum wanted nothing to do with any of them.

The group joined him in the conference room, apologizing for an unexpected, highly important conference call. Blah, blah. Callum didn't care. Introductions were made, and he explained that Grace would be back momentarily.

A scream poured down the hall.

His blood ran cold. The chatter stopped. He took off at a run with the murmuring of confusion trailing behind him as he hauled toward the sound of a woman—not Grace—screeching at the top of her lungs. "What's wrong?"

The group barreled in behind him. The screaming woman was on her knees, untying another woman on the ground, and his heart faltered.

"Who is she?" Callum demanded.

"My receptionist." Mr. Bastamonti surged forward. "Carol. God. Carol, what happened?" He dropped to his knees to ungag the woman on the ground. "Get the cop at the front of the office."

Fuck. "There wasn't a cop by the door." He moved into the hallway. *"Grace?"* Callum turned to the lawyers. "Who's the tall Asian lady? The woman at the front desk."

Mr. Bastamonti stared at him blankly.

Damn it. They'd been played. "Call 911. Where's the bathroom?"

Another lawyer pointed Callum the way Grace had been directed.

Callum flew down the hall, calling her name, knowing damn well she would not answer. A few attorneys had followed him. He reached the bathroom door and pounded on it. The door didn't budge. "Grace?"

No answer.

Everything within him turned dark. He reared back and kicked the door in.

The bathroom was empty.

The window was open.

Blinding rage swelled in him like a wave so dark and powerful he didn't know how to direct it. Callum reached for his phone. Someone else had already called the cops. He called his boss.

Vivian picked up.

"Call in every favor you have to find her—"

"Hale?"

"And do whatever it takes to tell me who did this. Because I'm going to kill them."

Chapter Twenty-Eight

Titan descended upon the office park. They arrived in SUVs and helicopters. They by-passed police tape and trumped every official-looking badge. Rage rolled off Callum. He didn't know whom to talk to, whom to trust. He wanted to burn the goddamn world down, but couldn't until he used every resource to bring his woman home. Then he would kick off his revenge tour, taking out every single thing he deemed responsible for today.

The door smacked open. A man he'd never seen strode in. Dark hair. Dark eyes. Years of stress were etched on his face. All at once, Callum knew who he was and didn't know whether he should trust him.

"We haven't met since you joined Vivian's team. Jared Westin." The man held out his hand, eye ticking at the moment of Callum's hesitation before they shook hands. "We will bring your woman home." Jared held up a hand to block Callum's explosion of distrust. "I take responsibility for whatever caused this to happen. Now, sit down. I'm going to tell you a story."

His hands balled into fists. He didn't have time for this bullshit corporate ass-covering. "I don't have time for fuckin' story hour—"

Jared paced to the window overlooking the circus in the parking lot. He rubbed a hand across his forehead. "It's not an easy story to share, but you need to hear it. And you'll trust me when I'm done."

Doubtful. Callum yanked back a chair and forced himself to sit. If this was the next step to getting answers, he'd momentarily follow directions.

Jared cracked a couple of knuckles and stared out the window. His face darkened, as if he were reliving a bad memory. "Years ago, there was a man who nearly destroyed my world. His name was Buck Baer." Jared's eyes narrowed on Callum. "Ever heard of him?"

Callum shook his head. "No."

"Yeah, didn't think so. He's been dead for a while. Good fuckin' riddance." He pulled out a chair at the head of the table. "We were battle buddies. But Buck Baer was in it for the glory. Then, after the Army, he wanted the money. Not a bad thing, but he took it too far."

"Great story, but we're wasting time." Nothing Jared had said made Callum believe Jared was any more invested in finding Grace than any other client.

"Baer pulled strings and orchestrated my fucking nightmare. He captured the woman I was going to marry." Fury flexed in his square jaw. "After I found Sugar, *I took his everything*. His property. His company. His contracts. Everything. I cleaned out the dirty and kept what didn't stink like shit, and I turned that into this. The division of Titan Group that you work for today."

The similar betrayal, fury, and panic resonated. As did Jared's revenge.

Jared pushed out of the chair and stalked to the windows again. He studied the activity below and turned to Callum again. "I have been burned by the people closest to me and the people who fought beside me. I get it. I know what's in your head right now. Probably better than anyone you've ever met."

"So what?"

"I'm vouching for this team and the people who I'm bringing in as an additional layer of security. If you work with us, we will bring Grace home. I give you my word."

The confidence in his rough voice offered the first shred of hope that Callum had felt. His molars clamped, and he didn't trust his voice.

"*We will bring Grace home.* If I have to, I will personally deliver her to your doorstep—"

"I will be wherever she is."

"I get that, and I'll make sure it happens."

He wanted to trust this guy. But it meant he needed to trust his team. Callum swallowed hard and had never felt so helpless.

"It's a horrible feeling," Jared grumbled, "not to be able to manhandle your way to a solution."

"Like you're reading my mind." Callum moved to the windows and peered out next to Jared. Law enforcement canvassed the office parking lot. He didn't know what they might find that would help. Investigators were interviewing everyone in the surrounding offices. He scrubbed a hand over his face. "I feel fucking helpless."

"I did too." Jared clapped him on the back as though to say it would be okay. "Now that you know why you should trust me, let me give you what I've learned. The feds believe they have what's needed for a grand jury indictment. They wanted to avoid subpoenaing her."

"What could she possibly know that is worth this much effort?"

"Marino is in deep with a Triad out of Shanghai. On paper, they look like Vegas investors who dabble in crypto trading. But actually, they've got an entire hedge fund propped up like a Ponzi scheme, laundering crypto. There's enough money moving through their entities to theoretically never stop grifting unless someone pulls a cog out of their well-oiled machine. If that happens..." Jared let out a low whistle. "Lots of everyday people around the world will have their investment portfolio disappear in an instant, and lots of criminal enterprises will find they don't have the money they thought they did."

Callum blinked. "What on earth could Grace possibly know about that?"

"Prosecutors believe Marino used her aliases, VPNs, and communication network to hide his tracks. She was the front and didn't know it while she was so-called dead."

Callum connected the dots between what Jared said and all of Grace's concerns, the way she lived, and her paranoia. "Marino knew where she was the whole time?"

Jared nodded. "Probably, and he was also using her as a third-party aggregator of sorts, laundering through accounts that she opened and thought she closed before opening new ones. She was staying hidden because the world thought she was dead, and it was a fantastic solution for Marino."

Every possibility ran through his head. Dean had said her skills erasing her tracks had been beyond what one person could do, and he hadn't been wrong. Callum had asked about it, and she didn't explain the complex layers of hiding her tracks beyond VPNs and ghost accounts. "He's not behind the Molotov cocktail or the safe house breach. Forget that those are two wildly different approaches to keeping her quiet. It would serve no purpose to endanger the communication network he built through Grace. If she's actually dead, his system disappears."

Jared nodded. "The different approaches tell me there's disagreement in the Triad."

"They know what the DOJ is investigating. But why take her now? She has nothing with her. She can't access her VPNs and emails. Just to keep her quiet?"

He raised his shoulders. "Sure, and keep her accounts away from the DOJ. The faction that wants to kill her probably has a shakier relationship with Dominic Marino than the group that abducted her."

His eyebrows lifted. "Then... that's good news?"

"Relatively speaking." Jared rubbed the back of his neck. "Look, there could be multiple bogeys in this shitstorm. The AG's office could have empaneled a grand jury without Grace. They obviously needed access, and given what happened today, where it happened, the Triad has a mole embedded within the feds' ranks."

But not Titan's?

"Our intel also leaked," Jared said, as if reading Callum's thoughts. "I don't know how yet, but I assure you that I'll tear everything apart and make sure that never happens to us again. Because it is an *us*, Callum. You're Titan. That means something. Maybe you don't realize it yet, but you will."

Callum didn't trust a soul here—yet part of him yearned to be so interwoven into a team again that it felt like family.

Jared tilted his head toward the office door. "I'm going to introduce you to men from our central headquarters team. They're older. They're experienced. They've been through this before. Every move will be redundant. Just to double-check that nothing shady is going on with your team. I trust them, but you don't have to until this is done. Are we on the same page?"

Callum thought over the offer and Jared's transparency. The man had been down a similar road with his wife's abduction. He understood the stakes. He trusted his team. Callum sawed his jaw but nodded. "All right."

Jared turned. "Let's go."

They passed conference room after conference room, each filled with attorneys and their office staff, law enforcement, and investigators, until they reached the farthest conference room. A man approached them from the opposite direction.

"Turbulence out of Boston was a nightmare," he said to Jared and then introduced himself. "Parker Black. I've had my eyes on this since Boss Man said go."

They entered the conference room. Dean offered Parker an appreciative look. "Took you long enough."

Gage sat with two men, introduced as Rocco and Roman.

Jared pulled Vivian and Gage into a separate conversation, leaving Callum with Dean and Parker in a huddle near Rocco and Roman.

Dean leaned back from the table. "Callum, give me a second?"

"Yeah."

"I understand where you're coming from. I get the distrust. I want you to know I run sweeps on my assets. I trust my people." He grimaced. "But there's obviously a breach. I see it. I believe it. You need to know it didn't come from me."

Callum held his stare a beat longer, searching for a lie in the way Dean spoke, but didn't find it.

"We'll find the problem," Parker promised. "But our highest priority is finding Grace. Agreed? We chase shadows and problems later. We find her now."

Callum nodded. There were leaks and moles, but based on what Jared said, Callum believed it wasn't the people in this room.

He waited while Parker and Dean compared notes, then looped in Titan's hierarchy of Jared, Vivian, and Gage. Rocco and Roman made small talk, but Callum wanted to climb the walls. Investigators pulled him in and out of the conference room several times. Each time he recounted the same thing, he wasn't sure how that information fed into the group working in this room.

Finally, Jared called everyone to the table and said to Callum, "You're not going to like this."

Callum steeled himself.

"We have a plan, and you're going to talk to Marino. Face to face. Explain what you know. What's happened. Lean into the idea that something Marino sees as a possession is in danger."

His chest tightened. He forced his voice steady. "Are you joking?" He shook his head. "He won't meet with me."

"Yeah, he will." Jared pointed to Parker and Dean.

"He's unaware of what's happened to Grace but knows the groups within his network who have expressed varying ways to keep her from speaking to the DOJ," Parker said.

Dean added, "The chatter's only been getting more heated. No one is showing their hand to him yet. He can open doors we can't."

"Think it through," Jared demanded. "He sees Grace as his property *and* as a source of his laundering network. He doesn't have all the information, which has got to be a kick in the nuts. He'll talk to you, and we'll figure out a way to track his next steps."

Callum would have to keep his fists at his side. "Fine. Set it up."

"Already done," Vivian said. "Gage is going in with you. Rocco and Roman will be on site. We'll probably place others throughout the meeting location."

Callum's frozen trust was thawing. He could trust these people. He had to. "When?"

"Chopper's outside waiting to take you to the airport. There's a jet that will take you to New York City. You'll meet Marino at a hotel."

"We already have Delta team tracking his every move," Rocco added. "You'll know if he does anything suspicious before you get there."

"And, Hale?" Vivian crossed her arms. "Don't kill the fucker after you have what you need from him."

Chapter Twenty-Nine

Dominic Marino was their enemy, but as much as Callum did not want to admit it, he was also a resource. That didn't negate Callum's absolute disgust of the man.

Rocco and Roman had arrived thirty minutes before Callum and Gage planned to walk in. They couldn't use comm pieces, and that was just as well. Callum didn't need chatter in his head. He was working too hard to follow Vivian's order.

They arrived at the swank hotel. The lobby was too trendy. The decor matched the people who milled about. Stationed somewhere in the lobby and bar were Delta team members. Callum eyed a guy with dark hair and tattoos, haphazardly scrolling on his phone. That guy looked like he could take everyone in the lobby out in a fistfight.

Callum checked his watch and caught sight of a blond surfer type assessing the lobby. He had his back to the wall, a suitcase by his side, and a deadly glare.

Across the lobby, Rocco waited by the entrance to the hotel bar, scrolling on a phone, eyes darting around the open space.

Where was Roman? There he was, kicked back on a sectional near the elevators.

"See anyone you know?" Callum asked Gage. "Think I've pinpointed a few."

"Not Marino, and he's all I care about."

Callum made eye contact with the street fighter but went about his business with Gage to the rendezvous point. All of Titan had his back. He didn't know who they were, might never see them again, but he sensed their unquestioning support. The feeling of camaraderie surged.

Damn, he'd been missing it.

He and Gage posted at the designated spot in the lobby. Callum checked the time again. Gage eyed his phone. They both received a message:

Marino arrived. Entering lobby.

Callum casually pivoted. His teammates covertly moved positions. All of them versus Dominic Marino, who wasn't an idiot. Marino likely had his own people in the lobby scouting for them.

He spotted Marino approaching across the lobby. "There he is."

"I see him," Gage confirmed.

It had been many years since Callum had sat across from Marino on the Willoughbys' deck. Marino had aged in the way wealthy people did: possibly a nip-tuck, a face full of filler, maybe even a hair implant. Expensive clothes, a smarmy smile. Callum expected nothing less.

Marino walked over and greeted them with his pearly white veneers. "Nice to see you again, Callum."

He shook the man's hand when he would rather have slugged him for all that he had put Grace through.

Gage's greeting leaned friendlier. They would play good cop, bad cop, though Vivian had reminded Callum not to take it too far. He needed to employ a solid dose of diplomacy if this meeting was going to be worth their time.

Callum turned toward the bar where they could grab a table near their backup team and still have privacy.

"I reserved a conference room," Marino offered. "I thought more privacy would be better."

He and Gage shrugged in agreement. The move wasn't entirely unexpected. Marino would have power players up his sleeve to assert dominance in a conversation he probably did not want to have.

They followed him toward the escalator that led to the second level. The conference room was nearby, and they settled around a large table.

What was Gage's first impression of Marino? He'd been up to speed on the basics: who Marino was to Grace and in business, what the Bureau of Prisons had to say on his time in the system, and before that, what was in the prosecutor's presentencing report.

In theory, Gage knew more about Marino than Callum. But Callum knew what mattered most: his obsession with Grace.

Callum cut to the chase. "Where's Grace?"

He held up his hands. "If I knew, I would have told your colleagues and saved us this time." Marino inclined his head toward Callum. "No one mentioned you would be here. I didn't know you had retired from the Army."

"I've been here since you pulled that stunt at the grocery store."

His lips pulled down as if trying to hide a smile. "I'm not sure stunt is the right word." He shrugged. "The interaction between a man and his wife is complicated—"

"You're not married anymore."

"What's a little paperwork to complicate a lifelong commitment?" His sleazy smile exposed too many teeth. "Why act like that? I thought you wanted my help."

"You're so hung up on your ex," Callum muttered.

Gage cleared his throat. Good cop. Bad cop. If they were going to meet their operating objectives, they would have to get under Marino's skin.

"Hung up on her like you?" Marino volleyed.

That caught Callum off guard, but he kept a straight face. In no way would Marino learn anything about his relationship with Grace. "Which of your business partners took her?"

"If someone has her, they won't hurt Grace."

Callum wanted to throttle his face in. "Actually. We're not so sure about that."

"Why's that?"

He pulled out his phone and pulled up aerial footage of their decimated safe house. "Do you know where I was this morning? I'll give you a hint. It's not there anymore." He thumbed through the images of what remained. It wasn't much. "Grace was about sixty seconds short of blowing up."

Marino's cocky demeanor shifted ever so slightly.

Callum noted it and pressed on. "So if you think one of your associates has simply taken her to ensure she doesn't have a conversation with *your friends*, as you called them, I'd say someone has blown smoke up your ass."

His focus narrowed on the screen. "Subpar Photoshop skills? I expected more."

Callum shrugged and scrolled through his saved photos until he found the one of a dead man lying next to his truck. "The way your associates are trying to keep Grace quiet doesn't work for me." His expression tightened. "And I suspect, it doesn't work for you either."

The tiniest flicker of doubt registered in Marino's conceited gaze.

"Look, Mr. Marino," Gage said, "I get you think you have everything under control. That you're pissed that someone firebombed Alicia Jackson's house to scare Grace, but you're wrong. This has spiraled."

Callum swiped his phone's screen and showed the pictures of the shooter at the safe house and the SUV with its shot-up engine and unconscious thugs. "These two are still breathing."

Gage hooked a thumb toward Callum. "You don't like him. From what I hear, the feeling's mutual. But if Grace is yours, you have lost control. In a sense, we'd like to give that back."

Good cop. Bad cop. Callum repeated the mantra in his head and would rather cut off his arm than even suggest Marino could *have* Grace after they found her. But Gage was speaking Marino's language and acting like she was a possession to find.

"I don't know what you're talking about."

"Sure you do," Gage pressed. "We already know you and the Triad have a man on the inside—that's obvious. You know when things are happening. You know what the meetings are about. You told Grace to keep her mouth shut. And we know it's about the money laundering through her communication network. We don't care about that. We're not the feds. Check us for wires for all we care. We want to know where Grace is." Gage waited, then tacked on, "You knew she was alive the entire time, didn't you?"

Marino pursed his lips, waging an internal battle.

"You want to keep her that way?" Gage asked. "Tell us where we need to go; we'll find your woman before the safe-house-exploding-faction finds her first."

Marino lifted his hands as if he didn't know, then dropped them to his lap. "I don't know anything."

The pressure building in Callum's head might explode.

"You really think nothing will happen to her?" Callum asked, grinding his molars.

"Why would anyone I know hurt Grace? They wouldn't dare."

"They already did."

The smug, conceited smirk fell. Callum wouldn't call Marino's expression worried—not by a long stretch—but there was something there. Not fear. If he had to guess, it was a lack of control. "Bullshit."

"No, he's telling you like it is." Gage shrugged. "Tossed her right out a window and into the trunk of a car. Look, I don't have a dog in this fight. No reason to lie. I get paid whether or not you give us anything. We just want to find her. Alive preferably."

Someone knocked on the door, and a uniformed waiter rolled in a catering cart.

Marino swallowed hard as if surprised by the interruption, then in a less steady voice, "I'll have to confirm that." He cleared his throat. "I ordered coffee and pastries." He gestured, distracted as he pulled out his phone.

Callum didn't want any fucking coffee, but he took Gage's lead and filled up a mug. Gage moved the platter of pastries onto the table. Was this some kind of power play? God, he hated games. He just wanted to get Grace back.

"Don't waste your time," Gage said to Marino around a mouthful of Danish. "I have a video that confirms it."

He didn't wait for Marino to ask and connected his phone to a Bluetooth flat screen. "Here we go." Gage chomped on another Danish. "These little fuckers are delicious."

A grainy CCTV video from the parking lot where she was taken was displayed on the screen. Callum hadn't watched this yet. His gut twisted. The window went up. Grace fell out. The landing had been hard, yet she fought to get to her feet before two people put her in the trunk.

"Pretty crazy, huh?" Gage tossed another piece of Danish in his mouth. "If she's yours, you should do something about it. Because that is fucked."

Marino frowned. His smug conceit had disappeared. "I have nothing else to say to you."

"Want the footage?" Gage offered as he slugged back coffee. "Man, this isn't too bad for hotel crap, is it?" he asked Callum. "Mind if I take another one of these for the road?"

"Send me the video," Marino demanded through clenched teeth.

Gage sent the link to the number Marino recited. As soon as it came through, the crypto king was on his feet and blasted out the door.

Callum wanted to tear the hotel down.

Gage hooted, and after they were out of the conference room, muttered, "That couldn't have gone better."

They walked across the lobby and departed the hotel, climbing into the waiting SUV.

"Hook, line, and sinker," Gage said as Roman pulled away from the curb.

Rocco glanced over his shoulder at Callum. "You don't think so?"

"We didn't get names."

"That was a long shot," Rocco admitted. "The video link?"

"Like I said: hook, line, and sinker."

A phone call rang through the SUV. Rocco answered it so that the speakers picked up.

"He clicked the link. We are live," Dean announced. "Job well done."

Marino had downloaded the video infected with a phishing virus. They had access to his keystrokes and communications. All they had to do was wait for him to make a call.

Chapter Thirty

With a dry throat and pounding head, Grace forced herself still and kept her eyes closed. *Don't panic.* The walls hummed around her as if she were sitting in the center of a power plant, but she couldn't hear her abductors or anyone moving or talking around her.

Carefully, she tested her arms and legs. They were bound. Not tightly, but enough that she couldn't fight or run away. She squinted her eyes, carefully opening them—and met the gaze of an older man.

Grace jerked back but couldn't escape.

"Easy," he said without getting up from his chair. "Easy. Calm down."

She searched her surroundings. Tied up and placed on a cot on her side, Grace twisted around and saw nowhere to go. The small room was almost like a storage closet, except hundreds of wires ran along the walls. Grace turned toward the man again. Older with graying hair, he was half the size of the man and woman who had taken her.

"Good," he said. "Stay calm. I won't hurt you."

"What do you want?" She memorized his hairstyle and the scar on his right cheek. He wore a crisp white button-down shirt, loosened at the collar, and loafers without socks like he would rather be on a sailboat than wherever they were.

"You're here for your own protection."

She shook her head. "I want to go home."

"Your husband is a very dangerous man."

"We're not married anymore. I don't know anything about him. I promise. I haven't seen him in years. I don't know—"

"Many of our associates are dangerous men," her captor continued. "You're safer with me."

Their associates? Her stomach turned. He worked with Dominic? Her mind raced to understand what was happening. "You're not going to hurt me?"

"No. I'll give you back to your husband, and everything will be fine."

Her heart seized. "I don't want to."

He looked at her curiously but lifted his shoulders. "This is where we stay until I hear otherwise."

He returned to his phone and ignored her until he brought her food. He untied her hands and feet and gestured behind her. "If you need the facilities, otherwise, good night."

Her meal consisted of several granola bars and bottled water. Hours ticked by, and eventually, unable to fight it any longer, Grace fell asleep on the cot.

She woke up to footsteps on the cement floor.

"Darling."

Wide awake but frozen in place, Grace prayed this was still somehow her nightmare.

"I know you're awake, Grace."

She opened her eyes, and there he was. Still handsome as ever with slicked-back dark hair and impeccable clothes. Clean-shaven and sporting a familiar cologne that made bile rise into the back of her throat, he smiled at her. "Nice to see you again."

"What do you want?" This was so much more than prohibiting her from speaking to the investigators and attorneys. Maybe he was after revenge. She'd taken so much of his money in the divorce. Most of it ended up with charities, but he didn't need it or care what she'd been given in the divorce. He would relish stripping it away.

"You look good for a dead woman." His nose wrinkled. "Even in these circumstances. In those clothes."

She gathered her knees to her chest. No one knew where she was. He could do anything to her, and no one would stop him.

"Stand up," he ordered.

Shaking her head, she couldn't swallow. Her throat dried like the moisture had evaporated from the room. Her eyes itched even as tears burned, but she didn't want to give him the pleasure of crying.

Dominic grabbed her hair and yanked her up until she was on her feet.

She stumbled but kept her footing. "What do you want?"

"In truth, I didn't want this for you, but here we are."

"I want to go home—"

His backhand slapped with an unexpected crack. The pain flared. She should have expected it. Her tongue probed her stinging cheek. Her tears fell. She wiped them away with the back of her hand.

"I'll decide where home is." His anger vibrated. "It's your fault you're here. Do you know that? I reminded you who you belong to, told you to keep your mouth shut." His irate frown pulled down. "I honestly thought you would, but you could never follow directions the first time. They were right to take you."

He paced the small space.

"I've known where you were every single day." He steepled his fingers and let his greasy grin surface. "You were more tenacious than I expected. I have to give you that. Entertaining, especially when I was in prison. I should thank you for the diversions, but little did you know how much you helped me."

She watched him stalk around her and didn't know what he wanted. Should she defend herself? Explain?

"The mishmash of LLCs and VPNs you used to hide from me is literally the only reason you're still alive." He cocked his head, studying her. "Honestly, you're far smarter than I gave you credit for."

It sounded like he might need her in some way. She could use that to her advantage if only she could ignore her fear. "I'm sorry."

She could tell he hadn't expected that. His lips pressed together, and Dominic let the silence hang as though there were more she should say.

"I've had time to think while everything played out around me," she said.

"About?"

"Death do us part," she repeated the words he'd mailed to her.

His cold demeanor remained unaffected.

"You would never hurt me," she lied, but knew he had always believed that to be true. Dominic never thought that sharp words, psychological coercion, or physical pain hurt when it came from him. He was missing a part of his brain that made sense of reality. "Everything I've been through, running from what I didn't know, wouldn't have happened if I were with you."

His disgust snarled. "You weren't alone, though. Were you?"

Her heart stuttered.

"I had a conversation with Callum Hale." Disdain dripped as he spat the words.

Grace might be sick. "That's my brother's doing. I can't help it. I've never been able to control them."

"He's always wanted you. That was clear from the first day I met him."

Could everyone see what she and Callum hadn't been able to? Why hadn't she seen it? But no, Grace had fallen for Dominic during the onslaught of lavish attention. "I… I, uh, don't know."

"You didn't then. You don't now. You're an idiot, Grace."

Oh, thank God. He didn't see the way she loved Callum. "Why did you talk to him?"

"He wants to find you. Everybody wants to find you." He rubbed a hand over his face and sighed. "I'll deal with them later. This is how everything will go."

She bit her lip and nodded.

"You come home. I'll let you pick the place you want to stay. The penthouse in Las Vegas is easier. But New York works for me as well. Not DC. Not Miami."

"Why?"

"You'll continue to communicate with the family and friends who know about your situation. Your life will continue exactly how it was, except you will stay in that one place. No resurrecting your life. You will continue to work on your little hobby job." He paused. "I actually like some of your work."

"I don't understand."

"You don't need to."

"Dominic—"

"Las Vegas or New York? Which will it be?"

"I, uh…"

"Grace, choose. I don't have to give you the option, darling, but I'm trying to be magnanimous here."

"I would be… a prisoner?"

"You would be safe. You will have everything at your disposal. You can stay in contact with your family. Though if you say a word or stray from our agreement, I'll kill you and bury you in the grave people already think you're in."

"New York."

"Fine." He turned for the door. "Time to go."

Grace followed Dominic through a maze of humming hallways. His expensive shoes echoed on the polished floor. The building seemed alive around them. She hadn't seen another person as they moved through the surreal labyrinth of matching walls and doors devoid of identifying characteristics.

"What is this place?" Its liminal space made her dizzy.

"A data center."

A windowless behemoth of the internet and artificial intelligence. She'd driven by the looming plain buildings that had popped up over northern Virginia. Their nondescript security presence was uniform, with fences and guards and tiny parking lots. From what she knew, few people actually worked inside the buildings that covered the size of several football fields. At least now she understood the hum.

And she knew they wouldn't run into a soul.

How was she going to escape?

Maybe she could peel down the hall, run into a room with massive servers—or whatever was in data centers—and tear out wires and press buttons on a wild ride. If she happened to shut down the internet for half of the United States or bring global banking to a halt, someone would know where to find her. That was better than somehow stealing Dominic's phone to call 911. She wasn't sure that a cell phone signal would transmit beyond the strumming sound of technology churning around her.

But for all she knew, any door she pulled open would lead to a broom closet, and Dominic would be pissed. For now, he only seemed aggravated that someone else had taken her. Not that she'd pretended to be dead to hide from him.

Her stomach turned at the thought of anything related to being his wife. "When we get," she caught herself from saying New York, "*home*, I need to go shopping."

"Obviously. I don't understand what you're wearing. Pick what you need, like always."

Like always, as if they hadn't been apart for years.

Even after his bank accounts were frozen, his residences were staffed, and his lifestyle remained. As a crypto broker, he had hidden money where laws hadn't caught up yet. Untraceable. There was no telling how wealthy he really was.

The people who worked for him were discreet and wouldn't breathe a word if Dominic's dead wife was suddenly in need of a personal shopper. He'd supply her with a fitness trainer, chef, stylist, and makeup artist by the end of the day now that he knew she'd chosen New York City. None of them would care that she was supposed to be dead and never left his property.

If he got her there, she would never leave. She couldn't do this again.

Grace turned and sprinted.

"Grace."

She kept running. The corridors blurred into a disorienting emptiness.

"Grace!"

She cut down a hallway. Then another. A red light called to her like a homing beacon. Dominic's bellowing voice echoed around her, growing quieter, but she didn't think for a second that she'd lost him. If he had access to this building, he might know its blank walls and featureless paths. Maybe he could pull up video footage and track her like a mouse through a maze, smiling and laughing at her ineptitude.

Her legs burned. Lightheaded, she needed to catch her breath. *Don't stop.* She drew closer to the red light. An exit sign, maybe. She ached to slow down but couldn't. She refused. Even as the sameness of the walls, the ceiling, and the floor twisted each stride into a dizzying trial.

Grace reached the end of the hallway. The exit sign directed her down another endless hall. She spotted another red sign and followed it until she reached a stairwell.

Stumbling down the stairs, she twisted around to the next flight, struggling to keep moving until the stencil-painted words *first floor* promised salvation.

The first floor was the same as the other. A liminal labyrinth, but with the slight difference of exits. She assumed the front entrance, at the top of the signage, was closest and took off.

Sweat poured down her back. Her aching arms pumped. The dozens of cat scratch scabs had their own pulses. Her exhausted body couldn't handle any more of this—then she saw Dominic dead ahead, running from the opposite direction.

She'd never seen that man run after anything in his life.

The front entrance was between them, splitting the distance evenly.

"Grace, goddamn you, stop."

Gritting her teeth, she called upon energy she didn't have and poured herself into escape. The world around them slowed as if she were running on the bottom of the ocean floor, pushing through a wall of water she couldn't see.

Grace reached the exit corridor first. His footsteps pounded behind, closing the distance, but she reached the front glass door—slamming into the glass at top speed and bouncing back like she'd run into a tree.

Dazed, unable to breathe, she lay on her back and stared at the featureless ceiling.

Dominic leaned over her face. "You stupid cunt."

Chapter Thirty-One

Callum eyed the tall iron fence that wrapped around the data center as Eli sped down the road on the outskirts of suburbia. This place never seemed to end. "Are you sure?"

"You want the statistical analysis?" Dean barked through the speakers.

"You've already heard what you need, Hale." Gage checked his ammunition. "Take a deep breath and check your gear. Make sure your head's in the game when we go in."

"Already there." Callum spotted the helicopter on the chopper pad. "Visual on the helo."

"Good," Dean muttered.

"There's all the confirmation we need. We're right on time for a rendezvous with the dickhead." Eli smacked the center console, hyping himself up. "You ready to get your woman?"

"Yeah." Callum had been waiting for this moment since Dean tracked Marino's movement and communication. Then the bastard had gone dark, and Titan had to rely on analysis and educated guesses, not the hard facts that Callum would rather sink his teeth into when it came to Grace.

A second SUV of his teammates followed behind as Eli turned off the main road and slowed at the security gate. Tire spikes and retractable bollards stood between the road and the data center's inner lot.

Eli lowered the window and painted on that southern charm that opened more doors than it should.

A suspicious man in a security uniform, a weapon on his hip, slowly approached them. He eyed their backup vehicle and rested his hand on his sidearm. "Can I help you?"

"Yeah," Eli drawled out his Louisiana accent. "We have an appointment with Mr. Marino."

"I don't know who that is, and we're not accepting visitors." He eyed the group in the vehicle, then again glanced at the SUV behind theirs. "You need to back up and leave the property."

"Why don't you radio whoever you need to and—" Eli smashed his door into the security guard and was out, gun in hand, before the other man got his bearings. "Don't move."

"There's a live feed—"

"Don't care."

Wes popped out of the backseat, disarming and zip-tying the security guard. He dragged him into the booth and, a moment later, the retractable bollards rotated toward the ground. The tire spikes flattened. He jumped back in. "He'll be cozy for a bit."

"Intercepting outgoing alarms," Dean announced. "They're canceled. You're good to go."

Their SUVs rolled in. Maybe someone would notice the gate had been left open, but by the time that happened, Titan should have been in and out with Grace. If she were in there. If they didn't miss her board the helicopter.

The facility blueprints were on file with the county, and they'd done their best to memorize them. The space they had to canvas was enormous, and they didn't have a hard plan. Just general guidelines from Dean and Parker based on best practices and whatever other bullshit they used to conjure up plans.

Callum had to trust it. He couldn't get over the size. They could walk from one side to the next and probably cover half a mile.

The other SUV peeled off toward the helicopter.

Eli stopped at the front entrance and parked on the yellow curb. They had the bells and whistles to get through the front door, and Dean would intercept outgoing alarms the way he handled calls from the guard shack.

"Let's go," Callum jumped out.

His teammates followed. Eli and Wes fell in close behind them. Gage pulled up the rear, communicating with the other team as Decker, Roman, and Rocco moved toward the helicopter.

A dozen yards from the glass doors, Callum stared at the woman running toward him like he was watching a movie. "*Grace.*"

Then she crashed into the door and catapulted backward, hitting the floor.

He hauled ass toward her—then saw Dominic reach her first.

He towered over her, hands on his knees, red face full of fury. Callum yanked the door. It didn't budge, and as Dominic turned his head, Callum pulled out his Glock. The answer to all of his prayers unfolded in that moment. He could pull the trigger and end every worry and fear Grace had ever had.

He pulled the trigger.

The glass shattered. Dominic cowered. It would have been too easy to kill him. Too horrible to do it and have his piece-of-shit body land on his woman.

Callum didn't know who moved in on Dominic. He didn't care if he ever saw him again. Gage issued orders, but Callum dropped to his knees at her side. "Baby. I'm here. I've got you." He peeled the hair off her sweaty face. Grace's chest heaved as though she'd been running for her life. He realized she had been.

Her eyes focused on him. "Callum." She propped onto her elbows, wincing. "Ow, oh, that hurts."

Had Dominic hurt her? She could have broken her wrists or arms with the impact of hitting the glass door. "Take your time. You're safe. Everything's fine."

"Does she need EMS?" Gage asked.

Grace slowly shook her head. "I just..." Her breath shook. "Need a minute."

"You can have all the time you need."

Her eyes watered. "Do you promise?"

The pleading in her expression told him they weren't talking about catching her breath. "I promise."

Grace squeezed her eyes shut and curled her legs to her chest. She wrapped her arms around herself and hugged. He couldn't let her sit in a pile of glass and cry. Callum scooped her into his arms and took her away.

She nuzzled against his chest. Glass crunched under his boots. They stepped outside and into the hot air of a long August day, and he placed her in the back of the SUV.

Eli had turned the engine on and left it running. Cool air poured over them. Callum crawled in behind her. "We'll take you to the hospital and get you checked out."

"I'm fine. Really."

"Precautionary."

"What then? Do I have to go back and talk to the attorneys?"

"No. Maybe later. But not right now. They figured out what they needed to know."

"What was that?"

"You don't really want to talk about this now," he suggested.

"I do. I promise."

"That Dominic and his business partners knew you were alive the entire time and utilized the network you created to funnel money."

Her jaw hinged. "That's what he meant..." She looked to the side, lost in thought.

Eli returned behind the wheel.

Gage retook his seat. "Rhys will handle Dominic with Decker and them until the FBI shows up."

Pulling a U-turn, Eli said, "Then that's our cue. I don't want to be around for the paperwork that's going to come." He paused at the security booth and rolled his window down. "You okay down there, partner?"

Partner sounded like pod-nah.

"He's from Louisiana," Callum explained. "I'll translate anything you can't understand."

"Hardy har." Eli scoffed, then laid it on thick, "*Ma cher*, don't believe a word dat one say."

She quietly laughed, and thank fuck, Grace wasn't totally broken. Callum would spend the rest of his life making her right again, but if they didn't have to deal with that, it was for the better.

They drove for longer than Callum would have expected, finally pulling into a small hospital where the staff met them at the door. The nurses had already been briefed on their arrival, and their lack of questions was telling. They were well-versed in working with Titan.

A man in a white coat walked into the hospital room. "I'm Dr. Tuska. You must be Grace."

She nodded.

"Sounds like you've had a horrible day." He turned to Callum. "Would you mind stepping out? Jared Westin is down the hall, waiting for you."

Callum double-checked with Grace. "I won't be far."

"I'm fine."

Callum shut the door behind him, wandering toward the nurses' station, and saw the man who owned Titan Group speaking to a young lady. He held back, not interrupting, and anticipated his boss's boss would probably demand that Callum spend the rest of the day being interrogated by the FBI.

The young lady noticed him and nudged her head. Jared said something to her, then patted her back before she retreated. The man whom some called Boss Man lifted his chin. "How's Grace?"

"Good. A little numb. But physically just banged up and bruised."

"Thank fuck for that, right?"

Callum nodded.

"Well, I told you I would make sure your woman came home."

"Thank you."

"We're still working on how and where the leaks came from. That's not taken care of yet, and I don't think it will be for a while. Keep your eyes peeled, and if something comes up again, feel free to contact me. I'll make sure Viv sends you my information."

Callum nodded.

"They'll probably keep Grace overnight. I'd say you should stick close, security-wise, but I think law enforcement has a solid handle on all the moving pieces. Dean could give you a more in-depth analysis, but I think this part of Grace's life is done." He hooked a thumb toward the young woman behind the nurses' desk. "That's my daughter. Volunteer candy striper extraordinaire. If you need anything, she's smarter than I am, so..." He shrugged. "She's a good resource."

The hospital kept Grace overnight. The stay had been dubbed precautionary. Prudent, Dr. Tuska had said, just to monitor her. She didn't think his reasoning was one hundred percent medical. The protective walls and constant flow of trustworthy people keeping an eye on her had probably been part of her overnight stay.

Callum and Vivian promised that her nightmare was over. They had meant Dominic, but the nightmare had continued when law enforcement descended upon her. Both her divorce and criminal attorneys had joined that conversation, in part, she believed, because they had felt bad for what had happened right under their noses.

The gist was simple. Dominic was in custody again. Initially, for unlawful imprisonment, but that was just to cover the paperwork for his initial arrest. Grace didn't want to know the details of the other investigations. She'd only wanted to know if he could get out.

As had been promised to her years ago, their verdict was not likely. Time would tell.

Either way, Dominic was done with her. Her usefulness was depleted, and he had bigger issues than her to worry about. Like a Chinese Triad—essentially, an Asian Mafia crime syndicate. She hadn't known what a Triad was until the investigators explained. Triads were a much bigger issue than an ex-wife.

The FBI had access to all of her secret accounts that she used while in hiding. Grace had walked them through the ins and outs of how she lived, without worrying about repercussions. She had immunity thanks to her lawyers.

Just as Callum had promised, she could let go of her aliases and LLCs and slip back into her own life. Even her Social Security number was back up and ready for her to be alive again.

That left her with the biggest decision of all. Callum.

He was the love of her life, and she couldn't say the words *I love you* out loud. It was as if they were physically lodged in her throat. The only thing her brain allowed her to do was count the days that had passed since she'd maced him at the library.

It hadn't been long.

Callum was absolutely, categorically nothing like Dominic. But the last time she'd been swept off her feet had been a disaster that had taken more than a decade to untangle herself from.

Hell, she wasn't actually completely untangled. She was sitting in the hospital because of her ex-husband.

Two knocks sounded on her door before Callum walked in. He held an iced coffee for her and a takeout bag from the Mediterranean place down the street that Asal, the volunteer assigned to her who had finished her freshman year in college nearby, had recommended. Asal was smart, a little sassy, and, Grace suspected, ordered to watch her in case she needed anything. As hospital stays go, this one rated like a nice hotel.

"Did you decide what you want to do?" Callum pulled out the takeout containers and placed them on the rolling table at her bedside.

She tucked her legs under her and positioned the table between them. "I talked to Mari about an hour ago and convinced her not to drive here. That I would go home later today."

She could tell that Callum wanted to ask, "And then?" She wished she had the answer.

He handed her a plastic fork. "I talked to Hayden after you went missing."

"Oh..." She winced. "I bet that wasn't a great conversation."

Callum waffled his hand. "We last talked again right before we geared up for the data center. I sent him an update but haven't heard from him since. Between shitty connections or being sent out on assignment, he's difficult to get a hold of."

She nodded, knowing that all too well.

"But be prepared for your overly protective big brother to talk your ear off when he gets you on the phone."

Callum opened the lids. Steam wafted, and they dug in, eating in silence. The nurse and Asal popped in with Grace's discharge papers as they finished their meal.

He lifted his eyebrows and shoved his hands into his pockets. "Ready to go home?"

The worst feeling of losing him came over her. She wasn't. He was still by her side. Literally, her ride or die. But there was a chasm she couldn't explain. "Yup. Let's go."

Chapter Thirty-Two

Callum pulled his new truck into the driveway and tried to hide the dread creeping into his bones. He glanced from the Willoughby house to the one he'd grown up in and back to Grace's. It had been so long since he had stood on her parents' front porch and watched her sit in the passenger seat of Dominic's car. Their lives would be so different if he had walked down those stairs and told Grace how he felt.

He'd done that now, and it was time to give her the space she needed. His body physically ached to let her go.

"Are you going to visit your dad?" she asked, fingers tugging at the hospital bracelet on her wrist, which she hadn't been ready to cut off.

"Yeah. I'll pop in for a minute if he's home."

Her head turned. "You didn't call?"

Callum shrugged. "I'm not that far from here. I can always come back."

He needed her to understand that the offer was always on the table. He would come back for her, without question, at any time. He'd be anything she needed, and right now, she'd made it clear he needed to return her to her family and the start of a stable life lived on her own terms. "I'm a phone call away."

"This feels... strange," she admitted. "We've been together every moment since I knew you were back."

"Now that you're alive," he gave her what he hoped was a lighthearted look, "we can do this whenever we want."

What did he expect? It's not like they would finish a couple of crazy weeks and, what, move in together? The truth was, they had both been on shaky ground before they collided. Not exactly logical to think they should cement themselves together and pretend life would work out unless... he didn't know, they did *work*. Work on themselves. Work on staying together. Yet, he wasn't sure when he would see her again. That was shredding his insides. "You need some time to pull your life together."

She nodded, tugging her lip between her teeth.

"Grace, this isn't goodbye."

"I know."

"Hang out with your parents. Ease into permanent decisions." *Like him.* "Figure out what you want without fear forcing those choices." *Want him.*

She did. He believed that, and knowing it made leaving her harder.

"I will," she said. "I haven't seen them in so long."

Another car pulled up in front of the house.

Hayden jumped out, blindsiding them both.

"Oh my God," Grace cried. "Hayden!" She turned to Callum, eyes wide and smile hinging into jaw-dropping territory. "Did you know?"

"No. I haven't been able to get a hold of him." Callum should have been thrilled, but the arrival of his best friend was the final nail in the coffin. The conversation was over. They couldn't stay in his truck any longer.

"I can't believe it." She jumped out and ran to her brother.

Callum scrubbed a hand over his face, took a deep breath, and followed. It made sense. Of course, Hayden would haul ass back home. Callum hung back on the sidewalk and watched the reunion. His heart swelled for them. Hayden swung his little sister off her feet in a hug.

Hayden set Grace down and strode to him, pulling Callum into a backslapping greeting. "Thanks, man. I owe you everything."

"Of course. Good to see you."

"The team's not the same without you," Hayden offered. "Actually, it kinda fucking sucks. It's working out for you at Titan?"

"Yeah. It's good." Titan brought him Grace and into a new fold. New teammates. New life. New everything—almost.

Grace didn't move to Callum's side as she had for the last few weeks. Callum didn't take her hand. By some unspoken agreement, they weren't sharing what had happened between them and fell into the roles they'd always had. Older brother's best friend. Best friend's little sister.

"Have you seen Dad and Mari?" Hayden asked.

"Not yet. We just pulled up."

"Then let's go." Hayden hooked an arm over Grace's shoulders and looked back. "You coming in?"

"Not this time. I'll let you catch up."

Grace ducked under Hayden's arm. Callum's heart seized. She closed the distance and wrapped herself around him, hugging him so tight he was terrified they'd never see each other again. He wanted to bury his face in her hair and memorize the way her body pressed against his. Instead, Callum held her like she might break, dropped his chin on top of her head, and fought every urge in his body to kiss her goodbye.

Not in front of her brother.

Not right now.

Not until... he didn't know.

He hung on to her for another moment, pressed a kiss to the crown of her head, and spun her back to Hayden. "Say hey to your folks."

His throat hurt, and, fucking hell, if he spoke again, his voice would break. Callum tossed up his hand to say goodbye, jumped in his truck, and drove and drove and drove.

Miles and time passed. He didn't realize where he'd been driving until the house came into view. The front window had been replaced, and a familiar car waited in the driveway. Callum parked and knocked on the door before he even thought of what to say.

With Argos and Toto flanking her side, Alicia swung the door open and scowled as she scrutinized him like only a librarian might, then her face softened. "Well, fuck. You didn't break her heart. She broke yours."

He pinched the bridge of his nose and didn't have shit to say.

"Come inside. You're letting all the air conditioning out." She directed him to the living room and walked away, letting him pull his act together. "Lemonade or iced tea?"

He sat on the couch that had been his bed and took in the room. The rug and drapes had been replaced. New books sat among her plants and knickknacks on the shelves. If he hadn't known better, he would have thought Alicia's living room always looked like this. She worked fast.

Alicia returned with lemonade. "If you don't speak up about what you want," she handed him a glass, "then you can't complain."

He took the lemonade. "This is great."

"As if there's another answer." She sat across from him and signaled the dogs to lie down. Sherlock pounced onto the couch, nuzzling his leg. "Guess he still likes you. Grace, on the other hand, might never be forgiven for dragging him outside and into that car."

"There's a chance some of his scratches will turn into scars. Maybe that will make them even."

"Petty logic to a cat?" Alicia harrumphed. "Spit it out. Why are you here?"

He took a long drink because he didn't have an answer. "Just sort of ended up here without thinking."

"Is Dominic in jail again?"

"Yeah. He's got bigger problems to deal with than Grace. He won't bother her again."

"Good. He can burn for all I care."

"We see eye to eye on that. One of the many reasons I like you, Alicia."

"I'm not very likable."

He laughed. "I've liked you since the moment you hit me with a pen. You're a good friend."

"Grace is, too, which leads me to ask again, what put that look on your face?"

He honestly didn't know. They had lived in a bubble, just as Vivian had said, and he was heartbroken that it was over. "Real life called, and I don't know where that leaves us."

"Did you ask her?"

"Well... no."

She rolled her eyes. "You're an idiot."

"What was I supposed to ask? I said everything I needed to say. She knows it."

"You know what she's been hiding from, and now, the world is her oyster. What comes next? What's she seeking? What does she want?"

"I don't know."

Alicia snorted. "That's bullshit."

"She's back with her family, figuring out what life should look like. I mean, come on, coming back from the dead isn't easy."

"That's not all she wants, and you know it. She's one of the strongest, most creative people I've ever met. Dominic stole her life from her. I didn't know her before, but I can imagine it."

"I've always known her, and... yeah. She is." He threaded his fingers through his hair and rested his head in his hands, elbows on his knees, and lost himself. He was grieving. He'd had and then lost the woman he'd always wanted. "She needs to be home."

"No. She needs to reconnect with her family. In a way, similar to how she reconnected with you."

He gave her a look. Maybe Alicia had missed exactly how he and Grace had reconnected.

"No, not like that, you weirdo. I mean, she needs to be around them. Be with them. And then…"

He waited for whatever wisdom Alicia would throw his way.

Instead, she threw a pillow. "*And then*? Come on, Callum. And then what?"

"I don't know."

Alicia tossed her hands in the air. "God, you are dense. Think it through. What does she need now?"

"Her family."

"Brother, *you are her family*. Not in the same way as her blood. But you have to understand that. Whatever happened between the fire in my living room and today when you trounced back in here, there was a transformation that surpasses whatever game of footsie you two had been playing in my kitchen. Can you see that?"

He could feel it for damn sure. "She needs time."

"For what?"

Callum tipped his head back and stared at the ceiling. It had been repainted. He couldn't find the lines on it that he'd fallen asleep staring at, knowing that Grace was sleeping directly above him. "To learn how to stay in one place."

"Not a bad answer," Alicia muttered.

He snickered and straightened to look at her. "I know what she wants. But I don't know how to get it for her."

"That's the tricky part. You don't. Dominic got her everything on earth. But he stole her magic, her power. You're what she wants. Staying in one place is what she wants. Not panicking about how to hide is what she wants. You are her solace. The place she goes to settle down." Alicia cocked her head. "My question for you is: can you handle that?"

He didn't hesitate to nod.

His phone rang, and he didn't know the number. "One second," he said, then answered.

"Hey," Grace said on the phone. "Guess what?"

A smile curled on his lips, and a warm light like the glow of sunrise dawned in his chest. "What?"

Alicia excused herself to the kitchen.

"I have a new phone number," Grace explained. "Not a phone number that forwards to another number and then another number."

"Nice work. How's that feel?" He leaned back. It had only been a couple of hours, but he needed to hear her voice more than he realized.

"Strange—Callum, I miss you."

He ran a hand over his face and rubbed his eyes. "Miss you too, babe."

"I wish you'd gone to your dad's."

"I had to run."

"Work?"

"No... just errands."

"How does this work? Us?" she asked quietly.

"I'll visit you whenever you ask me to."

"Like a long-distance romance?"

He hadn't found the words to describe what he wanted, and those fell short. Callum wanted so much more. "If that's what you want to call it."

"It's ridiculous, but I want everything to go back to how it was." She half-laughed. "Except for the part with the guns and fires and abductions."

He loved her more than he knew how to explain. They could be together. Live together? Why not? He didn't know—but he knew Dominic had rushed her, and now everything needed to slow down. "That's not ridiculous."

"Can I call you tomorrow?" she asked.

She'd gone from stripping off her clothes and demanding he fuck her to her asking if she could call. "Call me a hundred times a day. Any time you want."

"Are you still my white knight savior?"

His lips quirked. "I'm your everything."

"You are."

She ended the call. Callum let out a heavy breath and petted Sherlock after he jumped onto his lap.

Alicia padded back into the living room. "How's our girl?"

"Excited to have a real phone number."

Alicia rested her hands on the wingback chair. "Believe it or not, that's one step in the right direction toward permanence."

That was a good way to look at it. He gave Sherlock another scratch and stood. "Thanks for listening to me."

"Of course. Where to now?"

He thought about his crappy apartment, which could use a serious upgrade, and his job. In the last few days, he'd given his colleagues his complete trust and was rewarded with teammates in something far deeper than name only. They were a team, and for the first time, he felt like a part of Titan. "Home."

Chapter Thirty-Three

The first day without Callum sucked as much as the twentieth. Though "without Callum" was a misnomer. Grace had all of him. There was no question about that.

But she hated the distance and hadn't discussed him with her family. She wasn't concerned that they would doubt Callum was a good guy. They knew him, and any of her bro-code concerns with her brother had faded. But she was scared they would think the same thing Vivian had thought. That she and Callum were a white knight-damsel-in-distress collision of adrenaline and hormones.

Every morning, he called her to say good morning.

Every night, she called as she fell asleep.

He had visited her four times in twenty days. Each time they'd stayed in an extravagant hotel room, staying in bed while he promised he loved her, saying everything except the ways he would take care of her for the rest of her life. She knew he would, and that he was giving her the space to reclaim her autonomy.

But staying in hotels wasn't nearly enough anymore.

Grace sighed and studied the design she'd been sketching. It was done. Any further work would spoil the concept. She set her stylus down and would submit it to her client later today.

Mari walked in and plopped on the couch next to Grace. "Working on anything good?"

"Just finished." She positioned the screen to show her stepmom. "It's the third book in a series. I really love the way the stars pop in the sky on this one."

"Gorgeous."

Grace beamed. "Thanks." She tucked her feet under her legs. "I'm going to be gone for the day and will be back tomorrow afternoon."

"I'll tell Dad not to make too much dinner then."

She fortified her insides and fidgeted. "I'm going to be with Callum."

"That's what we figured. Things are working out well at his new job?"

Her lips parted. They knew? "Why did you figure?"

Mari tilted her head with a knowing eyebrow lifted. "Why wouldn't we?"

"*Mari.*"

She laughed. "Apparently, even grown adults forget their parents always know what's going on."

"I don't think you *always* knew."

"He's been watching you almost as long as you've watched him. He was less obvious than you, of course."

"I wasn't obvious."

Mari snorted. "You? As a teenager? Not obvious? I think you cried when he and Hayden took a set of twins to the prom."

"I did not." Well, actually, she had. "Are you going to tell me to give myself time, that whatever I feel is because I had a hellacious adventure with him?"

"Nope."

"No?"

"No. That wouldn't take into account all those years where you ignored him because he ignored you, and he was too worried about what Hayden would say."

Grace's frown deepened. That pretty much described their teenage years into their twenties.

"You two weren't meant for first-love heartbreak. You were meant for forever love."

"Oh my God, Mari." Her eyes stung. "I didn't say anything about forever. I said I wasn't spending the night here."

"Soon as you're ready, he's waiting for you, Gracie."

Grace already knew that, and quietly admitted, "I'm in love with him."

"I know, and when you're ready, you'll make sure he does, too."

She was ready and had been thinking about how life would work with Callum since the moment he had left her and Hayden in her parents' front yard.

Grace packed an overnight bag and loaded it into her car. A permanent car. One that she'd picked out, negotiated, and signed the paperwork for without asking for anyone's input. A silver sedan. Practical. Comfortable. Not flashy but had a good vibe.

She drove to meet Callum in the parking lot, and they checked into the hotel not too far from her house. She ignored the uncomfortable feeling that these meetups were too similar to untethered trysts. She had nailed everything else down. Now she was ready for the final touches of permanence.

Callum opened their hotel room, dropped their bags, and wrapped her in a kiss that melted rational thought from her mind.

"Wait, wait, wait," she said against his lips. "I want to show you something."

"It can wait."

"No. It can't." Grace dissolved into a fit of giggles as he tossed her onto the bed, covering her with his body. "It will just take a second."

"Fine," he grumbled with his lips against her neck.

The amount of internal strength required to roll away from his mouth astounded her. But it would be worth it.

She rifled through her bag and retrieved the paper. "Look."

His lazy gaze laser-focused as soon as he saw the picture printed at the top corner of the page. "What is this?"

"A real estate listing."

He snatched it from her, read, looked up and down again, then held out the paper. "You want to see it?"

"I don't even need to see it." The little white Craftsman house was within walking distance of Main Street in Granite Creek. "The pictures are cute. There's a garden in the back. Flowers in the front. Just looking at it makes me smile."

"It's everything you want."

"Almost." She tossed the real estate listing aside. "I want to be there with you." Her heart slammed in her chest. She didn't doubt he wanted that too, but saying it aloud nearly stole her breath. "We could make it our home."

She didn't need Callum to find her a house or to make that decision. She needed to find herself. He'd understood that before she had and given her the space.

Callum was everything her ex hadn't been. More than that, he was everything without comparison.

He sat on the edge of the bed and squeezed her hips and pulled her close between his legs. "Is that what you want?"

Nearly eye to eye, her grin hitched. "I mean, that's not all I want. But it's a start." She lifted her arms into the air for him to strip off her shirt. "Back to our regularly scheduled programming?"

His fingers toyed with the hem, and his stormy bourbon eyes reflected the two meanings of the here-and-now in the hotel room and their life together.

Their life together stayed in his mind; she was sure of it. Callum undressed her like a present, taking his time with every touch and tease until she ached for his mouth on hers again. His clothes came off with significantly less fanfare, and she didn't care.

His hands roamed her body. His mouth tasted every part of her until he'd wound her tight enough to scream. This was insanity. The craving for him. The desire for the way he filled her, fucked her, brought her to the edge of the universe, then gave her more.

Gloriously naked, he covered her with his body of carved muscles, and caged her, pinning her between him and the bed.

She moaned for more. "I need you."

His cock rubbed against her tender flesh. She needed Callum in every sense. The heavy weight of his erection stroked against her wanting pussy. Grace lifted her hips and locked her legs around his thighs. She did everything to coax him into her. Nothing changed the torturously slow teases.

"All mine."

She nodded desperately, silently begging for more.

He took her mouth, working his thickness into her, inch by inch, stealing her breath with each soul-touching thrust. She stretched around him, breathing his name as he stilled, deep-seated inside her body.

His ragged breath mirrored hers, and all she needed was him to fuck her until white lights and fireworks exploded. His forehead pressed to hers. Their eyes locked.

Her heart swelled, and she couldn't believe this man was hers. "I love you, Callum."

"Fuck, baby," he whispered hoarsely. "I love you too."

Then he unleashed everything he'd been holding back. An onslaught of kisses fell. His hips moved. He drove into her, biting, kissing, loving her neck. She gave him all of her. Every part. Her pussy. Her body. Her mind. Her trust.

She buried her face in the crook of his neck. The taste of him, the smell of him, he was everything she could ever want.

The building madness of an orgasm drew tight. She and Callum moved in an all-consuming rhythmic drive that turned her gasping moan into a delirious cry of impending release.

The fireworks and lightning of her orgasm hit. Grace bucked against him, dragging out the beautiful, blinding explosions until he forced another mind-numbing climax that shattered what she knew possible of pleasure.

Callum slowed, panting against the nape of her neck, promising all the ways she would moan like that for the rest of her life.

He captured her mouth again. The kisses flowed like the easy roll of his hips. Her fingers flexed into his powerful back. He set a pace so dangerously slow that she begged him for more.

Callum eased her into his arms and rolled onto his back, giving her the more that she didn't realize she wanted. "Use me."

Straddling him, she arched back, in control of the way she moved, of how they fucked.

He cupped her breasts. His hooded eyes drank her in like a man dying of thirst. Callum was everything she had always wanted. She let go of all her inhibitions.

"God." He groaned when she lifted, then took him again. "Just like that."

Her eyes shut. She filled herself with him over and over until the perfect cadence of bliss dictated how she rode the thick length of his shaft. Each invasion dropped her jaw more until her head tipped back and she cried his name.

Her pussy pulsed around him, and, clamping his hands onto her hips, took over the way they moved. Deep inside her, Callum rocked her hips, grinding her against him, moving their rhythm to a frantic pace. Her orgasm built, and he strained into her, arching his back as she fell apart again.

She dropped to his chest. Their heartbeats slammed together. His arms hung heavily over her back, wrapping her close as he promised her the future she'd always dreamed of.

Epilogue

One Year Later

The summer sun baked down on Grace. She squinted from behind her sunglasses, wondering how it was still so bright even under the shade of the canopy umbrella. The smell of burgers and hot dogs rolled off the grill, and the sound of laughter and banter made her heart swell.

Her dad, Hayden, Mari, and Alicia relaxed across the table from her. Her brother, with a beer in his hand, recounted tales as her stepmom swiped through photos on his phone from his time on leave, and Alicia tried in vain to get Grace's puppy Pickles to listen. Pickles was far too interested in Argos and Toto, who couldn't care less about an annoying puppy.

Grace's husband manned the grill, a sexy sight as he took a long pull from his beer, then removed the burgers and hot dogs. "Who's hungry?"

"I am," Dean called as he rounded the corner into the backyard, followed by some of the Titan crew. "How are you going to start without us?"

"This meal waits for no one." Callum placed the tray on the table and began introductions to Alicia and her family. "Dean's the former NSA guy."

Dean saluted.

"Eli's the Cajun."

Eli made a face. "Dean gets a job title, and I get what my accent already tells you? Anyone else think that's crap?"

Callum laughed, ignoring him, and continued, "That's Rhys. He's got a photographic memory, and this is Scarlett, who goes by Scar. She and my boss Viv keep everyone in line."

"I don't think I do," Scarlett said. "But that doesn't stop me from trying."

"If the rest of our crew gets back in town," Callum explained, "they'll head over."

Grace wondered if that would include Gage. She suspected that even if Wes and Decker made it over, Gage might not if Vivian didn't. Callum thought Grace was nuts, but she couldn't help but notice the way those two meshed when they weren't needling each other.

Everyone piled food on their plates. Callum made sure Grace had the burger with double cheese.

Callum and Hayden bantered and bullshitted like they'd done their entire lives. The Titan crew joked and ragged on each other just like Callum and Hayden. Scar and Alicia fell down a rabbit hole about late-19th-century authors who secretly encoded women's suffrage messages into the male-dominated space of serialized mysteries. Dad doted on Mari, and Pickles, snubbed by Argos and Toto, returned to his empty bowl to lick where Callum had dropped bits of burger and hot dogs while grilling.

Grace ate her ginormous cheeseburger and thought about everything she'd always wanted and now had.

Granite Creek had enveloped Callum and her just as Titan had pulled them into its tight-knit family.

Pickles perked up and barked, scampering under the table and through everyone's legs, until he reached the edge of the patio. The rest of the crew arrived—including Vivian and Gage, who didn't walk near each other.

Maybe Callum was correct.

Introductions were made, and the fun began all over again. Food. Laughter. The occasional dog barked, mostly from Pickles.

Vivian pulled Callum aside, and Grace watched out of the corner of her eye. She didn't want him to be called out on an assignment, but she'd become used to the ebb and flow of his job. Sometimes he had to leave in the middle of the night. Other times, he was gone for days without contact. No matter whether Callum was gone for an hour or a week, he returned just as in love with her as when he'd left. Maybe more so. This was the life she didn't know she could have. All she had to do was let go of her past and grow.

Callum and Vivian finished up their conversation.

"Everything okay?"

"Rhys' past is coming back to haunt him. But we don't have to deal with that right now." He wrapped an arm around her waist and kept her close.

If the younger Grace could see this Grace now, she would trip over herself. Not just because her husband was as in love with her as she was with him, but because she had embraced her life and let Callum be part of the future she'd only dreamed of.

Promises made. Promises kept.

What to Read Next

Run and Hide, Titan Protectors, Book 2

She's Hollywood royalty. He's the ghost in the shadows. When their worlds collide, the spotlight could kill them both.

Jules Lowry should be basking on her honeymoon, not hiding from paparazzi—and a stalker—after discovering her fiancé's betrayal. She walked away from the altar, determined to disappear. But when the threats escalate, her powerful family brings in the one man she can't trust: her former bodyguard.

Rhys can't stand red carpets. After years spent in the shadows protecting lives, he prefers personal protection assignments to celebrity drama. Still, when the Lowrys call, he answers. With a photographic memory and a relentless edge, he's the best in the business... even if it means faking a relationship with the woman who can shatter his control.

Bound by a dangerous lie and tucked away in a small town, Rhys and Jules ignite a chemistry that's all too real. But as the enemy closes in and buried truths unravel, they must decide: is their romance just an act or the fight of their lives?

Releases on June 16, 2026 at all major retailers.

Lost and Found, Titan Protectors, Book 3

The third book in the Titan Protectors series is expected in Fall 2026!
Visit www.CristinHarber.com for more information.

About the Author

New York Times bestselling author Cristin Harber packs her military romance, romantic suspense, and new adult romance novels with steam, sizzle, and action of all types. Whether you want fireworks in the bedroom or a hunky ex-military team that saves the day, her bestselling romance novels will make you swoon and smile.

The Aces Series

The Savior
The Protector
The Survivor
The Guardian
The Defender
The Bodyguard
The Saint

The Titan Series

Winters Heat
Sweet Girl (prequel to Garrison's Creed)
Garrison's Creed
Westin's Chase
Gambled and Chased
Savage Secrets
Hart Attack
Sweet One
Black Dawn

Live Wire

Bishop's Queen

Locke and Key

Jax

Deja Vu

A Very Titan Christmas

The Delta Series

Delta: Retribution

Delta: Rescue

Delta: Revenge

Delta: Redemption

Delta: Ricochet

The Only Series

Only for Him

Only for Her

Only for Us

Only Forever

Only for Love (Box Set)

Titan Protectors

Hide and Seek

Run and Hide

Lost and Found

7 Brides for 7 Soldiers

Ryder - Barbara Freethy

Adam - Roxanne St. Claire

Zane - Christie Ridgway

Wyatt - Lynn Raye Harris
Jack - Julia London
Noah - Cristin Harber
Ford - Samantha Chase

7 Brides for 7 Blackthornes

Devlin - Barbara Freethy
Jason - Julia London
Ross - Lynn Raye Harris
Phillip - Cristin Harber
Brock - Roxanne St. Claire
Logan - Samantha Chase
Trey - Christie Ridgway

Each Titan, Delta, and 7 Brides book can be read as a standalone (except for Sweet Girl), but readers will likely best enjoy the series in order. The Only series must be read in order.